LOVE & RUM

DANI MCLEAN

LOVE & RUM

DANI MCLEAN

LOVE & RUM

Book 1 of The Cocktail Series

Copyright © 2021 by Dani McLean

First edition: July 2021

Print ISBN: 978-0-6451624-1-7

Ebook ISBN: 978-0-6451624-0-0

Cover Design by Bailey Designs Books

Edited by Olivia Kalb Editing

Author photo by Rachael Munro Photography

Tinder is brutal.
Wine is forever.

1

AUDREY

I checked my messages as I entered the bar.

Nothing from Will yet, but I was early. Tiff would have scolded me for not being fashionably late, but I'd never been late to anything in thirty-one years, and I was hardly going to start now.

The bar was cute, or it might have been if I could have seen anything past my own hands. Tiff had said dim, but this was more like an 1820's Victorian cellar. The low, two-seater tables flickered with the ambient light of a few battery-operated candles, and the best I could say about the rest of the decor was that it was black. Or looked black in the darkness.

As I waited, I fiddled with my phone. At least scrolling Instagram distracted me from being nervous. I cursed my dress choice as the hem rode up my thighs, and no amount of pulling would keep it in place. My legs looked amazing, though, so that was a plus.

I'd chosen a seat where I could watch the door and threw a glance in that direction whenever I thought Will might have arrived.

I was liking a photo of a pug in a onesie when movement caught my eye. I looked up in time to see a tall man in a dark leather jacket. Maybe it was the confidence that was emanating off him or how the jacket showed off his broad shoulders and strong biceps, but I found myself wishing that it was him I was waiting for.

I shivered as he approached, flattered and a little nervous.

"Can I help you?" I asked.

"I was about to ask you the same thing." The darkness masked his face, but there was no disguising the suggestive tone in his voice.

"Is this where you tell me you can make my dreams come true?"

His voice was velvet smooth, amused by my skeptical response. "I thought we could start with a drink, but it really depends on the type of dreams you've been having. Do you often imagine yourself in an uptight bar surrounded by a dozen strangers?"

Damn, he was kind of funny. Ok.

"Sometimes. Usually, the lighting is better."

His laugh was a shot of warmth in the dark.

There was no way to get a read on his features in this light, not while he was towering above me, but I still felt myself flush under his gaze.

Then, a body slid into the seat next to me. "So sorry I'm late. Traffic was crazy," Will said, leaning in to kiss my cheek.

Strange, traffic had been pretty quiet for me, but I shrugged off his excuse. Hardly enough to be a red flag.

I turned back to where Mr. Tall and Sexy had been only to find he'd already left. Probably off to try that line on someone else. I hid my disappointment.

Will and I made small talk until a server arrived, and Will went ahead and ordered for the both of us. A protest stirred on my tongue, but I bit it back. He was hopefully trying to be chivalrous. It wasn't his fault he didn't know that this was the exact kind of thing Brad used to do.

Talk for me. Speak over me.

The drinks arrived, followed swiftly by a few small plates, and I was pleased to find that the conversation flowed easier tonight than it had at coffee a few days ago.

So far, it was going much better than I had expected. He was the right amount of chatty and flirty. Cute, too. Shaved head, which wasn't normally what I liked since I preferred something I could run my hands through, but it suited him.

After a drink and an amusing story about the time Will went on a road trip with his brother only to be stranded with a flat tire in the middle of nowhere for an afternoon, Will paid the bill, and we wandered out to the street, walking with no particular destination in mind.

It was a balmy night, the summer humidity clinging to my skin, typical for Chicago in July. But it was nice to be out enjoying the night air and the company.

As we rounded a second block, I'd begun to wonder what came next. Was he waiting for me to make a move?

Sure, we'd been flirting tonight, but I was so out of practice.

We continued along in silence before I bit the bullet. "Where do you want to go now?"

He shrugged. "I'm open. What do you want to do?"

Shit. Well, that backfired. "Uh, I could go for another drink. Did you want to find another bar or …?" I hated that I wanted him to make it easier on me. To take the next step so I could know where this was heading. It made me feel like Brad hadn't left my system yet.

"My place is close. We can have a drink there. No pressure."

I considered it. I was having a fun time and wasn't ready to go home yet.

"That sounds nice."

He led me up to his studio apartment. The tiny space was decorated so dully that I found it hard to believe it wasn't a show home. Everything was white, from the walls to the cabinets to the couch. At first glance, there didn't appear to be anything personal.

Finally, I spotted a series of six black and white photographs hanging in matching frames on one wall. One appeared to be a historical image of his building. "This is a cool picture. Where did you find it?"

"Oh, that just came with the apartment. Whole place came furnished when I moved in." He handed me a glass of wine and sat on the far end of the couch, leaving me with a decision to make.

Based on how well the evening had gone so far, I felt good about taking a small leap of faith, and so I took the closest spot on the couch to Will, allowing our bodies to touch knee to hip. His arm came to rest naturally behind my shoulders.

Ok, this was good.

"So ..." he said.

"So."

"I've had a really good time tonight. Most of the people I've met through the app haven't turned out so well."

"Oh really? I only just joined recently, so I don't have anything to compare to."

A finger lightly traced a line on my shoulder, sparking goosebumps along my skin. He leant closer. "You know, I'm a bit surprised that you're single, if I'm completely honest. What made you join the app?"

Oh, God, do I tell him? I didn't want to lie. Firstly, because that's no way to start a potential relationship, and who the hell knew where this would go? Secondly, I was terrible at it. I couldn't maintain eye contact and ended up feeling sick.

Guess it was now or never. "Well, about a year ago, I got out of a long-term relationship that ended pretty badly. Only recently have I been ready to get out there again, so here I am."

"How long were you together for?"

"Almost ten years. We met in college and moved in after we graduated."

He looked shocked, and I couldn't blame him. "Wow, that's a long time. I'm surprised you didn't get married."

Immediately I broke eye contact, and his reaction was physical as he leaned back and moved his arm away from me. "Are you still together?"

Understanding what I'd accidentally suggested, I rushed to reassure him. "No! No, we ... got divorced a year ago." It didn't seem to reassure him at all. Instead, he moved farther away, shifting on the couch even though there wasn't enough space for it. The message was clear; this date had officially gone south.

"Who left who?" His voice was as distant and cold as the rest of him, and I found myself staring at my hands, now awkwardly twisted in my lap. Why would that even matter?

"He left me."

One thing was for sure, I wasn't interested in going over the details, and as Will stood up and crossed the room, it seemed he wasn't either.

"You know, I'm actually pretty tired. Maybe you should ..." Wow. Talk about getting the cold shoulder.

So, after gathering what was left of my self-esteem and my bag, I stood and walked out.

2
AUDREY

As soon as his door closed behind me, I messaged Tiff. No way was I going home to wallow, and I knew she'd want the play-by-play.

I watched the three little dots confirming her reply before they stopped, and she called me. "Right, get your ass over here so we can rip him to shreds over cocktails and ice cream."

I laughed out loud. Tiff was a tough love kind of woman, and I loved her all the more for it.

Fifteen minutes later, she was buzzing me up to her apartment, and when I walked in, she was already preparing a cocktail.

"Tiff, you're off the clock; you don't need to." Even when she wasn't working, she was playing bartender.

A stern look crossed Tiff's angular face, her features as sharp as her tongue. "Fuck off. We're celebrating."

I dropped onto her couch. "Ok. What are we celebrating?"

"That I get the pleasure of your company instead of that loser."

Tiffany poured an amber liquid into two short, thick tumblers that I knew from experience were as heavy as they looked and then added a fat, square ice cube to each. Honestly, I'd never met anyone more born for their job than Tiff. She was not only a fantastic mixologist, but she was a great listener with a directness I appreciated. Working in sales for so many years had given me a keen sense for bullshit, and Tiff was as blunt as they came. There was compassion beneath it, which she'd deny, but I knew her to be loyal and protective.

Her apartment wasn't huge, a converted loft space with a single bedroom and exposed brick. But the open living and kitchen area was cozy, and Tiff had replaced the dining table with a bar cart and liquor cabinet. There was no real rhyme or reason to the decor, lots of brass and copper and bottles, and I knew her couch was scored second hand from an apartment block downtown. But it was comfortable and real, precisely like Tiff. No pretense, no time-wasting. There was nothing in her apartment that wasn't functional. Tiff didn't care for useless trinkets or having anything "just for show" as she said. During the summer, we'd sometimes visit the markets, and she'd spend at least seventy percent of the time complaining about every decorative piece I bought until she came across some antique cocktail shaker, and then she'd be in heaven.

She brought the drinks over and sat next to me on the couch. We mirrored each other with our feet tucked up, and our bodies turned towards each other. As she settled, a strand of her thick, long blonde hair fell into her face, and she brushed it back into position. She'd added a geometric design into the asymmetrical undercut on the left side of her head.

"Your hair looks good."

"Thanks, I just did it today." She traced over the lines, pleased. "The design took forever, but it turned out pretty great in the end." Her glass clinked against mine. "Cheers."

Rich, velvety bourbon spread through me as I took a sip. It was good. Really, really good. Familiar, but not. "Old fashioned?"

"Yep, with a spin. I swapped out the angostura and syrup with creme de cacao and peach bitters. I also tried that new bourbon you gave me."

"The Grumpy Sailor?" The distillery was one of my clients and another reason Tiff and I got along so well. I provided the spirits; she crafted the drinks.

"That's the one. It's got a good flavor profile. I'm telling Harry tomorrow we're adding it to the shelf."

Harry owned The Basement but had done the smart thing and left the running of it to Tiff, who was a one-woman show. I mean, you don't get crowned Chicago's best bartender three years in a row for nothing.

Besides, Harry might have been good with numbers, but he knew shit about drinks. How he came to open a bar was anyone's guess.

I took another sip, recognizing the flavors more clearly now. "It's amazing. As is the company. Thank you for rescuing me from my date."

She waved me off. "It's the least I could do. So, what happened?"

"The divorce happened." I grimaced.

"Brad still fucking things up for you even from the afterlife?"

"He's not dead, Tiff."

She gestured with her drink, voice firm as she spoke. "He's dead to us." After another sip, she asked, "So, he got weird about the divorce?"

"That's putting it mildly. He went from sixty to zero as soon as I mentioned it."

"What an ass."

"I don't know. He genuinely seemed like a nice guy before then. I just wish it didn't matter. That I could be honest and not play any of these dating games." My head dropped back against the couch. "It's so exhausting."

"Amen to that."

"Maybe I should just keep being single. I don't know if I have it in me to date."

"Uh, excuse me, but fuck that. I could go to the bar right now and find at least five guys who would easily sleep with you. One idiot shouldn't turn you off completely." Her smile turned sly. "You know, it's still early. You could see if someone's up for a booty call."

I laughed. "Okay, I've only just started getting out there again. I hardly think I'm ready to be double-dipping in a single night."

"Please, you need to get laid, simple as that. And it wouldn't even be that hard. Sex is easy. It's relationships that are the problem."

As long as I'd known her, Tiff hadn't had a relationship last past a couple of weeks.

I hummed in agreement. "I'm not even thinking about a relationship right now. Work is crazy. It's only been six months since we started, and David's keen for me to launch the new MacMillan rum." I wiped off a line of condensation from the glass. "Did you know it'll be a year next week since the divorce?"

"I remembered." She placed a warm hand on my knee. "How are you feeling?"

"Good," I answered, honestly. "The only thing about it that worries me is if tonight is any indication, it's going to keep me single forever."

"Don't be like that. It was one date."

I scoffed, frustrated by how tonight had gone and my situation in general. "I might as well just buy shares in an adult toy store now. I'm pretty sure no man may touch me again." Tiff barked out a laugh, and I continued. "Which is all I really want. Do you know how long it's been since I've been kissed? I mean, like, really made out. Let alone touched, and God, just forget about being fucked."

I knocked back the last of my drink, then said, "It's all I dream about."

Tiff's voice dripped with disdain. "After ten years with Brad, anyone would feel that way."

I laughed, handing over my drink so she could top me up. "Oh, I'm talking beyond the typical repressed horniness of a sexless marriage. I feel like a teenager in heat half the time. I swear to God, Tiff, I saw a YouTube comment the other day about an actor's long fingers, and my mind went straight into the gutter. I practically had to shut the computer down to stop myself from mentally accosting a man I've never met." I covered my face in my hands as she chuckled.

Tiff bumped my hand with my now refilled drink, still laughing as she sat back down. "Stop being embarrassed. I think it's great you're exploring what you want. Now you just have to find a guy to give it to you." She added a wink for good measure.

Nodding, I knew she was right, but I had no idea where to start. "I just don't ever want to feel like I did with Brad. I finally feel like myself again, you know? I barely even knew who I was after the divorce, and the last thing I want is to lose everything I've built over the last year just to traipse after some guy."

"But …?" Damn, she could read me well.

"But I'm so ready to get laid."

"Atta, girl." She downed the rest of her drink and slapped the glass onto the coffee table before fully turning toward me. "Look, if sex is all you're after, then easy! One-night stands are a dime a dozen. But you can't treat it like you would a normal date."

"Why's that?"

"Because you're not interested in finding out their views on politics or their favorite childhood memory. It's not about long conversations or a deep emotional connection. You're just looking for someone who you're attracted to and who is down for something quick and dirty."

"But what if they're a dick?"

She pinched her lips together. "I so badly want to make the obvious joke here. Look, if they're an ass, you leave. Simple as that. But come on, haven't you ever just seen someone who turned you on and wanted to know what their skin tasted like?"

I remembered the man in the leather jacket and felt heat rise to my face. "Of course, I can name at least ten celebrities right now who top that list."

"Ok, and they're great inspiration for some quality you time, but I'm talking about a purely physical relationship with someone you just met."

"I mean … it's not like I'm opposed to the idea, but I don't know if I'll be any good at it."

"Good?" She shook her head. "Auds, you're thinking about it all wrong. It's not something you're good or bad at; it's just about being upfront. Make sure you tell these guys that you're only after something casual, and they'll pretty much do the rest."

"Really?"

"Usually. But never do anything with anyone you don't want to, always text me where you're going, and don't fuck anyone who doesn't respect you. I don't care how big their dick is. If they don't come prepared, they can go fuck themselves. Literally."

"I don't know …" On the one hand, the idea was exciting. On the other, the reality was terrifying. "I do want to try something new … but where would I even start?"

"Oh, that's easy. I can help with that." Oh God, there was no backing out now, not if Tiff had anything to do with it.

And yet, I couldn't deny the thrill that ran through me, a buzz that went beyond the alcohol.

3

JACKSON

Bryson's voice rang out across the room. "Ok, everyone, take your seats. Let's get started."

I readied myself.

In the center of the room, a series of tables were arranged in a large U shape, with enough seats to accommodate the main cast, a handful of writers and producers, some key people from the network, and Bryson, our show runner.

From my seat, I watched as the rest of the room took their seats, and I smiled across the space at my good friend and co-star Wesley.

Next to me sat Olivia, who played Meira, co-lead and center of the love triangle that was the norm for these types of shows.

Keeping close to the room's edges was a small camera crew and photographer, busy capturing behind-the-scenes footage that would get spliced into the promo stuff. I was sure the show's Twitter account would be trending in under an hour. I'd already been warned that we were expected to participate in more publicity this year.

Liv nudged me in hello while Bryson cleared his throat. "Welcome to the first table read for season three of The Guild." Claps and a light cheer echoed around the table.

Bryson began reading aloud. "Interior. Night. Laying on the ground is Meira, unresponsive. Ares is crouched over her, his bloodied hands cradling her face. Cut to a wide shot of the both of them alone in the darkness. The destroyed house around them is still. Silent."

"We hear a gasp and come back to a tight frame as Meira awakens. They stare into each other's eyes, and Ares smiles, teeth bloody ..." Bryson pointed to Wesley, who then said his line, "You took your time, sweetheart. Thought I was going to have to come down there and get you."

Wes continued, and I sat back, making myself comfortable. Despite being the lead of the show, I didn't have any lines until page ten.

The show was based on a series of extremely successful books and unsurprisingly focused on a love triangle between Wes, Liv, and myself. I played Ryder, a detective with The Guild; Liv was Meira, a witch ingenue I'd rescued in season one from the god Ares, who was played by Wes, villain turned anti-hero over the course of season two. We had gods and magic and ridiculous fights with CGI. We also had the highest ratings of any show on the air right now.

Yes, it was as campy as it sounded. I absolutely loved every minute of it.

The table read stopped and started throughout the morning, allowing the writers to tweak certain lines as they heard them, and we were only a third of the way through before we broke for lunch.

I turned to my left, glad for a chance to finally catch up with Olivia. "Hey, Liv, how are you? Busy summer?"

Liv looked refreshed and relaxed with her honey-colored hair thrown up in a loose bun. She dropped her glasses onto her script and smiled brightly. "Hey! Yes, it was a busy break. I shot a small indie feature up in Toronto last month, then flew out to LA to do the rounds out there. Fit in a trip to Hawaii with some friends. The usual."

"Oh, of course, totally normal activities," I said, sarcastic, and her light laugh chimed throughout the room.

She leaned in conspiratorially. "A little birdy told me you were caught creeping out of another model's hotel last weekend." It didn't surprise me that she'd heard. Gossip traveled fast in this business.

"I'm not one to kiss and tell," I said, but Liv knew me well enough to read into my smirk.

"Unlike Wes," she said, moments before a hand sharply slapped down on my shoulder. "Talking about me already, Liv?" Wes said.

When I stood to hug him, I was freshly reminded of our physical differences—the four extra inches he had on my six-foot frame, his long, lean limbs wrapping around my broader muscular body, and his grown-out black curls contrasting with my short, blonde cut. "Hey, Wes, how are you?"

He looked every bit the devilish rogue the show sold him as. "Great, man! I'm fucking ready, you know?"

"Tell me about it. This season is looking good."

"It really is. Did you see the fight we have in episode three? It'll be nice to kick your ass for once."

"Only in the fakery of TV magic would you ever be able to beat me, so enjoy it while it lasts."

"You wish, man." Wes laughed, clapping me on the shoulder for the second time. "Hey, what are you doing later? We should catch up properly. There's a bar downtown I gotta take you to. It's totally weird, looks like the inside of my grandma's house, but the drinks are killer, and the bartender is hot. Called The Basement."

"Sounds interesting, but I can't tonight. I've got a wardrobe fitting first thing in the morning."

"Next week then. Let me know." And then he was off to chat with one of the film crew, who, from her giggling response, definitely had a crush on him.

Before the break ended, I checked my messages, noting two missed calls. One was from Sarah, my baby sister, and the other from my agent, Terry. I dialed his number without listening to the message.

"J! Glad I caught you. I've got good news; we finally got the offer on that teen movie series. It's a three-picture deal, lead role,

filming in Vancouver next year." Terry's ever-present optimism
wasn't dulled by the phone connection.

"That's great, Terry. Any word on the Michaels script?"

"Not yet, but don't worry, I've got my feelers out there. Are you
free for lunch tomorrow? We can go over this offer."

"I should be. I've got the fitting at eight, but I should be done by
noon."

We arranged to meet for lunch near his office before I was given
the sign that the break was over. I'd have to call Sarah back tonight.

Terry was a great agent, persistent and clever. It helped that he
was a genuinely nice guy on top of that, a rare trait. Plus, he
understood what I wanted, and he was good at pushing me to think
about what I was going to do next. Not that the show wasn't going
great, but it was not going to be around forever.

Having a hit show these days didn't guarantee anything.

I wasn't ignorant enough to think I had the luxury of time in
this industry. Here today, gone tomorrow, was very much a job
hazard.

By the time we finished the reading, I was tired and ready for
home. During the last scene, Wes had texted me "Your fly's
undone". It wasn't, and when I'd looked over to scowl at him, I
knew he'd done it on purpose, as the film crew was directly behind
him, and they'd perked right up when they saw me giving him the
evil eye. Bastard loved pulling shit like this.

From his smug grin, he could tell which finger I'd imagined
giving him.

I only hoped I'd hidden it well enough that I didn't get scolded
by the PR team.

Despite my exhaustion, I loved days like today. The work, the
process, the thrill of another season. Working like this, surrounded
by the creative team, always felt like a real collaborative effort. The
cogs all working together.

That said, I was looking forward to getting home. It probably
wasn't the smartest idea to go to a bar the night before the read. It
hadn't really been worth it; the dim atmosphere made it impossible

to see anything. Which, yes, had the benefit of helping me keep a low profile, but it had made it difficult to catch the eye of anyone who wasn't three feet in front of you.

Still, there had been one woman. A good sense of humour and incredible thighs. Pity her date had rocked up when he had.

4

JACKSON

Once home, I returned Sarah's call, shucking my leather jacket over the back of a chair while it dialed.

"There's my favorite brother," she said. It was Sarah's custom to answer my calls as if we were already in the middle of a conversation. Somehow it made me love her more.

"I'm your only brother."

"That just means I'm obligated to love you. Not to like you."

"And yet you manage it anyway." Her giggle was swift and made me miss her.

There were six years between us, but Sarah and I had always been close. Growing up, our parents both had to work long hours to make ends meet, and I'd taken it upon myself to look after Sarah to help them out, even if Sarah had treated me more like an annoyance than an authority figure. We'd spend hours watching movies and arguing over our favorites. Sarah must have made me watch *Notting Hill* a million times until I finally had to embargo any Julie Roberts or Hugh Grant film for at least six months. Then I repaid the favor by forcing her through a Wesley Snipes marathon.

We'd lost touch a little bit when I'd first started acting. The grueling schedule of audition, audition, audition had left me little time for a life. I felt guilty anytime I wasn't working towards my goal, which meant missing time with my baby sister. Once I'd signed with the show, she had been the first person I'd called, and we'd arranged to meet for brunch every Sunday. It was by far my favorite part of the week.

"How was your first day back?" she asked.

"Good, good. It's good to see everyone, you know. Good to be back."

"Sounds like it's … good." She emphasized the last word, playfully mocking me.

"How did it go with the celebrant?" It was still hard for me to believe that my twenty-three-year-old sister was going to be getting married in two months. Whereas I couldn't remember my last long-term relationship. Or even my last short-term one.

"It was wonderful. He's given us homework to fill out, like questions on our favorite things about each other and stuff, so that he can start putting them in the ceremony. Matt's already stressing about it. He's probably going to have it finished by tonight." Hearing how happy she was made it easier not to worry that she was rushing into this.

"That's great. Dad gave the green light then?" Our father didn't hold too many traditional values, but he stood firm that the father of the bride paid for the wedding. It was sweet, but considering our parents didn't have a lot of money to start with, both Sarah and I had tried to talk him out of it many times.

Needless to say, we hadn't managed it yet.

Of course, that didn't stop me from going behind his back and helping out. It had taken some convincing on my part, but I was earning enough from the show that my own expenses were taken care of, and even if they weren't, I would have made it work so that Sarah could have the wedding she wanted.

This year the cast was planning to ask for a pay raise, and my first act would be to repay Dad all the money he'd spent on the wedding. After all the years he and Mom had spent making sure Sarah and I had what we needed, I wanted to make sure they were able to retire comfortably.

"Only after Mom threatened him," she laughed.

"Whatever works. Hey, so Mom mentioned the dishwasher broke last week. If they need any money, I can—"

Sarah cut me off. "Jace, you know they won't take it. Anyway, it's fine. They already got one of Dad's friends around to fix it. So don't worry."

"Ok, ok," I conceded.

There was a solid beat of silence from her end. "So ..."

Uh oh. I knew exactly what came after that sound. There was only ever one reason Sarah said, "So ..." like that. And it was right before she asked about my love life.

"How is Katie? Or is it Felicity? I can hardly keep up these days." And there it was.

"Sarah ..."

"What?" She said with fake innocence, probably twirling a strand of her shoulder-length bob like she always did.

"Don't start, okay. We've talked about this. I'm not leading anyone on. In fact, I'm very honest about-"

"Only wanting in their pants?"

"That's not how it is at all."

"That's exactly how it is."

"Sarah."

"Okay, okay. Fine." She sighed. "If you want to go whoring around Hollywood, who am I to stop you. Don't even get me started on the fact you've slept with your co-star."

"I don't need to get you started. I've heard all your thoughts on it before, and you'll remember it started and ended over a year ago; we're good friends now."

And a good thing, too. Liv was a nice girl and sexy enough that she'd landed hottest actress titles in most teen magazines. We dated for a short while when we first met on set, but despite her good looks and my respect for her as an actor, it had never worked out between us. And it had nothing to do with the five-year age gap.

I work hard and I love what I do, but I'd never enjoyed talking about work all the time. If I was going to be in a relationship, I wanted someone who brought something different to the conversation. So that pretty much ruled out the cast, the crew, and most of the industry. And was exactly why I preferred one-night stands.

The good thing in my line of work was that casual encounters were business as usual. No one working a full-time TV schedule could commit to anything else unless you managed to be one of the rare couples who could work and date. Too many egos, too many hours together, and depending on the show, too many conflicting emotions. And God forbid the audience didn't like the pairing. The PR team loved the free promotion that came with dating rumors but hated established relationships in case it didn't work out. So, relationships became the exception, not the rule.

Luckily, once the show had taken off, I had no time for a proper relationship, so I'd never had to worry about what I would do if the right person ever came along.

Work was my priority right now, and that suited me just fine.

"I didn't realize you felt so strongly about my virtue," I playfully replied.

"Please. You haven't had any virtue since you were caught with your tongue down Ashley Johnson's throat in middle school. I just … worry, is all."

"What are you worried about?" Only my baby sister would feel the need to worry about me. Our family had a serious case of overprotectiveness. It didn't bother me; I was as bad as the rest of them.

"Jackson, don't you want a girlfriend? In the last five years, I can't remember you seeing anyone for longer than a weekend. Don't you want what Matt and I have?"

"A life sentence?" I joked.

"Come on, be serious."

"Ok, maybe someday I might want to settle down." Someday far, far off in the future. "But I'm happy with the life I have right now. You really don't have to worry; I'm just enjoying myself, safely. Besides, the show keeps me so busy that I barely get a moment to myself, so even if I wanted something serious right now, which I don't, it wouldn't be fair to put someone else through that."

"I know, Jackson. I'm just trying to look out for you."

"I think that's my job, sis."

"Well, you're doing a terrible job," she retorted, making me laugh. "Just … think about it, will you? I've gotta go. I'll see you Sunday. Love you."

"You, too."

I ignored the creak of my spine as I flung myself onto the couch and toed off my shoes. Then I considered Sarah's point. It was true I hadn't dated anyone serious in a long time, but it wasn't because I ultimately didn't want to get serious with someone; I just couldn't see it working right now.

I was extremely busy with the show, especially now that filming was about to begin. Shooting was incredibly unpredictable. We mostly had nights and weekends to ourselves, but it depended on the script and the schedule. One disorganized day could have you filming into the next, and other times we would shoot three episodes back-to-back because a particular guest star was only available for those exact dates, and we needed to get as many scenes filmed with them as possible, meaning the rest of the episodes were filmed out of sequence or weeks later.

It was hard to maintain a relationship when you couldn't make plans too far in advance or had to cancel last minute. It was why most actors dated in-house. They understood the chaotic hours and hectic responsibilities. That you could be in the middle of a romantic dinner, but if your publicist called out of the blue, you damn well better pick up, unless you wanted whatever media shit storm to railroad you without having a game plan.

But, if I was going to be really honest with myself, and I did prefer to be, I was lonely. Sex was great, and I could always find someone to satisfy me, but I wondered what it might be like to see someone for more than one night. To wake up next to them, spend a lazy day together, or come home to them after filming.

The whole 'one-night stand' dance was getting a little old. What I wouldn't, couldn't, admit to Sarah was that she was right. I did want a relationship. I wanted someone to come home to, someone to talk to, someone who made me laugh, supported me, and built me up when I felt like an imposter. I wanted to have someone steady and familiar to anchor me when the press was driving me crazy, someone down to earth but interesting, someone with their own life but who wanted me as much as I wanted them.

I thought of my dad and the life he'd built for my mom and us, and I wanted that for myself. I wanted to be the kind of man he was.

But until I could offer any kind of stability, what sort of partner could I really be? What sort of future could I offer someone?

I sighed, scrubbing at my dry eyes. Where the hell was I going to meet a gorgeous, smart, interesting woman when I spent all my time between sets? And even if that woman existed, would she really want to put up with all of this?

And was I ready for it if I met her?

5

AUDREY

One year.

A whole 365 days since I'd been officially divorced. It almost felt like yesterday that Brad and I had gotten together, and yet I couldn't be further away from the person I'd been then.

We'd met in college. It had been my first time out of my parent's grasp, though even from a distance, they had found ways to hound me over poor grades or my choice to have a life outside of school.

Meeting Brad had been a breath of fresh air. He'd been confident and enthusiastic. I'd enjoyed being attractive to someone who seemed as interested in knowing my mind as they were my body. The sex was decent, too. Much better than the handful of encounters I'd had up to that point.

Although he was always far more ambitious than I ever was, it had been a nice change from my parents' overbearing pressure always to do better. Be better.

Hindsight was a real bastard. Looking back, I saw it for what it was, a sideways move from my parents' hovering judgment to the guilt trips and control of my husband.

The weight that lifted the day the divorce was official was beyond what I could describe. The best I could manage was some clichéd metaphor about light and dark, and there was probably a Katy Perry song about it, but mostly I just felt free.

For the first time in ten years, I had no one but myself to please, and so I did just that. Tiff helped me find a new apartment, and soon after, David had come up with the money to get his start-up off the ground, allowing us both to leave Empire Distributions behind for something more passionate and personal.

I'd just gotten myself comfortable on the couch when Tiff messaged me.

Tiff: Where are you?

I contemplated calling her back before I remembered she was working.

Me: At home, why?

It was a Tuesday night; where else did she think I'd be?

Tiff: You know why. Today is D-Day.

Meaning, divorce day.

Me: I know what today is. I just don't want to make a big deal of it.

Her response came seconds later.

Tiff: Fuck that plan. Come to the bar. Dress very sexy.

Immediately, I knew she was trying to set me up.

Me: Sorry, can't. Tonight's the night I'm having dinner with the president.

In a word, she leaves no room for argument.

Tiff; Reschedule

I groaned to myself, knowing I was going to give in. As comfortable as I was, getting dressed up always boosted my confidence, and frankly, I could use some of that today.

Me: Fine. Be there in 15.

As quickly as I could, I freshened up, skipping the shower in favor of a quick spritz of my favorite perfume. I slipped on the only lace underwear I owned and pulled out a comfortable sleeveless turtleneck dress that hit me mid-calf.

It wasn't what Tiff would call sexy, but it was soft and loose, and I felt good in it. It went back into the wardrobe a minute later when I read Tiff's next message.

Tiff: Put that damn black turtleneck back and wear the slutty red mini I got you for your birthday. Then get your ass here. QUICK.

After slipping into the strappy red dress, I grabbed my purse and headed out the door.

When I arrived, I found the bar predictably quiet. It was only eight p.m. on a Tuesday, after all. A handful of people were scattered around, tucked away in the private booths along the back wall. The main bar was empty save a single man talking politely to Tiff as I approached. His back was turned to me, and the breadth of his shoulders feeling vaguely familiar. He appeared to be my age, with a clean-cut look and sandy blond hair.

I walked to a chair farther down the bar, but Tiff turned her head and motioned to the seat next to him. "It's easier if you sit here, gorgeous." She was using her customer voice, but there was a dangerous glint in her eyes.

Easier, my ass.

Hiding the roll of my eyes behind closed lids, I took the seat next to him and hoped to God I looked casual doing it.

Tiff began mixing me a drink, and I became acutely aware of two things: one, the man beside me smelled incredibly good; smoky and sweet, like a vanilla pod held over a flame; and two, how intimately close we were sitting, making my nerves spike.

I chanced a look at him without fully turning my head. Even from this odd angle, I could tell his looks went beyond just conventionally attractive. Both his sleeves were pushed up, and I cast my eyes down to where his bare forearms were leaning on the bar next to me before tamping down the desire I felt as I admired the strength of his hands. There was a vein flowing from his wrist that I was itching to trace.

Suddenly, I was self-conscious. Tiff's intentions might be good, but even I knew when I was out of my league.

Before he could notice me looking at him, I focused on the drink Tiff had placed in front of me. Crushed ice filled the glass, surrounded by a mottled brown concoction. Of all the things Tiff had put in front of me, this ranked low on the display factor.

My nose wrinkled. "That might be ... the ugliest thing I've ever seen."

One delicately arched brow was raised as Tiff slid the drink closer to me. "Well, you can shut the fuck up because it tastes amazing."

Next to me, the man tried to cover up his laugh with a cough, and I had to stop myself from instinctually turning to him, like a moth to a flame. "The last time you said that, I regretted it."

Tentatively I brought the glass to my nose for an experimental sniff and had to admit I was pleasantly surprised. "Mmm, is that cinnamon?"

She hummed her acknowledgment. "And star anise. It really offsets the gin."

Immediately, I put the drink down and eyed Tiff. "You know how I feel about gin."

From beside me, the man spoke, and there was a teasing note to his voice. "And how is that?"

We both turned towards him. Thankfully, Tiff answered his question. I was too lost in my first direct look at him. Handsome didn't even begin to cover it. Gorgeous, maybe? Beautiful, definitely. The basics registered somewhere in the back of my mind, but it was his eyes that mesmerized me. They were small but kind, emanating warmth and sparkling with undisguised humor. Bright, bold, expressive. So damn expressive. Devilish even. They shined as he met my gaze.

"She can't stand it." Tiff reached forward and moved the drink over to him. "You look like an adventurous man. Care to try something sweet and spicy?" I somehow held back my groan.

Holding my gaze, he took the offered drink and raised the coupe to his lips, giving a small nod to both of us. "Cheers"

His mouth was plush and pink as a fresh rose, like a shade of Mac lipstick I was sure I owned but hadn't worn in years.

When he lowered the glass to lick his lips, I had to avert my eyes.

"That's pretty good. Not what I'd normally drink, but good."

Tiff was unsurprised. "Thanks, I know."

Turning to me, he said, "And she is right, you can't taste the gin at all. You should try it." He held it out to me.

It was tempting, but I had a strong feeling I was going to need my wits about me tonight, and gin was not the way to do that. "Oh, no, thank you."

"Go on, Auds, weren't you just telling me how you want to try new things?" Tiff was not so subtly nodding in his direction. "Come on. I'll make you a fresh one. Or would you prefer something special tonight?"

I know what you think you're doing; I wanted to say to her. But the best I could do with the gorgeous man next to me was glare at her and hope she understood.

From her barely disguised chuckle, I knew she did.

"Just a glass of the prosecco will be fine. Thank you, *Tiffany*." The use of her full name always annoyed her.

She moved gracefully behind the bar to get my drink. "You're lucky I love you, refusing a perfectly good drink like this. But since we're celebrating, I'll allow it."

"What's the occasion?" The man beside me asked.

"Um," I stumbled. Thanks, Tiff. Well, it was nice while it lasted. "It's … an anniversary." My throat tightened. "A year since I got divorced."

"One year since you were free," Tiff corrected me, a glass of prosecco now placed in my hands.

"You're divorced?" He sounded curious, surprised even, but not judgemental. Still, I couldn't help but recall Will's accusing tone from the other night.

Swinging on my seat to face him, I asked, "Are all men scared of a woman who's been in a long relationship before, or are you all expecting us to just wait patiently as virgins until you show up to rescue us?"

Oops. Might have gone too far there. I fully expected him to huff and leave, so I was shocked by his hearty laugh.

I apologized. "Sorry, I shouldn't have said that. I had a bad experience recently."

"Any man scared of a woman with experience isn't worthy of you," he said, sounding genuine. Which was unfair because I knew it was a line, yet it worked on me anyway.

"I'll drink to that," Tiff said, holding up a glass of water. She wouldn't ever drink while she was working, but I appreciated the sentiment. "To freedom."

"To new experiences," the man added with a wink, and I hid my blush by taking a sip of my drink.

"I wish dating were easier," I admitted, repeating the thought I'd had since I decided to put myself out there again.

Tiff leaned against the bar. "I keep telling you. Casual sex is the way to go."

There was movement in my periphery, but I kept my eyes on Tiff. Sarcastically, I responded, "Sure. As long as I don't mention the divorce, I don't have anything to worry about."

Tiff regarded me with a smirk like she knew something I didn't, and then she'd pulled away to attend to a customer at the other end of the bar, leaving the handsome stranger and me alone. My fingers traced the slender stem of the glass before I finally gave in to the urge to look at him again.

That sparkle was still in his eyes as he watched me; a small curl set in the corner of his mouth, the faint indent of a dimple visible beside it. It was new, having someone wait. Having the time to decide what I wanted and the space to act on it. Unfortunately, all my thoughts were fairly singular right now, mostly just a growing list of all the places I wanted to touch him.

Small laugh lines appeared as if he could read my thoughts before he turned pensive. "Can I ask what happened with your ex?"

I sucked in a slow breath. Where did I begin? "The short of it is, we fell in love, we fell out of love. Then he left."

"Any particular reason?"

"Any particular reason you're asking?" I challenged.

Those eyes smoldered. "Just wondering what would make a beautiful woman like you fall out of love." He slowly took a sip of his drink, not breaking eye contact, "I wouldn't want to make the same mistake."

Heat crept up my cheeks, and without really thinking and definitely without meaning to, I gave him the honest to God's truth. "It wasn't working for a long time, but we kept it going even though we were both miserable. Brad wanted someone who could give him more."

"And what did you want?"

His question took me by surprise. I knew the answer, of course, but it wasn't anything I'd allowed myself to voice out loud. My eyes darted over to Tiff, who was far enough away that I knew she couldn't hear us. Quietly, I said, "To be enough."

The power of those eyes hit me hard. They were blue, I could tell now, but it was the force of them, the way he looked at me like I was something precious, something wondrous; it was too much. I turned back to the bar and swallowed another sip of wine to steady my resolve. "What about you?"

"I've never been married."

"Not for you?"

"Not yet. I'm too focused on my career right now and don't have time for a relationship beyond something casual."

"And you enjoy that?" I was genuinely curious.

"Absolutely. I like women, and I like sex, and I've had a lot of both. I know that sounds cocky, but it's true."

"Actually, I find your blatant egotism refreshing."

"Really?"

"God, no." It felt good to laugh this freely. Despite his cockiness, something was disarming about him. I couldn't put my finger on it, but I was drawn in, addicted to his piercing gaze, like he was trying to decipher me. "Although I do like your honesty. If there's one part of dating I hate, it's the half-truths and fake personas everyone puts on to impress. It's exhausting. If casual sex means not having to worry about all that, then sign me up."

He leaned in. "I like it. It's fun to figure out how to get under someone's skin, and even better to get under their clothes." We weren't touching, but the closeness of him was making me light-headed.

"Jesus."

"That's usually what they say."

"Oh, my God."

"That, too."

"Stop, seriously," I said, laughing and pushing him back.

Tiff returned to top up our drinks, and as they talked to each other, I enjoyed a moment to observe him and appreciate how open he was.

That openness was reflected in everything about him. The relaxed outfit, dark jeans and a navy sweater, fit his form to a T but weren't showy. He knew how attractive he was, and while he didn't seem to flaunt it, he absolutely owned it. He was comfortable in his skin, and my hands twitched against where they had been resting between the short hem of my dress to keep it from riding up and hiding the soft curve of my waist. I pulled my hands away with effort and tried to muster up the same confidence that he exuded so effortlessly.

When he caught me admiring, he winked before turning back to Tiffany to finish his point. "It's the kind of TV show where everyone is young and beautiful, and the storylines range from unrealistic to ridiculous. But it's a great crew, and I get paid to act, so I can't complain."

Of course. That explained why he looked like he'd come out of a catalog. "Oh, so you're an actor?"

"Audrey." Tiff sounded scandalized, "Please tell me you're joking. I hate television, and even I know who he is."

Well, now I felt sheepish. "Sorry," I offered to both of them.

"Don't apologize. It's refreshing." He held out his hand, "Jackson Ward. Nice to meet you."

"Audrey Adams." I slipped my hand in his, and if my mind was distracted by desire before, touching him ratcheted it up even further. Now I wasn't just thinking about all the places I wanted to touch him, but all the places I wanted him to touch me.

I cleared my throat. "So, tell me about your job."

He proceeded to describe the banalities of show biz, and I was listening, I was. There were a lot of similarities in our industries. But mostly, I was entranced by the passion he had for his work. Those hands—those hands!—kept jumping into the space between us as he spoke, occasionally brushing against me and setting my skin aflame.

But, by far, his jaw was his most distracting feature. I couldn't help but notice the way the muscles flexed and moved, telegraphing his thoughts even when he wasn't saying a word. I could have lost myself watching them shift and change, studying his face like a sculptor.

"Sounds a lot like my job," I said, hoping that if I kept him talking for a little bit longer, I could figure out the next move.

"How so?"

"It's like performing a mating dance every time I meet a new client, and anytime you see them after that, there are smiles and hugs and 'how is the misses?' But a lot of it is only for show."

"A lot of wank is what it is," Tiff added.

"I mean, it's not that bad," I couldn't help adding defensively.

"Auds, please."

I relented. "Ok, fine, yes, it can be terrible. At a certain level, the niceties aren't real, and if you aren't careful, it can lure you into a false sense of friendship with people, which can backfire big time. But as long as you remember it's a professional relationship, you can avoid problems."

"You're right; that sounds exactly like working on TV." Jackson gestured between Tiff and me. "You two seem to be friends, though? Actual friends, I mean."

"Hard not to be after how we met," Tiff said, and Jackson looked at me, curious.

I felt my ears heat up as I explained. "I caught her naked in the office with the delivery woman. I came back the next day because I still needed some paperwork signed, and she looked like she wanted to fight me—"

"I thought you were going to get me fired," Tiff interjected.

"And I was so afraid of her that I told her with an ass like that, I didn't blame her for wanting to get in their pants."

Jackson's head tipped back as he laughed, and a new wave of heat passed through me.

"And we've been friends ever since."

My smile was wide. "Tiff was the first person I'd ever met who was fearless at being herself. At first, I think I just wanted her to rub off on me."

Tiff leered across the bar. "The storeroom's free, wanna go for it?"

I leveled a look at her. "I'm not fucking you in the storeroom. It's disgusting in there."

Beside me, Jackson coughed out a laugh. Damn, that sound was addictive.

Tiff feigned offense. "Oh, I see, you only have eyes for the pretty boy now, do you?" She cocked a brow.

Embarrassed, I cleared my throat. "Don't you have something to clean?"

Tiff's giggle and wink as she walked away did not go unnoticed but were quickly overshadowed by the deeply interested look Jackson was sending me.

It left me unmoored.

His hair, almost brown in this dark light, fell in a disgustingly charming way. I imagined I wasn't the first to picture how soft it would be between my fingers, which pushed other images into my mind, of both gentle and filthy measures.

Again, it seemed from the gleam in his eyes that he could guess where my thoughts were. "You two seem pretty close, are you …?"

"No," I assured him. "No. Tiff is bi, but I'm not, and she might like to make jokes, but we'd never …"

"And do you have eyes for … what did she call me?" He was teasing, feigning innocence, but wow, that mischievous glint in his eyes made me want to kiss the grin right off his face.

"Pretty boy?"

"Right. So do you?"

Beneath the litany of nerves, a spark flickered on in me. An urge to be bold. Maybe it was adrenaline. It was so unlike anything I'd experienced before. And here was my chance, right? To have that night of casual sex that I'd been wanting?

A thousand tingles scattered across my skin as his hand brushed against my arm. Maybe I'd be embarrassed tomorrow, but right now, I wanted to get out of my head and take a chance.

To new adventures, right?

I slid off the stool before I could talk myself out of it and moved into the space between his thighs. From a place of confidence I may never have again, I placed one hand at his knee and lightly trailed my palm up his thigh. Just far enough to watch his eyes darken with hunger. At this distance, I knew the exact moment they flickered down to my lips. The fact that I was having this effect on him made me heady with desire.

"My place is nearby," I said.

I hadn't answered his question. Hell, I barely remembered what it was at this point, but those four words had been chanting through my head for the last twenty minutes or so, and now that it had left my mouth, I was mostly just relieved I'd had the guts to say it out loud.

He covered my hand with his own and leaned in, his breath warm against my cheek, and I knew he noticed my shiver in response. "Lead the way."

6

AUDREY

Holy shit, this was happening. Okay, I could do this.

I threw a look over my shoulder at Tiff, who was already waving us out with a smirk. Yeah, she was going to be all over this tomorrow.

Thankfully, my place was ridiculously close to the bar, as in, two blocks, around the corner close. Jackson's hand practically seared a brand over my lower back; our bodies walked so closely together that I was hyper-aware of every scant inch between us. I couldn't think about anything else.

I barely remembered getting from the bar to my place, so caught up in my thoughts. I couldn't believe I'd just asked this stunning man to come home with me, and he'd said yes. As I opened my front door, my nerves kicked in.

Was I really about to do this? Was it too late to back out?

I mean, I didn't want to, not really. But this was crazy, right? I'd never done this before. I barely knew anything about him. He followed me into the apartment before turning to face me, frozen in place against the entryway wall. Now that the moment was here, I was at a loss. Did we just go for it? Damn, I was so unprepared.

My nerves must have been written all over my face because

Jackson gently closed the distance between us until our lips were only inches apart.

Jesus, he smelled incredible. Decadent and smoky, like an illicit treat. I might pass out before we even did anything. Oh. His lips looked fantastic, and I wondered what it would feel like to taste them. I bit my lip, anticipating.

My breath hitched as I gazed into his eyes, and every inch of my skin tingled. Why had I even thought about backing out of this? My thoughts chanted loudly, 'kiss me kiss me kiss me' as though I was hoping they would somehow telegraph themselves to him.

"Can I kiss you?" His voice was soft. Nothing had ever sounded so good.

"Yes." Please.

And, wow. Jackson's lips were better than I had imagined. Was kissing always this incredible and I'd forgotten? I couldn't remember any other kiss making me feel so blissed out. His lips moved confidently against my own, and I leaned into him, tentatively exploring with my tongue.

I was rewarded with a low moan, and oh, I wanted to hear that sound again and again.

Soft kisses traveled across my cheek to my neck, and then I was having an out-of-body experience as he began to nip and suck at the sensitive skin.

Holy hell.

My fingers curled against his shirt, and my head fell back against the wall behind me while his hands grazed my ribs, brushing along the outline of my breasts.

His lips brushed my neck as he asked, "Is this ok?"

My thoughts were a haze of feeling and lust, but I managed a shaky nod, my heart racing as fast as my mind was. I took a deep breath in a futile effort to calm both.

Pulling back enough to make eye contact with me, he waited, his eyes questioning. A swell of gratitude threatened to engulf me. He wanted to make sure. Who was this man?

I wanted him more than I'd wanted anyone else before.

I nodded again, more controlled this time, arching into him as I said, "It's more than ok."

The hunger in his eyes sent a shiver of anticipation through me, and then his hands were reaching below my hips, gripping the backs of my thighs and picking me up, guiding my legs until they wrapped around him. And, wow. That had never happened to me before, but damn, did I like it.

I moaned faintly, "Oh." The sound left my lips before I realized it. All I could think was that I really wanted him to press me into the wall right now, crowd me between the cool surface and his smooth, hard warmth. But I couldn't bring myself to say the words. I could barely think. Jackson had replaced every thought.

His chuckle was a deep rumble, and I was sure he was about to tease me, so I cut him off with a kiss. Wrapping my arms around his neck, I tangled my hands in his hair. The same hair I had been itching to touch earlier, and I was pleased to find it as soft as I imagined it.

My moan was lost between our mouths.

7

JACKSON

I relished the feel of her body wrapped around me as I picked her up. The hem of her dress slid farther up her thighs, and I felt the material shifting under my fingers, which ached to free her supple skin.

Thankfully, the wall kept us both steady because the sexy sounds escaping her drove me crazy. I would love to have her like this, and from the way she clutched and ground against me, she wanted it. It wouldn't take much to undo my jeans and ease into her, but I wanted something else right now. I wanted to see what other sounds I could get out of her. I wanted to touch and taste all the beautiful skin that had been teasing me all night.

I needed to see the full extent of the lacy bra that had been driving me wild since she had first sat down next to me.

My hands gripped her thighs, and dear God, I needed a second to enjoy the feel of the firm muscle. I imagined running my tongue along the inside of her thigh as I breathed in her sweet scent.

As if she sensed where my thoughts were, her legs tightened around me, and I moaned as she ground against my hardening cock.

Fuck, I really needed to take this to the bedroom; otherwise, we wouldn't make it out of this hallway. And I really wanted to get naked.

I pulled us away from the entryway wall and walked forward toward the open living area. It was light enough that I could make out the shape of the couch but too dark to make out much more.

She hadn't had time to turn the lights on when we'd entered the apartment, and I snuck a look around while stopped in the middle of the room, trying to decide whether to use the couch. It looked comfortable enough, but the thought of it irked me.

So that left me with one option.

"Um," I pulled back and chided myself for feeling remotely nervous. "Which way is the bedroom?"

Audrey, looking kiss drunk, considered the question. She relaxed her legs, making it clear she wanted to get down. "Right! Sorry." She sounded bashful, and it only made her more attractive.

I set her down, and she took my hand, "This way." When we reached the bedroom door, she looked back at me, her eyes gleaming with playful intent. Here, again, was another view into this hidden side of her, seductive and exciting. I wondered if she even knew she was doing it.

Her nerves were back in force when she reached the bed and sat down on the edge. She eyed my body hungrily but didn't quite meet my gaze. I watched as her fingers absentmindedly trailed the hem at her thighs, dipping under the fabric to stroke her skin.

Fuck, she was sexy.

I licked my lips, and her eyes jumped up to meet mine, sparkling in the low light. Usually, I wouldn't have waited, but I wanted to take my time, enjoy her reactions. She seemed caught in the middle of herself—half the time, she was patient, waiting for me to take control; and the other half, she was a live wire, primal and demanding. I honestly didn't know which I liked more, but not knowing what to expect from her had me more worked up than I'd ever been before.

I could spend hours just taking this woman apart, and God, I wanted to.

I brought my hand up to my chest and ran it down my shirt; her eyes followed the movement. I grabbed the material of my sweater and hoisted it over my head, leaving me shirtless before her.

She averted her gaze, dropping it to my crotch, her bottom lip caught in her teeth. I was straining against the material. I'd meant to tease her, and sure, it was working, but I felt she was having more of an effect on me than the other way around. And she hadn't even touched me yet.

I stripped off my pants and underwear, enjoying the way her breath hitched at my nakedness. Then she surprised me again by giving me a wicked look as she undid the zip of her dress, standing briefly to let it fall to the floor.

Unbelievable. One minute, she was nervous, and the next, she was commanding. I was captivated.

That same lacy bra that had tormented me earlier looked as enticing as I imagined. "Beautiful," I told her because it was true.

She said nothing, covering herself with her hands. That wouldn't do. Before she could get too self-conscious, I slipped my arms around her waist and lowered her onto the bed, kissing her thoroughly.

She relaxed underneath me, and I became addicted to the sounds of her whimpers. I needed to do whatever I could to keep her making them. I wanted to make her feel as good as possible.

Breaking the kiss, I asked. "Tell me what you like."

"Um …"

There was a long pause. I felt her fingertips softly stroke my shoulder. "We can stop," I offered, in case she was having second thoughts.

This time her response was immediate. "No." A soft smile played on those perfect lips, and I wanted to kiss her nerves away.

"How about this, I'll do something, and you tell me if you like it or not."

She bit on her lip as she nodded. "Ok." That breathy answer washed over me. I'd bet she didn't even realize how sexy she was right now. She could ask me to do just about anything, and I'd do it. Give her whatever she needs.

Kissing her, I pulled that same lip between my teeth, and she rewarded me with a moan. Ok, she liked that. Trailing kisses across her cheek, I tried the same on her neck, just below her jaw, sucking a kiss before I lightly scraped my teeth against the reddened skin. She arched into me, exposing more of her neck.

She definitely liked that.

Nuzzling into her, I breathed her in and followed the smooth line of her neck with my lips. Curious, I bit into the mark with a little more pressure.

"Good?"

"Mm-hmm." She nodded.

"So, I should keep going?" I teased.

"Please."

With her back arched, I unclasped her bra, then trailed my fingers lightly down her arms as I removed it, feeling goosebumps flare across her skin. She was so responsive. I couldn't help but wonder if she wasn't able to tell me what she liked because she didn't know or because she was scared to say.

"You know you can tell me to stop anytime."

"Ok."

I lifted my head, holding her gaze, "I mean it. You don't like something, you tell me."

"I promise. Can you …" She swallowed and licked her lips, drawing my attention there. They were already red and swollen. "Can you do that again? With your teeth?"

A low growl left me. She was going to kill me slowly.

"Like this?" I repeated the action and delighted in the reaction it elicited. She was getting louder, more confident in her responses.

"Yes." The word disappeared into a hiss.

Her skin tasted clean and sweet, unbearably soft everywhere. I kissed along her neck to her chest, marveling again at the swell of her breasts as my hand came up to cup them. I stopped short of touching my lips to her skin and peered up, waiting for her to meet my eyes. When she did, I held her gaze and slowly circled my tongue around her nipple, continuing with licks and kisses while it peaked.

There was a momentary pinch of her brow, gone before I really noticed it, but I could guess what it meant. I wanted her to say it, though. I wanted her to know that she could—she should—tell me when she didn't like something.

Lifting my head again, I arched a brow in question, watching as she fought to get the words out. But I was a patient man, and I'd stay here all night if I needed to. Not that it would be that hard of a sacrifice.

Eventually, she said, "They're not very sensitive." Adding, "My nipples." Then, "It doesn't really do anything for me."

It came out in a rush, and she looked apologetic, even though she absolutely shouldn't be. My smile widened, and I repositioned myself a little lower, kissing below her breast. "Good to know." I nipped at the soft swell of her stomach, feeling ravenous for her. "What else?"

Her voice was a whisper. "I, um, I like what you're doing."

"Mmm, I can tell." After leaving another mark by her navel, I surged up and met her lips with mine.

She was incredible.

Her nails dug into my back, gripping at me as she moaned.

She turned her head to kiss me passionately then surprised me by running her nails along my back, ratcheting up the fire racing through my veins. Did I mention this woman was incredible? I'd been with women who were shy in bed and women who weren't, but none seemed to go between the two states the way Audrey did. And it was really working for me.

Anytime I thought I had her under my spell, she turned the tables and had me under hers.

Her lips were intoxicating, her tongue swirling against mine and filling my mind with filthy fantasies. If the way she sucked on my lower lip was any indication, I wasn't going to be disappointed with her if and when she got her mouth on me.

Kissing down her body, I slowed as I settled between her legs, taking a moment to settle myself as well.

I kissed along her inner thigh, as soft as I'd imagined it earlier, pausing when I reached her center, and I teased her by letting out a long warm breath against the thin material.

I buried my nose against the fabric and breathed her in.

Rewarded with a shuddered plea, I basked in the view of her breasts as they rose with her heavy breaths, her eyes fiery with lust. My smile widened.

"I wish you could see how gorgeous you look right now," I said, kissing the inside of her thigh.

Her face turned against the pillow; her quiet words almost lost. "Thank you."

I couldn't understand how someone so clearly stunning could ever be shy in hearing it. Surely she had heard this before? Or had that asshat of an ex-husband lowered her self-image?

"You really are. So fucking gorgeous." I kept my eyes on her face as I trailed a finger along the damp trail on her underwear, earning me a moan and a wiggle of her hips. My hips ground against the mattress, urgent for some friction.

"I bet your pussy is just as beautiful." I lowered my head until my mouth hovered over her, our eyes locked. "I wonder if it will taste as good as the rest of you?" Without waiting, I ran my tongue along the seam of her panties.

"Jackson." My name came out as half breath, half moan.

"Yes?" I ran my fingers up the back of her calves, teasing her.

"Please."

"Hmm?" I smirked as I raised up, waiting.

She growled. Fucking growled. One of her hands found its way into my hair, gripping the strands, and I couldn't have gotten harder if I tried. She was definitely going to kill me.

And it would be a sweet, sweet death.

"I want you to …"

Her eyes closed as she took a deep breath. I reached up and ran a thumb over her hand, offering some support.

"I want your mouth on me. I want you to make me come."

Nothing had ever sounded sweeter or had me harder. I hooked a finger under the band of the lace and pulled.

Once removed, I slowly slid my hands from her ankles to her waist, enjoying the way she writhed under my touch as I settled back between her thighs.

"You're so fucking sexy." I trailed my fingers along her lips, humming in approval of how wet she was already.

She moaned above me, and I couldn't wait any longer to taste her. My grip firm against her thighs, I slowly lapped at her, sucking and keeping pace as she rocked her hips towards me, seeking out more.

Her fingers brushed through my hair tenderly, in stark contrast to her other hand, which was braced on the top of her thigh, nails scraping over her skin. I grasped her hand in mine, linking our fingers together on the sheets, my other palm holding her hips down as she bucked against my lips.

8

JACKSON

After she came, I crawled back up the bed to lie beside her, still hard but not in any great hurry to deal with it. I liked these moments between, watching as their breathing came back to normal, the glazed-over look in their eyes, the flush of their skin.

It was always interesting to see what they did next. Some women jumped to reciprocate, others went straight for sex, and one even tried a half-hearted hand job. I was curious to see what Audrey did.

Her head turned toward me on the pillow, eyes blown wide and lips plump and dark from where she bit them to keep from screaming. She was insanely alluring like this. I watched as her eyes traveled down my body to where I was hard and waiting, and a wicked grin spread across her face.

My cock jerked at the sight of it.

Despite our previous activities, she hesitated before touching me, her fingers skittering across my chest before landing on my right nipple. She began to tease it, first watching how my body reacted before looking up for confirmation that I was interested.

"Feels good," I reassured her. "You can use your tongue if you want."

She does, tentative touches like she hasn't done this before, or maybe in a long time. It made me wonder how long it had been since she'd been with somebody.

I guided her head up so I could look her in the eyes. "You feel amazing."

She lit up and surged forward to kiss me again, all the previous caution gone.

As the kiss deepened, she crawled fully onto me, a leg sliding over my thigh and brushing against my leaking cock. I felt her wetness against my skin, and it was fucking glorious. My head fell back against the pillow as I groaned.

She started sucking little open mouth kisses on the underside of my jaw, and I clutched at her hips, maneuvering her until she was on top of me. This time she pulled back, blinking at me while her breath escaped in quick soft puffs against my skin.

She was holding back or nervous, which wasn't good. I took charge, rolling us over, so I was on top, her legs falling open around my hips. I rested on my elbows to keep most of my weight off of her.

As quickly as I could, I grabbed the condom out of my pants and put it on before I returned to the bed. Her hands pulled at me greedily. It wasn't an effort to comply.

My head fell forward in a mix of pleasure and disbelief at how wet she was. It was an easy slide into her, and it took considerable effort to slow down. I wanted to last.

"Ok?" I asked because I needed to know.

Her urgent nod was accompanied by a drawn-out moan, encouraging me. To ensure I'd gotten the message, she wrapped her legs around me, digging her heels in to urge me forward. This woman was glorious.

Taking the hint, I pushed in all the way, reveling in the feel of her around me. There was hardly anywhere we weren't touching, yet I wanted more.

As I moved inside of her, her eyes fluttered closed. She bared her neck as she arched into me, pulling me closer. I buried my nose into the juncture between neck and shoulder, nipping at the heated skin.

She was gripping me. From her arms to her thighs to her sweet center, I was trapped, and it was fucking incredible.

Sweat started to collect between us, the sounds of our bodies moving against each other accompanying the rough chorus of our panting.

I was moving faster now. Pleasure building in my gut. Pulsing within me.

She was unwinding beneath me, head tossed back, taking and giving in equal measure.

My thoughts were frantic. They slipped past my tongue as quickly as they occurred to me. "Feel so good. So sexy. You don't even know, do you?"

Her breath was coming in gasps. In. Out. Quick. Shallow. She trembled beneath me. Powerful. Precious.

She tapped at my shoulder. Tried to speak through her whimpers.

I slowed, allowing her to catch her breath. Tried to catch my own.

"Can we?" Her head tipped back against the pillow. Licked her lips. "Can we take a break?"

"Of course." There was a bead of sweat collected at her collarbone, and I gently kissed it away, tasting the salty sweetness of her skin before I pushed up and fell beside her on the bed. There was a lingering shakiness in my thighs. Seemed I could use a break myself.

Her voice was barely above a whisper, but her gratitude was undeniable. "Thank you."

Turning onto my side, I let my eyes take in her naked body. Her chest quickly rose as she took in deep breaths, and her skin was flushed from the waist up. Lips red and swollen. Barely parted. Tongue reaching out to wet them. She was stunning.

The room was hot, sweat coating my temple, abs, thighs. "Would you like a glass of water?"

She nodded slow, half dazed. I stole one more kiss and then made my way into the kitchen. The first glass I quickly downed myself before refilling the glass and heading back into her bedroom.

One arm was thrown above her head, wiping the sweat from her brow, and one leg was bent, resting on the bed. She looked blissed out, and I swelled with pride, knowing I was the cause.

"Here." I slid into the bed, back against the wall, and she sat up next to me to take the glass, which she drank quickly, moaning her appreciation. I couldn't help but smile.

Even if we didn't do anything else, this might be one of the more enjoyable evenings I'd spent with a woman.

She finished drinking and placed the glass on the nightstand, taking a silent moment to breathe. "I can't believe you're in my bed right now," she said, her voice just above a whisper.

"I think I'm insulted." I chuckle.

"No, that wasn't …" She ducked her head, shy. "I don't normally get this lucky."

I discarded the joke that immediately came to mind and decided to be sincere. "I think I'm the lucky one."

"Ok." She laughed, blushing deeper. "You've already gotten me naked; you don't need to charm me."

"I'm just being honest, but I like that you think I'm charming."

She laughed and made herself more comfortable beside me, sliding down until her head hit the pillow. I watched as she trailed a hand along my thigh, mirroring the movement from the bar earlier tonight, with blatant appreciation in her gaze.

I flexed my thigh as her hand passed and chuckled as she momentarily jolted before firmly gripping the muscle and testing the feel of it. She moaned at the resistance, and God help me; the sound went straight to my cock.

Aware that she might still need to catch her breath, I slid down, laying on my side beside her, and pulled her in for a kiss. She deepened it immediately, her tongue exploring my mouth, and I gently pulled her in towards me. Our legs tangled, my thigh slipping between her legs, and she gasped as it brushed against her.

I took my time, just like this, trading kisses and touching her until she was underneath me again, thighs spread, and begging me, "Please."

It took all of my control not to grab her and fuck her until she was screaming my name.

Instead, I forced myself to slow down, even though I felt my orgasm building as I entered her again, her pussy spasming around me so tightly that I cursed into her shoulder.

As if knowing I needed the distraction, she pulled my head up and kissed me until I could barely remember my name and tilted her hips to get me to move.

So I did, encouraged by her enthusiasm. I gripped her waist, her hips, her ass. She met every thrust, welcoming me deeper, harder. And when she snuck a hand between us to circle her clit, I was undone; the sounds of her pleasure pushing me over into my release.

———

I COULDN'T TELL how much time had passed when I finally slid out of her bed, picking up my clothes and dressing in the near dark of the room. Audrey was sleeping, curled on her side, disheveled yet peaceful.

This certainly wasn't how I was expecting my night to go when I entered the bar, curious after Wes' comments earlier in the week.

Not that I was complaining.

To be honest, I was a little intoxicated by her.

I wasn't going to lie. I'd built up a healthy confidence in my skills. Many women had been satisfied, but there was something thrilling tonight about pleasing Audrey. Exploring her, discovering what she liked, coaxing reactions out of her when she seemed to be holding back, then being rewarded by all those little gasps and moans when I hit the right spot.

It was a huge boost to my ego. But more than that.

It had been fun.

And she was ... Unexpected. Mostly quiet. Tentative. Waiting to be lead, or maybe just expecting to be. Then those moments where she surprised me. Fire in her eyes and an underlying strength in her body. Like a lioness in wait.

Suddenly, I wished I had more time. I wanted to take hours to map out her body, wrapped up together with nowhere else to be.

But that wasn't what this was.

Once dressed, I paused, torn by indecision. I'd done this a hundred times but now felt guilty at the idea of leaving without saying goodbye.

My wallet, phone, and keys were tucked in my pockets. There was no reason I was still here. All I had to do was leave.

I winced as I looked at the time. I had to be on set in five hours. Today was going to be exhausting, yet I couldn't bring myself to be mad about it. In fact, I was probably more annoyed at the idea of leaving than the inevitable fatigue that would set in.

With a sigh and burying the nagging thought that I'd likely regret it, I tiptoed out of the apartment.

9

AUDREY

Jackson was gone when I woke up, and if it hadn't been for the slight ache in my body and the sight of my clothes strewn all over the floor of my bedroom, I would've wondered if I hadn't just had some incredible fever dream. I rolled over and buried my face in my pillow, breathing in deep, the smile on my face widening. I couldn't believe I'd had a one-night stand; wait, no, scratch that, that wasn't the part I was in awe of; I couldn't believe I had just had the most mind-bending sex of my life with a complete stranger. Who was I?

I laughed, feeling delirious. He'd … And I'd … Wow.

Remembering what had happened only served to make me smile more. Ok, now I could see what Tiff was talking about. That was incredible. Indescribable. Was it like this every time? Why hadn't I been doing this all along? Or maybe the better question was, why had I stayed miserable with Brad for so long and missed out on this?

A small voice reminded me that it probably had more to do with Jackson himself; that sex with everyone was unlikely to be this good; that Jackson had been incredible in a way beyond just sex. He'd been patient, and he hadn't grumbled or made me feel bad when I'd needed a break. He'd made me feel like I was beautiful, treasured. It made me want to believe it.

It made me want more.

I jumped into the shower, a little regretful that I had to wash away the memories of last night but not wanting to walk into work smelling of sex. Smelling of him. I buried my nose in my shoulder, hoping for some lingering memory, but all I could smell now was my lavender body wash. Oh well, I still had the memories. And boy, was I going to be replaying them as often as possible. I could barely wait to tell Tiff about it. I resolved to text her to confirm her schedule so I could head over after work if she were free.

Dressing, I spotted my discarded lingerie on the floor and remembered his reaction to the lace. I opened my underwear drawer to assess the situation.

When was the last time I bought something that wasn't plain and practical?

As I took in the collection of comfortable cotton pieces, I realized I'd forgotten how good it was to wear something for myself. To see myself as sexy.

I'd have to go shopping.

Later that morning, I couldn't keep the smile off my face as I entered the office. As usual, I beat the rest of our small team by thirty minutes. And, as usual, David was already there.

It was my first favorite thing about working here: having a boss as passionate as David. The second was the space itself. There were only a dozen of us in total, so the office wasn't large by anyone's standards, but we made the most of it. David had sourced local artists for photographs and artwork of the city, a celebration of all things Chicago, which built on his, or I should say our, mission statement of supporting local vendors.

I rapped my knuckles on his open door, smiling at the picture he made; chin in hand, brow furrowed in concentration, the bright colors of his Hawaiian shirt utterly ruining any sort of seriousness that he might otherwise have hoped for.

David looked up from his laptop to greet me. "Morning, kiddo."

Even my dad never called me that. But I'd never minded with

David. In the last two years of working for him, I'd come to respect him greatly. He'd been the only part of working at Empire Distributions that hadn't made my soul want to shrivel up, and when he'd asked me to join him here at Bespoke Beverages, I'd said yes without hesitation.

"Morning, David." I made myself comfortable in one of the two armchairs facing his desk, noting how his beard was almost completely silver now, though still trimmed and groomed to perfection.

He shut his laptop and clasped his hands over it. "Ready for today?"

I nodded. "Absolutely. I just wanted to come in and run through the notes again before I head out."

"Good. Before you go, I wanted to let you know I'm in the process of getting us some help." He looked serious. Too serious.

"That's great. I know how busy you've been."

"How busy we've *all* been," he said, catching me with a shrewd look over the top of his glasses, looking even more like a concerned dad. "You know how much I've appreciated your efforts over the last six months, but you don't—"

"Need to work so hard. I remember." He was a broken record at this point.

"Which is why I'm getting us some help. It won't be much, but we're in a good enough position to lighten the load a bit."

"David, I think that's great. The team has been working hard, and I know they'll like having another set of hands around. But don't worry about me. I can handle it." I could, and I would.

Hoping to derail any further comment from him, I stood and asked, "Can I get you a coffee from next door? My treat."

"Thanks." He scratched his beard. "My usual."

I winced. His usual was laden with cream and syrups. "I still don't know how Nicky lets you drink that stuff. Isn't it sacrilegious?" I couldn't understand how someone married to an Italian drank coffee like that.

"What my husband doesn't know won't hurt him. Now get." He

waved me out the door. "And don't forget to get a receipt," he called out as I left, laughing.

———

THE DRIVE OUT to Westchester always made me happy.

The warehouse stood on the corner block like an old guard dog, imposing in size but calm and comforting in its protection. The building was a stalwart of the area, part of the rich history from the builders who had made this town what it was.

Jeff MacMillan was no different.

The MacMillan Distillery was our biggest client and the first one we'd landed after leaving Empire. A small-scale distillery specializing in rum, it was exactly the kind of place David and I wanted to focus on at Bespoke Beverages—local, with a focus on flavor and creativity.

Jeff and Julie MacMillan were an energetic couple in their late fifties. Jeff had been a carpenter in his previous life but a lover of liquor for longer. After Julie suffered a health scare ten years prior, he'd decided to stop waiting and finally do something he loved.

A sentiment I could get behind.

I smiled as I stepped into the open warehouse, the air filled with the smell of oak and yeast.

"Audrey! You're here!" Julie's voice called out across the floor as she moved towards me, catching me in a tight hug.

I really loved my job.

"Julie, how are you?"

"Wonderful. Thank you again for coming all the way out here to see us." She said as if a twenty-minute car ride from the city was a burden.

"Of course, you know I wouldn't make you and Jeff trek into the city. And I like the drive." Jeff had made it abundantly clear he hated the city, which meant meetings were onsite instead of the office.

"How you put up with all that I'll never know, but we do

appreciate it. Now come, can I get you a drink?" She herded me into the small office tucked in the back, Jeff nowhere to be seen.

"Yes, thank you. Just some water."

"Alright. I'll go find Jeff while I'm at it." She flashed me another warm smile, then journeyed back to the warehouse, calling out to Jeff to "get your ass in the office."

I snorted a laugh in the empty room, then set myself up in a visitor's chair with my laptop ready.

Jeff hurried into the office moments later, sweaty and out of breath. "Miss Adams, good to see you again." Jeff dropped unceremoniously into the chair behind the desk and looked at me expectantly.

"You, too, Mr. MacMillan." We sat in mildly awkward silence as we waited for Julie to return.

Thankfully, the wait was short. "Here you go, hun." I nodded in thanks as I took the glass of water from Julie and waited as she made herself comfortable before beginning. I was here with a proposal, after all.

"So firstly, thank you for letting me come by today. I know how busy you both are, so I won't take up too much of your time. We've talked previously about expanding distribution and how we might promote the new style."

"The dark, yes. It should be ready for transfer from the casks in a few weeks, all things considered."

"Fantastic. I can't wait to try some. Now, I've already started talking to customers and bars that I know will be a good fit for the new style, but I wanted to suggest a launch event. Something small and tasteful with a mixed guest list of industry professionals and general patrons. It would be a way to build up the brand and generate some good word of mouth. But it would have to be self-funded, and I would need your go-ahead."

I watched as Jeff considered this, then shared a look with Julie that I was too nervous to decipher. It wasn't dismissive, but it wasn't overly enthusiastic either.

"And how much is this going to cost us?" Jeff asked.

Ah. I knew this would be the sticking point. Luckily, I'd come prepared, and I moved to place my laptop on the desk, facing them. "Well, that is entirely up to you. I have some examples here of some events I've prepared in the past with itemized budgets so you can see what's possible." I paused, giving them a moment to scan the details on the screen. "If you agree, then you tell me what the budget is, and I'll work within that."

Jeff sighed, looking conflicted. "If you think it will help in some way, then I'll consider it, but I'll need to know more before we can make a decision."

I nodded with understanding, already filing away some initial ideas that might work.

He continued, sounding apologetic about his reticence. "I can't deny I'm nervous about this, but I guess we need to trust that you and David know what you're doing. Say what, send me this," he pointed to the screen, "so we can look it over, and we'll get back to you."

———

MY ADRENALINE RAN out in the early evening, and I surprised myself by clocking out at six p.m., hours earlier than usual since we'd started the company.

Part of the problem was proximity. My apartment was walking distance from the office, and the area wasn't prone to dangerous encounters, so I could work as late as I wanted and be home in the same amount of time it used to take me to get to the station.

Really the problem was a severe perfectionist streak that meant I found myself working more than was probably wise.

So it was a novelty to leave work before the sun had set.

I headed straight from the office to Tiff's apartment, knowing she would be eager to get the details about my time with Jackson.

Actually, knowing Tiff, she was more than likely dying to tell me, "I told you so," since she'd practically engineered the whole thing, but I didn't care. I'd had the best night of my life, and she could take the damn credit.

"Normally. I'm more of a parade girl, but I'll settle for a national holiday," she said by way of hello as she opened the door.

"Ok, yes, get it all out now. You were—"

"Right? Fantastic? The best wing woman ever?" she said, thrilled.

I wanted to roll my eyes, but I couldn't. Not with the shit-eating grin that took over my face.

Tiff actually looked impressed. "That good, huh?"

"Incredible," I answered.

"I do know how to pick 'em."

I shrugged off my blazer and draped it over my bag before dropping onto her couch. It may have been sourced off a street corner, but the thing was insanely comfortable. I did not want to think too hard about why that was. "Yes, thank you. I would never have even left the house if you hadn't invited me."

"I know."

"And I wouldn't have even met him if you hadn't forced me to sit next to him and been so annoying trying to get us to talk to each other."

"I know."

"And I probably would have left without him if you hadn't—"

"Audrey, I know!" she grumbled. "I take it back. I don't want the parade anymore." For all of Tiff's swagger, she actually didn't enjoy people heaping too much attention on her. It was one of her most endearing qualities and a big part of why I loved her. She was confident enough in herself not to need anyone else's validation.

"Good, because that's all the credit I'm giving you."

"Now tell me everything. How big was he? I'm guessing above average."

"Oh my, God, I'm not telling you that!" I paused. "What's average anyway?"

Tiff lost her breath laughing.

10

JACKSON

I was an idiot. Two weeks had gone by, and I was still thinking about Audrey.

It wasn't unusual to think fondly of a woman I'd slept with, but this felt different. I felt compelled to see her again.

I'd thought about that night endlessly, and while I normally wouldn't pursue something beyond a single night, I hoped there could be a middle ground between the one-night stands I'd had and the "forever" that I should probably start aiming for. Especially since Audrey had been pretty adamant that she didn't want anything serious either. It could be perfect for both of us.

But how? I didn't know her last name, and all I could remember about her job was that it was in alcohol sales, or was it marketing? Damnit, I'd been too hypnotized by her smile and the way she spoke her mind, not to mention the way that dress had hugged the swell of her breasts.

I'd been right, too. Every inch of skin that it alluded to looked better exposed.

And more than just wanting to get into her bed again, I wanted another chance to see those dancing hazel eyes, her crooked smile, and delicate features.

Jesus, I needed to pull my shit together.

"I mean, it's only my left leg. I can live without it." Sarah's casual tone pierced my thoughts.

"Wait, back up. What are you talking about?"

Sarah's glare told me she knew I hadn't been paying attention. Shit. "Oh, so now you're listening to me? What has you so distracted anyway?"

I shrugged, feigning ignorance. "Nothing."

She raised a single brow but offered nothing in return. Ugh, she was becoming more and more like Mom every day. Not that I'd tell her that.

I quickly debated whether to tell her the truth or not. I settled for not. "Sorry, it's just a work thing."

"Want to talk about it?"

"It's fine. Nothing I can't handle."

She picked up her coffee and carefully considered me across the table. "Ok, this can't honestly just be about work."

"Why not?"

"Jace, I've known you my whole life. I know work problems versus girl problems."

"I'm a grown man. I don't have girl problems."

She cocked that same eyebrow in response, mocking me.

"It's nothing," I said, nervously scratching my neck. "I might have met someone." I blurted out.

She sat up straighter, instantly intrigued. "And?"

"And nothing. It was a one-time thing. I didn't even get her number."

Sarah deflated, groaning. "Ugh, guys are the worst! You obviously like this girl enough that you're sitting there with heart eyes still thinking about her, and yet apparently you were either too horny or too stupid to get her details? I feel sorry for you."

I was still stuck on the heart eyes comment. "And why is that?"

"Because. If you'd done the decent thing and taken her on a date instead of banging her like some floozy—"

"Jesus, Sarah."

"Then you wouldn't look like someone who just lost the Oscar."
She took a bite of her toast. "You're the floozy, by the way."

"Yeah, I got that," I said wryly.

"So?" she asked, waving her toast towards me.

Was I meant to know what she wanted me to say? "So …
what?"

She huffed. "Are you going to see her again?"

"I told you—"

"So what, you have *no* other way of contacting her? How did
you even meet her anyway? An app? Friend of a friend?"

Ah. That was it: her friend, the bartender. If I went back to the
bar, maybe she would give me Audrey's number or some way to
contact her.

Sarah was a genius.

"Anyway, she must be pretty special to have you pining over
breakfast."

"Yeah …" I smiled. "Maybe."

————

I MET Terry at some trendy restaurant that looked exactly like every
other trendy restaurant in Chicago. With the show in its third year,
it was time to start thinking about my long-term goals.

Before the show had started, and for most of my career, the focus
had been on chasing the job that would put me on the map. Step by
step, audition by audition, inching towards a point where I didn't
have to worry about what would come next. Where I could pick and
choose the jobs offered to me and have the career I wanted, as well
as the financial stability to look after the people I cared about.

Terry was already seated when I arrived, but he stood to give me
the customary half-handshake half-hug that industry folk had
perfected. "Hi, Terry."

"Hey, my man! How are you?"

Terry didn't tend to use my name. It was always "my man!" Or
"there's the next McConaughey." No idea why; he was either being

ironic or he just really loved McConaughey. I'd known him for six years, and the closest I could tell? It was both.

"I'm good. Been back on set for a week now. It feels good."

"Good to hear." He sat back down and gestured to the chair across from him. "Sit! Do you want a drink? Coffee? Cocktail?"

A waitress appeared by my side as soon as my ass hit the chair. "Just a black coffee, thanks." She nodded and left.

"Now, I don't want to push," he started, but I knew he really did. It was his job, after all. "I still need an answer on that teen romance series. They're really vying for you. If you want it, we should act soon."

I sighed, avoiding his eye. That bland teen romance would probably be a cash cow, but nothing about it excited me. Minus the show's supernatural elements, it was the same thing I'd been doing for the last two years.

"I know. I just need a bit longer."

Terry rubbed at his jaw. "If you take too long, it'll be out of your hands. Are you sure you don't want to just jump on it? I could make some phone calls today. Get the wheels moving."

"I don't know, Terry."

"Hey, you don't have to take it. There's nothing wrong with just sticking with what you're doing now. There's plenty more buff leading man roles out there if that's what you want. You just need to tell me if you want to be Thor or you want to branch out like that weird-looking guy from those wizard films."

"Daniel Radcliffe?"

"Is that him? The one who played a glittering vampire."

"Robert Pattinson."

"Oh, yeah. Like him."

"You do at least remember my name, right, Terry?" I was only half-joking.

"Of course! Don't be stupid. But yeah, you probably want to tell me which way you want to go with these offers. I mean, do you want to go Hemsworth or Patterson?"

I didn't correct him on the name. Though the reference inevitably changed, he'd been touting that line for at least a year now, pointing out my two options: lean into the action hero slash heartthrob gig or start pursuing more serious indie roles.

"The show's not going to last forever, J. You should have a plan."

"I know. I'll think about it."

"Now for the good news." He placed a thick envelope on the table before me.

"What's this?"

"Take a look."

I opened the envelope and slipped out the first page. It was the Michael's script. The same one I'd been chasing since I'd heard about it. The same one everyone and their cousin had been after.

"Have I told you lately that I love you?" I said, which resulted in a belly laugh from Terry.

Subversive was a fantastic indie script, ripped from the blacklist. Addison Michaels, the writer and director, had become a studio favorite after last year's sweep at Cannes and Venice. His latest project was the hot new thing on everyone's wish list, a dark comedy attracting some serious talent if industry gossip was to be believed.

But I would have to fight for the role and really sell Michaels on hiring me. Even with the show at its peak—hell, probably because of it—I didn't expect to be his first choice for the role of a male submissive who plans with his lover to kill his mistress and steal her millions.

Because despite the buzz surrounding it, *Subversive* was a passion project at heart, and I'd heard Addison Michaels had full control on casting.

I also knew that I could kill this role, and I had no doubt I could convince Michaels to hire me in it. Still, it was a risky career move on my part. Hollywood was littered with stories of great scripts that became bad movies. Or worse, shelved movies.

And I knew the show likely only had another two or so seasons before the novelty wore off. Even if the audience was still there, I didn't want to be playing this role in another four or five years.

I had to get this job.

———

THE LOT WAS BUSTLING with various crew members when I arrived on set the next morning. I had barely set my bag down before Naomi, the production manager, spoke over my shoulder.

"I should have known I'd find you here." She stood a few feet away, at the edge of the padded area where we practiced fight choreo, and motioned towards the staff I was holding. "Did Felix bring out the surprise yet?" Felix was our props master.

"Not yet, but now I'm excited to see it." The best part about being on a vaguely sci-fi show? The cool fake weapons.

She moved closer. "Anything else you're excited to see?"

Naomi and I had been casually flirting on and off most of last season, but it had never gone beyond the occasional line and a handful of lingering glances for one reason or another. Her move from assistant to manager had been hard-earned last year, and I suspected she hadn't wanted to invite the inevitable gossip that would come if we were seen together.

So she'd kept it light, and I had enjoyed the flirtation. This seemed like more, though, but I now found myself not interested in following through.

She moved closer. "You look good. How have you been?"

"Good. You?"

"Busy. Exhausted. The usual." She chuckled, tucked a stray curl behind her ear. I'd often thought about running my hands through those curls, but it wasn't her silky strands I was itching to touch now.

"I could use a drink later. I need to unwind a little. You should join me if you're interested?"

"Thanks, but, uh, I can't."

"Well, if you change your mind, let me know."

A few months ago, I would have jumped at the chance, hell, probably even a few weeks ago. But then, I hadn't met Audrey yet.

I couldn't remember the last time I felt anything more than lust for someone, and I didn't really know what the hell to do about it.

Impulse drove me to many places. Some would call it recklessness. Sarah likely would. It was what convinced me to pursue acting, it had gotten me this role, and it was what led me back to The Basement that night to see if I couldn't convince a certain bartender to give me the number of her friend.

———

As I ENTERED THE BAR, I briefly considered tracing my steps to see if I could find Audrey's apartment again, but that felt creepy and unnecessary. As long as the blonde was here—what was her name again?—I was sure I could charm her into offering Audrey's details. I hardly thought I'd have to do much; she'd practically forced us together that night, so maybe she'd gladly help me out.

That said, I had snuck out in the middle of the night without even a goodbye.

I suddenly wondered if this was a terrible idea.

My chance to turn back disappeared as quickly as it had come because the blonde—Tiffany, that was it—in question spotted me. She was serving a couple who were standing at the bar, and as our eyes met, I tried a friendly smile, hoping that if she was pissed on behalf of her friend, the most she'd do was kick me out, not kick my ass.

Especially since there were witnesses here.

Although I somehow doubted that that would deter her.

My stomach unclenched as she waved me over, clearly suspicious. I took a seat at the bar while the couple took their drinks and moved to a booth across the room.

"Well, well, this is a surprise." Her tone was light, but her gaze cold, sizing me up.

I remembered how blunt she'd been the other night and decided to go for sincerity over charm. "I'm an idiot."

It appeared to work. She barked out a laugh and visibly relaxed. "That's for damn sure."

"I want to see Audrey again, and I thought you might help me get in touch with her."

If she was surprised, she didn't show it. She simply leaned back against the cabinet behind her and crossed her arms. At least she was smiling. "And why would I do that?"

"Because you're a good person who believes in second chances?"

"I don't know … Audrey is my oldest friend. I barely know you."

"What do you want to know?"

"What do you want with my friend?"

"I told you. I want to see her again."

"Why?"

I let out a breath. "Because I like her. And I can't stop thinking about her."

"And?"

"And?"

"I'm going to need more than that to go behind my best friend's back, pretty boy."

I'd known this was unlikely to be easy, but damn. She was enjoying this, I could tell. "I don't know what you want to hear, but I've met a lot of people, and I haven't met anyone like her before. She's just …" Interesting, incredible, the sexiest person I'd ever seen?

"She is." Something in my expression must have passed her test because she pulled at the strings of her apron and gestured to a booth in the corner. "I've got to handover to night shift. Give me a minute."

Ok, this was looking up. Tiffany wasn't exactly on board yet, but she hadn't told me where to go, and from the little I knew of her, she wasn't the type to mince words.

I moved over to the booth she'd directed me to. Being in the bar brought back memories of Audrey, and I wondered what the chances were of her walking in again tonight. Did she visit Tiffany here often?

I eyed the door as I waited.

When Tiffany returned, she set down a beer in front of both of us. "Looked like you could use one," she offered.

"Thanks." I tilted my chin upwards, feeling the need for some neutral conversation. "What's up with the roof?" I hadn't noticed it the other night, but now that I had, I couldn't avoid seeing the array of odds and ends adorning the ceiling. Was that a parasol next to a tricycle? "Did the decorator buy out a garage sale or something?"

"Or something. However, you're not far off. Story is, when Harry—that's the owner—when his parents died, they left a chunk of money to him along with all their stuff. And because he couldn't bear to sell off all their knick-knacks, he used them to theme the bar and pay homage to them, especially since it was only with the inheritance that he was able to open the bar to begin with."

"That's sweet." I meant it.

"Yeah. He's a sentimental old fool, even if he can't run a bar for shit." She spoke fondly. "Luckily, he has me for that."

A tentative silence settled between us, the kind that existed between two people who were new acquaintances. I wanted to bring up why I was here again but didn't want to push the subject. Thankfully, Tiffany did it for me.

"I'm not giving you her number."

I tried to hide my disappointment, but I suspected it was still obvious. "Ok."

"But I will help you."

"Oh." It occurred to me what she might be implying. "I know this is going to sound like a line, but I can't give you my phone number. No offense, but it's not a great idea for me to hand my personal details to anyone, and as you said before, we don't really know each other."

"No offense taken. Anyway, that's not what I had in mind."

"So, what do you have in mind?"

"That Audrey is her own woman, and I think she should get to decide if she's interested in seeing you again. She shouldn't be put into an awkward situation where she says yes to a date just because you've put her on the spot."

Well, damn. She had a point. I'd been propositioned enough by instant messages that I knew how uncomfortable it was when someone you didn't know expected something from you.

"So what do I do?"

"I guess it's time to prove you're not just a pretty face, isn't it?"

Tiff reminded me so much of Sarah, and I barely stopped myself from the automatic retort that came to mind. "I guess so."

"And just so you know, I love that woman. I'd kill for her." She hardened her gaze, shooting daggers at me. "I mean it. You hurt her; you lose something."

I appreciated her loyalty, impressed that Audrey had someone in her corner who would defend her as staunchly as Tiffany did. She was a hell of a good friend.

"Message received. Now, I think I have an idea …"

11

AUDREY

The MacMillan launch was definitely making it difficult to focus on my sex life. I had half a mind to just invest in a new vibrator and call it a day, but Tiff—as always—wouldn't let me give up. That said, even she was finding it impossible to work around my current schedule.

It was my third late night in the office, and while a normal person would be happy that it was a Friday, possibly going out for after-work drinks or planning a big weekend, here I was at nine p.m., trying to work out how we could launch the MacMillan's new dark rum.

I wanted unique. I wanted new.

Unfortunately, both of those cost time and money, and we weren't exactly flush in either.

But I was determined.

MacMillan's was an amazing little distillery whose owners' whole heart went into making something that spoke to them. I just wouldn't forgive myself if I didn't make this the best damn launch that I could.

Jeff and Julie had put their faith in us, signing on when David had first started this venture, and I felt obligated to repay that faith, to prove to them we were worth it, for David more than anything. I knew how much this meant to him.

And I called David the sentimental one.

I stared at the list of ideas that I'd written down, ranging from the traditional to the outright impossible—like a free celebrity endorsement. Two, in particular, struck me as both interesting and potentially possible: a themed cocktail event and a flight tasting tour.

I imagined the cocktail event as an exclusive one-night-only evening hosted either at a client's bar or a function space we used solely for the launch; we could include food and make it part degustation and part presentation.

Whereas the flight tour would be scaled down to the essentials and hosted at a number of bars—cross-promotion was always an easy sell—and I'd target the pre-dinner, pre-theatre crowds.

I marked the two ideas in bold and opened up a new worksheet so I could start to brainstorm what I'd need to make them happen.

Even though the launch would be on the smaller side, the magnitude of what was required settled in my bones. Familiar fears crept in like cold steel along my spine. I'd helped set up launches like this in the past, but this was the first time it was all on me. I couldn't mess this up.

Messing this up meant I wasn't ready. That David had made a mistake.

So, I had to work harder. I meant what I had said to David. I could handle this.

I *would* handle this.

Hmm. Maybe if I worked through the weekend, I could present to Jeff and Julie on Monday ...

Guilt sank in my stomach. I had promised myself I would start dating again, and I could hardly do that if I spent all weekend holed up in this office, could I?

I imagined what Tiff would tell me to do, and I knew I needed to embrace this crazy plan I had decided on. I still wanted it, but wanting and doing were far from the same thing.

Torn between work and my love life, I chose option three: procrastination.

Which is why I spent the next twenty minutes venturing down an internet rabbit hole looking at the vast array of images of Jackson Ward.

Who wouldn't, though? He was tall, lean, chiseled. Like an Abercrombie model.

Dirty blond hair that was probably cut by committee, always perfectly tousled in any number of ways. Those deep blue eyes glinting above the sharp, cocky grin that seemed to be his trademark.

And yes, ok, I may have checked to see if he had a girlfriend. I maintained it was only to make sure I hadn't cuckolded anyone. And if I happened to read a handful of articles that detailed his steady history of rumored relationships or confirmed flings, it was hardly my fault.

Apparently, he'd been seen on the arm of at least a half dozen models, and I gave myself a gold star for not comparing myself to them, for too long at least.

He certainly hadn't been lying when he'd told me he didn't do relationships. Not that I had gotten the impression otherwise, but it was nice to know he'd been honest. It meant I could keep my good view of him.

And considering the slideshow of memories I'd been left with, I wanted nothing more than to keep that view intact.

Images flashed across my mind of Jackson's fingers splayed over my hips, pinning me down as his mouth worked its wicked ways between my thighs. Just remembering it had my pulse racing and my muscles contracting in response. Talk about a feast for the senses.

Jackson had stoked a fire in me I hadn't even believed existed. My whole sexual experience before that night boiled down to a series of missionary-style fucks, always at night, before sleep, in a bed, usually with the lights off. I had thought that was all I would experience, and I was ok with that. I never figured myself as an adventurous lover. I'd had no clue how much a well-placed bite right in the crook of my neck with just enough force to leave a mark would drive me insane to the point that even the memory of it made me squirm.

Damnit, I really wanted to have that again.

I opened my dating app, reminding myself not to compare every man I saw to the handsome actor who took up residence in my fantasies.

It was more difficult than I anticipated.

Still, I managed to set up two dates for the weekend. One for drinks on Saturday night with a banker named Beckett; the second for Sunday dinner with Chad—who was a PT, because of course, he was.

It took effort not to back out of both.

And, by the end of the weekend, I firmly wished I had.

I also wished I had spent the entire weekend in the office because at least then I'd have accomplished something. But no, I had made this "get out and date again" bed, and now I was lying in it, annoyed and exhausted.

Tiff was, unsurprisingly, after all the dirty details. "Sucked literally or figuratively?" She asked over the phone Sunday night after I'd told her how well my weekend had gone.

I tensed from my sprawled position on my bed. I was starting to really rethink this whole sex thing, feeling hollower with every disappointing encounter. But Tiff's refusal to judge, or let me stop looking, kept me from falling into a shame spiral.

"We didn't even come close to literal sucking. After Jackson, I'm finding it difficult to be interested in anyone else."

"Maybe you should try and hook up with him again."

"Funny," I responded dryly.

"We could find a way." Her voice was innocent in a way that made me suspicious. And nervous.

"No. I was lucky enough the first time. The chances of seeing him again are about one in a trillion. A trillion trillion." I let out a long, harsh breath as I stretched my back, trying to ease out the stiffness that had set in. It was probably too late to go into the office. "I'll just keep trying with these apps and see if I can't strike gold twice."

12

JACKSON

"Cut!" Bryson's yell reverberated across the set. "Let's move onto the next scene. Olivia, I need you on your mark in five."

"I think I've got it, thanks." Liv's tone was dry, and from anyone else, Bryson probably would have cut them down, but from Liv, he seemed to let it go.

Done for the day, I checked my phone. Good. Plenty of time.

"J! Glad I caught you." Wes clapped a hand on my shoulder and walked with me as I made my way to change out of my costume. "Are you coming to this thing tonight?"

"The drinks? Yeah, Terry told me I had to. You're there, too, right?"

"Yeah, I'll be there."

When Tiffany mentioned that she didn't want to corner Audrey into an awkward situation, I'd started thinking of my options. I knew Tiffany wouldn't want me going to Audrey's office or her apartment, but the bar was fair play, as far as I could tell.

When Terry had mentioned they were planning a semi-formal schmooze fest to lubricate some deals, especially with some high-profile producers he wanted to get on the good side of, I'd seen my opportunity, and hey, had he heard of this bar downtown? Because I think it might be perfect.

Terry took care of the rest.

Now I just hoped Tiffany would get Audrey there like she'd said she would.

———

My PHONE RANG in the cab on my way to the bar, and I answered immediately when I saw the caller ID.

Sarah was already talking by the time the phone got to my ear. "You're not going to bring some airhead to my wedding, are you?"

"Oh, hello, Sarah, how are you?" I joked. Throughout the wedding planning, Sarah had been the picture of calm and collected. Mostly. Every once in a while, a little bridezilla would appear.

"Sorry, yes, hi, Jace, how are you, blah blah blah. You're not, are you? Because I have to confirm seating numbers tomorrow, and I know we gave you a plus one, but if you're thinking of bringing one of those side chicks you always seem to have around "–

"Now that's just rude."

She sighed. "I want to be supportive, Jace. I really do, but this is going to be our whole family, and it's not fair on them or us if you show up with someone who can't handle all that. You know how we are." I did. "And you deserve someone who can be one of us. Someday." Her voice was strained, and it helped reduce my irritation. With the wedding getting closer, her stress levels surely had been rising.

"It's ok, Sarah. I …" How to phrase this … "I don't know if I'll have a date, but I promise if I do, she'll be cool."

"Ok, good. Well, I'll keep you as a plus one, and then we can always stick one of the second cousins next to you if you don't have a date. Oh, hey! Whatever happened with your goddess?"

"My what?"

"The woman who had you brooding last weekend? The one you stupidly let get away?"

"I'm, uh, I'm working on it."

"Well, you better not mess it up this time."

No. No messing up this time.

————

THE AGENCY HAD DONE WELL. There were at least a hundred people here, some I knew well and others I only knew by reputation.

The first thing I needed to do was check in with Tiffany, who was overseeing the bar staff.

"Are you sure she's going to come?" I asked, nodding my thanks as she passed me a glass of soda water. I preferred to be sober at these types of events.

Tiffany let out a dry laugh. "Definitely. She's a bleeding heart. As soon as I told her we had two staff call in sick, she was offering to get down here to help." When she notices my surprised expression, she added, "It's not the first time."

Warmth bloomed in my chest. It fit perfectly with the impression Audrey had made on me so far. Smart, sexy, generous.

"Will she be annoyed you lied to her?"

"Are you kidding? This is like some shit straight out of a movie. Besides, it's kind of romantic, and she deserves a little excitement for a change." I didn't hide my smile at her kind gesture. "And if you ever tell Audrey that I said that, I'll use your balls as a garnish."

"Noted." I stifled my chuckle. I could definitely see why Audrey liked Tiffany so much. They were lucky to have each other.

While I waited, I made the rounds, chatting to a handful of people I recognized. Eventually, Terry pulled me away to introduce me to a producer working on a graphic novel adaption for Netflix and was interested in getting me on board.

The producer was nice enough, a stunning older Vietnamese woman who had an acerbic wit, which I appreciated, but I couldn't gather any real excitement for the project. Still, I wasn't one to burn bridges, so we chatted politely, and I agreed to look over the script.

I turned back toward the bar, snaking my way through the

crowd to ensure I was close enough to see Audrey when she arrived. A commanding voice stopped me.

"Jackson Ward. Terry tells me I should be talking to you about a role in my next film."

In the last five years of having Terry as my agent, most conversations started this way. I'd long learned to roll with it, but as I turned around to face the person who'd greeted me this way, I was momentarily startled.

Addison fucking Michaels was standing in front of me.

Holy shit.

I held out a hand. "Mr. Michaels, it's great to meet you."

His grip was firm. "And you. I should admit, I don't watch your show, but my wife seems to enjoy it. She said you're quite good."

Well, damn. Thank you, Mrs. Michaels. "Thank you, or uh, thank her."

"And you're interested in Subversive." It was a statement, not a question.

"I am. It's a fantastic script, sir."

"Thank you, I agree. What role, in particular, are you interested in? I wouldn't have expected someone with your … current trajectory to find anything of interest in a film like this."

"I can see why you would think that," I agreed. "But I would also argue that roles like Parker don't come across very often, and it's the exact type of character that made me want to act in the first place."

"What about him appeals to you?"

"The way I see it, his conflict doesn't stem from having to be in control, from what I've researched, that's a misnomer for d/s relationships. Instead, the conflict comes from betraying the trust built between them, which is so crucial for people in those arrangements. So he has no problem taking charge, never did, but he struggles with every decision that requires manipulating or lying to her because it goes against everything they've had up to this point."

"That's an interesting take." His expression gave nothing away, so I could only hope I hadn't completely misread between the lines in the script. Knowing how much this meant to Addison, if I'd missed the mark, it would be hard to convince him to give me a chance at the role.

Movement caught the corner of my eye, and I looked over to find Tiffany gesturing at me.

My pulse kicked up a notch.

I tried to scan the room for Audrey, but there were too many people, and I couldn't get a good look behind the bar. I'd have to get closer.

"Are you looking for someone, or am I boring you?"

Shit.

Here I was with one of the leading directors in show business, and he thought that I was ignoring him.

Terry was going to kill me.

"Of course not, Mr. Michaels." I scrambled to apologize. "Sorry, I thought I saw something. It's not important."

"I'm not so sure," he said, now looking in the same direction. And was that amusement I could hear in his voice? "Someone seems to be trying very hard to get your attention."

I followed his line of sight to where Tiffany was now motioning very tersely.

Addison chuckled, "A friend of yours?"

"More like a mutual acquaintance," I needed to get over there before Tiffany made a scene, but I didn't want to offend Addison by running off. Tiffany made a giving-up gesture while shaking her head and turned back to the bar. I made a decision.

Hopefully, Addison was a romantic.

"I, uh, there's a woman. Amazing, smart, beautiful. And a friend of my acquaintance over there. She's helping me fix a mistake I made, which it's hopefully not too late to make up for. But unfortunately, it means I'll have to cut our conversation short."

He considered me, and I wondered what exactly he thought of me at that moment.

"Love is a fool's game, and we are all fools for it." Addison's lips had quirked into a smile, so I didn't think I'd horrified the man beyond ever hiring me, but he was so hard to read it was impossible to tell.

"I wish you luck with your friend," he added.

"Thank you again. It's been great meeting you. I really hope we can talk again about Parker. It's a fantastic role."

He shook my outstretched hand, "It's been interesting, to say the least, Mr. Ward." Then he was off, presumably to talk to someone who wasn't too distracted to talk to him.

It was fine. Terry would no doubt kick my ass, but at least he didn't seem offended.

Fighting my way over to the bar, I sat. Tiffany appeared out of nowhere. "Time's up, pretty boy. She just walked in."

Adrenaline buzzed through me. I wasn't even bothered by the stupid nickname she refused to stop calling me. It was growing on me, not that I'd let Tiffany know.

Meanwhile, she'd already returned to the other end of the bar and begun talking animatedly to someone as she kept an eye on the servers.

No, not someone. Audrey.

Her hair was tied up, bringing sharp focus to her bright eyes and soft lips, which she'd painted a shade of red that sent my blood rushing south. She was as beautiful as I'd remembered.

Fuck, I'd really been an idiot to leave that morning. I needed not to mess this up.

Audrey's laugh cut through the noise in the room, a familiar sound I'd been replaying to myself since I'd last seen her, and I swear to God, my heart skipped.

It was the moment her eyes met mine across the bar that I felt my confidence restoring itself. Recognition, surprise, then thankfully, joy and lust played over her features, and I knew that no matter how this ended, I wasn't the only one who had been remembering our night together.

"Fancy running into you again." She shot an incredulous look over her shoulder at Tiffany. "Can I get you a drink?"

"Thanks. I have it on good authority that the drinks are pretty good here." What the hell. One wouldn't hurt. "What would you recommend?"

She hummed, making a show of thinking it over while smiling at me. "There's a rum-based one topped up with sparkling wine. It's one of my favorites."

"In that case, how could I refuse?"

I watched as she made it, enjoying having a moment to re-familiarize myself with the little details of her. That plush lower lip that I knew felt so good between my teeth. Nimble fingers that could be equally gentle and rough. That careful concentration that she appeared to give everything she did.

Damn, it was good to see her again.

When she passed the finished drink to me, I brought it up to my lips slowly and sniffed, but there wasn't anything discerning coming off the drink. Taking a sip, I tasted lemon and thyme, lightened by the bubbles and a tangy alcoholic twist.

"Good?" She asked hesitantly.

"Amazing," I said, taking another sip. "It's good to see you again."

Her smile widened. "You, too. I didn't think I would, after ..."

"But you hoped."

She rolled her eyes. "Still as cocky as before, I see."

"You wouldn't want me to change. You like me like this."

"Is that what you think?" She said playfully.

"It's what I remember. Among other things." I didn't miss the flush of her cheeks at that.

She moved to serve some others before Tiffany shooed her back in my direction.

"So what brings you back here?" She asked, leaning comfortably on the counter between us.

I gestured to the crowd. "Work does. The agency I'm managed by wanted to get a few people together."

"This is a few people?" The bar was entirely too packed.

"One or two." Her hands rested on the bar near mine, and I reached out to brush her knuckles. "What about you? Did you decide you needed a side hustle? Not making enough selling booze during the day, so you have to do it at night, too?"

Her head titled back as she laughed, sharp and light. "Shows how much you remember. I don't sell booze during the day. I market and distribute, thank you very much. Besides, I'm only here to meet cute guys."

"Oh, really? Any luck?"

She slumped down, playing up a resigned shake of her head. "Sadly, no."

We were interrupted as Wes arrived at my side, asking Audrey for a beer. He turned to me. "Oh, man, I'm going to split soon. Think anyone will notice?"

I shrugged noncommittally. "Probably not. Do you have somewhere better to be?"

"Yeah, if I can get out of here soon enough, I can get between two sexy numbers."

"Six and nine?" Audrey asked. She was back with Wes' beer, and we both looked confused for long enough that she clarified, "Two sexy numbers?"

Wes cracked up, laying an extra bill on the bar as a tip. He motioned towards her. "I like this one. Nice work."

I shoved him away with one hand, "Yeah, yeah. Get out of here."

After another hour, Tiffany finally managed to convince Audrey that she wasn't actually needed, and she joined me on the other side of the bar so we could talk without getting interrupted.

So, of course, Terry appeared. "There's the next McConaughey." He turned to Audrey, studying her. "You're cute, do you act?"

She shook her head. "No, I market alcohol."

"Pity, I could find you some really steady ad work." He stuck his hand out, "I'm Terry, his agent."

"Audrey Adams," Audrey said, shaking his hand with an open smile. "Can I ask why McConaughey? I mean, I guess I can kind of see a resemblance, the sandy hair, the blue eyes …" Even though she was referring to me, her attention never left him, her tone warm and friendly.

"He's a great actor, don't you agree? Largely made a career out of his looks until he was only really being cast as the romantic lead, not unlike our J here. But then he surprised everyone with a series of smaller serious roles that he knocked out of the park. Took his career in a whole new direction. Proved pretty isn't always all there is."

"Wow." Yeah, wow. How had I never heard this before? Probably because I'd never bothered to ask Terry why he was always using that comparison.

"Jackson is lucky to have an agent who believes in him so much." Audrey smiled, and I could see Terry was a little under her spell. Not that I could blame him. She must be a killer saleswoman.

"It's easy to be. There's a lot of potential there." Terry picked up a drink offered by a waitperson walking by, then pointedly added while looking at me, "He just needs to pick his next project so I can do my job and get him to the next stage of his career."

"Well, hopefully, some good news comes after tonight."

He hummed, hopeful. "Hey, I need to talk to Wes. Have you seen him?"

"Uh, yeah, he should be around. Somewhere." I said nonchalantly.

"I think I saw him in the corner booth," Audrey added.

Terry went off in the direction we'd mentioned, leaving Audrey and me alone again. Or as alone as we could be in a sea of a hundred people.

I normally hated these events, but it was surprisingly fun with Audrey there.

"So …" Audrey bit her lip, and I fought the urge to lean in and kiss her. "It's kind of loud in here."

I nodded. "Crowded, too."

"Yeah. I know somewhere nearby where we could go. Somewhere more intimate." A small dimple appeared in her cheek when her smile widened enough. I wanted to lick it.

"Lead the way."

13

AUDREY

This time, my lips were on his before we reached my door.

Seeing him again had felt a little surreal, although far from a coincidence if I knew Tiff. My heart had damn near stopped when I'd spotted him at the bar, looking like a three-course meal in those tight jeans and button-down.

I may not have thought I'd ever see Jackson again, but that hadn't stopped me from fantasizing about what I wanted to do with him. And now that I had the chance, I was going to go for it.

His body was a warm, hard wall against my back as I unlocked the door, and my own body buzzed with energy, my veins filling with a mix of excitement and nerves.

With my hair tied back, he had ample access to my neck, which he took advantage of, his kisses practically searing my skin. Need coursed through me, stronger than last time. I didn't have to worry if this would be good. I knew it would be.

I moved us quickly to my bedroom, and once there, I turned and pulled him close; my hand bunched in his shirt as his slipped around my waist, gripping tight. My senses were overwhelmed, everything in my body firing under his touch.

His eyes had darkened to a stormy blue as he dipped down to

kiss me, and I lost myself to the incessant crash of his lips on mine, his breath hot against my cheek. When his tongue slid across my bottom lip, asking for entry, I granted it, gripping his shirt tighter when my knees weakened beneath me.

I wanted and needed more. My other hand moved to his waist, and I tugged roughly on his belt, bringing him closer. There was little space between us as it was, but it wasn't enough. I wanted to feel his skin. I wanted to be enveloped in his strong hard warmth, driven to pleasure by his hands and mouth. I wanted too much at once, and I wanted it all right now.

I felt him smile against my mouth as I took charge and shuffled out of my pants, all the while steering us toward the bed. One pant leg briefly got stuck around my ankle, making me giggle between breathless kisses.

Once my knees hit the bed, I laid down and drank in the sight of him before me. Damn, he was sexy. His chest rose with rapid breaths; his pants strained where his erection made itself known. I licked my lips. I couldn't wait to get my mouth on him.

There was hunger burning in his eyes as they raked over me, studying my body before returning to my face. The corner of his lip quirked.

Slowly, as if he knew how crazy it made me, he stripped his shirt off, and I waited for him to remove his pants, but instead, he leaned in and buried his face in my neck while his hands gripped my waist, pushing my shirt higher. I pushed against his chest. "Wait, let me." Then I rolled us over so I could straddle his waist.

I pulled off my top in a move that was much smoother than I'd planned, exposing my—thankfully—matching navy underwear. They weren't as sexy as the black lace pair I'd worn last time, but I hadn't known I was going to be getting laid when I'd left the house earlier, and honestly, I was about ready to throw out every unsexy bit of lingerie I owned and replace it all if it meant getting a reaction from the gorgeous man under me.

But I was getting ahead of myself. Just because I wanted there to be a next time didn't mean there would be, so I needed to make the most of right now.

I dropped my hands to his chest, caressing the smooth skin before venturing lower to outline the contours of his abs with my fingertips. He was a work of art. I may never be able to look at a Greek statue again.

His grip on me was firm as he kneaded my thighs and ass while I explored. He was allowing me to lead, giving me control of what happened next. I wanted to tell him how much that meant to me, but I didn't want to ruin the moment, so instead, I showed him.

I took my time as I continued to map out his body with my hands, enjoying his stomach muscles quiver under my light touch.

He was solid, his skin intoxicatingly soft, and I wanted to taste it. I leaned down and closed my mouth over one nipple, sucking and smoothing over the peaked bud with my tongue, grounded by how real he felt, smelt, tasted.

He groaned, rough and raw, and his hands gripped my thighs and ass harder, driving my desire up. We weren't even naked, and yet I felt myself flushing from head to toe.

He tried to maneuver me back onto my back, but I clenched my thighs around his hips and held us steady. "Not just yet. There's something I want to do."

He smiled, but I wanted to make sure he was on board. "That ok?"

"Baby, that's more than ok."

I flushed, thrilled at the pet name. Definitely adding that to the list.

Unlike the past, where taking care of my partner's needs was the rule and an obligation, with Jackson, I wanted to do it because I knew it was reciprocated and not demanded.

When I was with him, I wanted to stop thinking. Just … act on instinct, trust my gut at the moment.

I trailed a series of bites and kisses down his neck, chest, stomach, touching and tasting everywhere I could as I shuffled backward. As I undid his belt, I looked up at him, feeling a rush at being in this position. At having him under my spell.

He lifted his hips and stepped off the bed to help me pull off his clothes. He stood before me, completely exposed, while I admired his incredible body.

The absurdity of the situation hit me, and there was a beat where I could practically feel my body fighting off my nervousness.

As the moment stretched out, I waited for the inevitable complaint. Or command. Brad would have told me to hurry up by now, thoroughly ruining the mood with his tense impatience.

But Jackson simply licked his lips, eyes raking over me, hungry like he wanted to devour me.

When his cock twitched in anticipation, I was startled out of my thoughts and huffed a short, embarrassed laugh, but Jackson's focus was still fixed on me with that hungry smile, and that was what finally set me back in motion.

I was driven by the need to see him undone. To break that calm exterior and see if I couldn't make him half as lightheaded as I felt right now.

Crawling onto the bed, I was of singular focus. My hands brushed along the fine hairs of his thighs, feeling how the thick muscles beneath twitched in anticipation. His cock stood strong, thick, against his belly, the tip shining.

I was continually humbled by his patience. The inherent power of feeling like I could have my way with him. The kindness in his patience made me want to be bold. To tease.

Following this desire, I kept my grip loose as I wrapped a hand around the base, just enough pressure that he would feel it. But not enough.

He cut off a moan, keeping still. The only sign I had of how affected he was, was the curling and unfurling of his toes. I was impressed with his willpower.

When I made no further movements, his eyes opened, and I waited until our eyes locked before slowly licking him from root to tip. His jaw clenched, eyes fluttering briefly before pining me with a hungry stare. Still, he remained silent.

A game, then.

Maintaining his gaze, I continued to lavish him with my tongue. Then, because I needed to get a reaction from him, needed to hear him, I sucked his tip into my mouth, enjoying the rich, salty taste as it burst across my tongue.

His groan was guttural, a rumble in the darkness. His body seemed to hum with it, and I felt myself getting wet.

I doubled my efforts, tightening my grip and taking him deeper into my mouth. My nose brushed against the damp curls at his base, just long enough to hear the grunted "Fuck" fall from Jackson's lips before I pulled back. My breath was ragged, and my lips were slick with spit, but I'd never felt more powerful, more in control.

"I fucking love your mouth," he said, and I knew he felt me smile around his cock. I moaned around him as I picked up the pace, loving the way he responded with a loud moan and a hitch of his hips.

His hand cradled my head, not grabbing, just holding there, caressing. His thighs trembled, a series of continual flexes that told me he was getting close.

And I loved how vocal he was about what he liked. Groans, grunts, curses … the lot.

The way his head fell back in a mix of pleasure and disbelief filled me with a unique kind of pride. Not to mention how fucking hot it was. I just knew I'd be replaying this moment in my fantasies later.

I lost myself to the pleasure of him. The heat against my tongue. The smell of sweat and sex. The wet sound as I pulled off away, panting against his thigh. The tender feel of his throbbing vein beneath my lips as I trailed kisses along it. The pure euphoria and delight when I brought my lips to his balls, discovering how much he enjoyed it.

From there, it was only a matter of time before he was coming in my mouth, and I lapped up what I could, wiping my mouth against his leg when it spilled from my lips.

Despite not finding my own release, I felt as boneless as he was. I crawled up his body and couldn't help myself from kissing his cheek and whispering, "I've wanted to do that since last time."

With the strength he had left, he crushed our lips together.

I laid down beside him, curled into his side, and watched

happily as he came down from his post-BJ high, harboring every contented sigh and locking it away in my mind for safekeeping.

I rested my chin on his chest, more than a little proud of myself at how glassy his eyes were with the bliss of the orgasm. I did that.

My confidence was so high, I teased. "I'll just give you a moment before the next round."

His chuckle was hardly more than a breath as his hands explored my body. I shuffled off my underwear, so we were both naked.

"I'm really glad we bumped into each other again," I said.

"Yeah, about that. It may not have been by accident." Jackson trailed a finger along my spine, and goosebumps broke out.

"I had a sneaking feeling that was the case. Tiff looked far too pleased with herself."

"Are you mad?"

I considered the question, putting aside my joy at seeing Jackson again and thinking over what they must have orchestrated to set us up again. "No, I'm not mad."

But maybe next time … The words sat on my tongue, and I paused, wondering if I should say them. Would he even want there to be a next time?

"I'm glad I got to see you again," I said instead, nervously repeating my earlier sentiment.

"Me, too. I'd like to keep seeing you. On purpose, this time." He tucked a stray hair behind my ear. "And maybe without Tiff there."

"I'd really like that." His fingers brushed my cheek, and I leaned into the touch before turning my head to kiss his palm. "Actually, I'm surprised Tiffany didn't just give you my number."

He groaned in frustration as he pulled me up, meeting my lips halfway and slotting his leg between mine so that we were tangled together more deeply. When I finally came up for air, I rested my hands on his chest.

"I want to be honest about something," I said.

He brushed a thumb over my cheek, and I was struck again by how handsome he was. Those sparkling blue eyes looked at me with a warmth I couldn't remember Brad ever having.

Before he could respond, I pressed on; I needed him to know … "I just … I have to tell you that I don't want something serious. I'm not interested in a relationship right now. Maybe I'm totally getting ahead of myself here, but I can't … I'm just not ready for that right now. It's got nothing to do with you—God, that sounds so cliché—I just—"

"Hey, it's ok." His hands were warm against my cheeks, and I took a deep breath, feeling myself loosen up on the exhale. "Audrey, I like you. I can't say I wouldn't be interested in more, but honestly, right now, I'm not looking for a relationship either. That doesn't mean I want to stop seeing you, but I can't promise anything."

"I don't need promises," I said firmly. Promises came with expectations.

"Ok, no promises. We just take it slow."

"Slow is good. How will it work?"

"How do you want it to work?"

"Exclusive, but casual. No commitments, no expectations. We just see each other when we can. Although I have to warn you, I don't get that much time to have a life outside of work. And I don't really want to give that up just for some …" I let myself trail off, suddenly aware I might be about to insult him.

"Some incredible sex?" he offered, teasing.

I playfully rolled my eyes but felt heat spreading over my face, strangely shy even though we were lying naked together.

His smirk softened. "And just for the record, I'm not seeing anyone right now, casual or otherwise."

Just me, my giddy mind reminded me. "I'm not either."

"So that just leaves one last question."

"Oh? And what's that?"

"Are you sure you're ready for round two?"

14

JACKSON

I was a walking cliché, but I couldn't really bring myself to care. My night with Audrey this weekend, and the knowledge that I'd see her again, had me grinning like an idiot as I walk onto the lot.

Unlike Wes, morning shoots had never been an issue for me. There was a routine to our schedule that I appreciated, even if the days were occasionally long and there were long periods of nothing in-between takes.

Anyone who'd ever worked on a set like this would tell you it was a lot of waiting. And sitting. We mixed it up by training as much as possible, even though they didn't really let us do the hard stunts, but we learned the fight choreography, and there were enough gratuitous ab shots that they liked us being in the gym for a few hours a day. It was better than sitting on my ass; I'd tell you that much.

Based on today's schedule, I had a few hours before I was needed in hair and makeup, so I teed up some time to see Felix, our props master, to get the low down on the new weapons for this season.

Despite the absurdity, I really liked being playing Ryder. I got to wear some amazing suits and wield a number of intricately crafted weapons that made me feel like a total badass.

Last year, I'd let slip to Felix that I had a thing for archery, just to see if I could get a chance to play with them this time around. Standing with Felix as he unloaded a series of large protective cases onto a long table, I had a good feeling when he slapped me on the shoulder and said, "Buddy, if you like these, you're going to *love* what we have in store."

Next to the array of rather nasty-looking guns, Felix opened a box and carefully removed its contents from the soft foam encasing, handing it to me, with expectant joy on his face. He was especially proud of this one.

"Oh, man, you were not lying," I said gleefully, holding what was by far the coolest, most badass weapon I'd been given on this show in the last three years.

The bow was light in my hand, and it looked like a mix of dark wood and metal but was no doubt some form of whatever plastic or rubber they used for these things. It was only as long as my forearm, and I couldn't see the limbs or string, but something told me they were hidden in there. Or maybe they'd be CGI'd in during post. I didn't know what kind of magic they weaved, but I was officially in awe of the prop masters.

"Glad to know you like it. It's one of my favorite things we've made." He took it out of my hands and pushed a small button that was hidden amongst the engravings. Limbs immediately extended from the center and locked into place, pulling a string taut between them. "I mean, there's no way it would hold up in the real world, but it looks frickin' cool if I do say so myself." He held it up and pulled back the string. "It locks tight enough that you'll be able to draw and release for camera, but try not to strain it too much." He handed it to me, and I tried it out. He was right; it was holding far steadier than I was expecting.

"Wow, J, I think you might be compensating for something." As curious as I was about the new toys, Wes had made his way over. Of course, he'd naturally gravitated toward the largest gun on the table.

He held it up and mimed stroking the barrel suggestively while leering at me.

Felix admonished him while taking the bow off me and laying it gently back in its casing. "Stop messing around, Wesley. Besides, that one is yours."

I laughed loudly as Wes wagged his middle finger at both of us. "Everyone knows I don't have anything to compensate for."

"God, do you ever stop talking about your dick?" Liv rushed by, not pausing as she passed us with her coffee in hand and sunglasses still on.

"Long night, Liv?"

She snorted. "Like you'd know anything about long things, Wes." Then she disappeared off into hair and makeup.

Wes appeared unfazed by her retort and turned back to the props table, picking up and admiring some modified handguns. "Got anything new for me, Felix?"

"Actually," Felix said as he pulled out an extra-long slim case that both Wes and I were familiar with. Inside was Wes' typical weapon, a spear with a series of engraved markings in the shaft. When Felix handed it to Wes, I could see that it had been altered. Most of the surface was blackened, resembling scorch marks, and the tip had been updated with a crude split, giving the whole weapon a raw, archaic look.

It was very fucking cool.

"Fuck. Yes." Wes tested out the feel of it with a few practiced moves while Felix explained the changes.

"Since the fight with Mars almost destroyed it, we wanted to really play up the wear and tear from that, and I also wanted to represent Ares' more vulnerable state this season. So you get a sense of that exposed anger in how jaded and rough his spear looks, and you kind of worry that either could break at any moment."

Wes nodded along, still admiring the spear. "Yeah, that's awesome. I love it." He hands it back to Felix, who promptly returns it to the case. "Great work as always."

I was checking over a few more props when Wes got my attention.

"Hey, J. I've got some thoughts on next week's script. You got some time to run lines with me?"

"Yeah, I've got a bit of time."

"Cool." He said, and I followed him into our designated rehearsal space.

The studio lot where we filmed wasn't as big as most, but Wes, Liv, and I did manage to sequester a small space for the three of us to unwind and rehearse between takes. We mostly used it to relax; days on set could be long and sometimes boring, so it was nice to have somewhere we could commiserate together.

Wes dropped into the chair across from me, one hand digging into his curls as he pulled out his script. I knew he could see my confusion when he tossed it aside.

"What's up, man?" I asked. From the pained look on his face, I already had the sense that this wasn't going to be about work.

It wasn't like Wes to brood, despite the villain he played on the show, so my confusion slowly morphed into concern. "Everything ok?"

Wes hunched over, his earlier cocky ambivalence nowhere to be seen. "Not really, J." He groaned. "It's been a tough week."

"Girl problems?" I joked, hoping to lighten the mood and immediately regretting it when he bristled. "Sorry."

"Let's just say I can relate to my storyline this year."

He was referring to the unrequited love angle between Ares and Meira, which surprised me because, as far as I was aware, he wasn't seeing anyone. "I had no idea."

"Yeah."

"Do you want to talk about it?"

"Yes? No. Honestly, I've been over it so many times in my head I'm a little sick of it, you know? I've never been here before, wanting someone who doesn't see me that way. Who only wants me as a friend."

"Have you talked to them?"

"I don't need to. I just found out she's in a pretty serious relationship, so I just need to get the hell over it already." He slumped back in the chair. "What are you doing later? We could hit a bar, wingman for each other?"

Now it was my turn to squirm. I hadn't been keeping Audrey a secret; it just hadn't come up before. Wes and I spent more time talking shop than anything else, although I realized now that I'd unfairly assumed he wasn't capable of a serious conversation. "Actually, I can't. I'm seeing someone."

Wes' smile appeared genuine, although tinged with sadness. "Bar girl, right? That's great, man. You deserve it."

"Thanks, Wes. You do, too. Things will work out."

He reached forward for the abandoned script, only offering me an appreciative look in response. I had trouble reconciling his usual boisterous facade with the sullen guy across from me, and I could only imagine what he was going through. "Anytime you need to talk, come find me," I added, wishing there was more I could do.

"Hey," I said after a long stretch of silence had passed. Wes looked up from where he was adding notes into the margins of his script. "Have you heard anything yet about the renewal?"

"Nothing concrete, but it's looking good. I just hope Terry can get that deal worked out. The extra money would really help set me up."

I hummed my agreement, knowing exactly what I was going to do with the extra money. What I didn't like, however, was that the whole thing felt out of our hands. Not that I didn't trust Terry to have our interests in mind, but something irked me about having to sit back and just wait.

We'd already been knocked back last year when we'd asked the same; the studio came back with some line about how the show was too new, none of us were famous enough to really demand that sort of money, blah blah blah. But we had one more season under our belt now, and the predictions were that our ratings were only going to get better, so I was cautiously hopeful that we'd be successful this time.

I just wished I could do something to move it along.

———

A FEW DAYS LATER, it was still on my mind as Audrey and I laid, happy and exhausted, in my bed.

She'd messaged after finishing work late, wanting to know if I was free, and since I was already home, I'd invited her over to my apartment, something I rarely did.

Damn, she looked good draped across my sheets.

I paused in my naked appreciation of her breasts to ask, "Do you often have to negotiate contracts in your job?"

"Almost always, why?"

"We're hoping to secure a better deal if the show gets renewed, but right now, it's all happening behind closed doors, and it's bothering me."

"I mean … it would be a completely different ballgame for your work, I don't know the first thing about it."

"I know. I guess I was hoping you might have some tips I could use to push the conversation in the right direction."

"Hmm. Well, it's all about context. Sometimes, you need leverage. Other times, it's more about influence. But I always start with getting to the heart of what the other party wants and then being clear on what I can offer in exchange, even if that means making a concession. Although it's win-win if you can find something that sounds like you're making a compromise on something you're actually happy to do." She shook her head. "Sorry, that was all a bit vague, wasn't it? I don't even know if that will help at all."

I considered what she'd said and the seed of an idea planted; but one I'd have to spend some time fleshing out later when I didn't have a naked, beautiful woman in bed with me.

"Ok, enough work talk."

"I can think of something else we can do."

"Oh?" I liked where this was headed.

"Mmm, there's a great show I heard about; you might know it. Apparently, I'm out of the loop."

"You must be; it's very popular," I said, enjoying the laugh it pulled from her.

"You don't mind, do you? That I haven't seen it?" I shook my head, and she continued. "It's not personal. I just don't really watch television. It wasn't something my parents liked me doing when I was growing up and it kind of stuck."

"No TV? I can't even imagine." Some of my favorite memories were in front of a television. "What did you do for fun?"

She blushed. "Ok, but you can't laugh."

"I won't."

"Really, you can't."

I held one hand up in a promise.

"Do you remember those maths problems where you knew, like, Tim was taller than Steve but shorter than James, so how tall is Lucy? Those."

My lips twitched around a joke before I reconsidered and settled into a fond smile. "That's really what you did for fun?"

She ducked her head. "I liked solving them. My parents didn't like games either, but I can play a mean round of solitaire."

"You don't have any brothers or sisters?"

"No. Just me."

"Were you ever lonely?"

There was a beat. "My parents worked really hard to be around, so I was never alone."

I could guess at what she wasn't saying and felt a wave of awe for this incredible woman who had spent her childhood lonely but refused to accept any pity for it. Remembering my childhood, I said, "I used to hate those maths problems. I always hoped for a multiple choice answer and just picked C."

She laughed, a little tension draining out from between the angles of her shoulder blades. "I bet you still passed every test."

"I was consistently lucky," I added, just to hear her laugh again. Then I gently asked, "Are you close with them? Your parents?"

"We talk. They live up in Madison and don't ever visit, but I try to spend the holidays with them." She smiled softly. "What about you?"

"Yeah, we're definitely close. I don't get to see them as often as I'd like, but we talk a lot, and I have brunch every weekend with my sister. They're the main reason I want to renegotiate the contract.

It'd be nice to give back to them after all they've done for Sarah and me."

Audrey considered me quietly, and I was held captive by her intense gaze. I took my time to appreciate the flecks of gold that sparkled in her eyes, hinting at a treasure I'd only myself started to glimpse. I hoped I would have the chance to discover all of it.

Eventually, she leaned in and kissed me. "They're lucky to have you."

I cupped her cheek in one palm. "I already told you, I'm the lucky one."

15

AUDREY

I knocked again.

Then, louder.

Finally, I called through the door. "I come bearing coffee."

"It better be strong." Tiff ripped the door open wide, her hair a wild mess where it had been thrown into a bun with little concern for how it looked. She was wearing her usual ripped jeans and tank top, which I could only imagine were thrown together in the same thoughtless fashion as her hair.

I held the coffee out to her. "Three extra shots. Your usual."

"Thank fuck. You ready to go?"

A naked body shuffled down the hallway behind her. "Uh, yeah ... Are you sure *you* are?" I gestured at the retreating bare ass.

"Oh, Diego knows his way out. Right, D?" She raised her voice as she called down the hall. A muffled response confirmed.

I shook my head in amusement as she shut the door behind her and took a long sip of coffee. "I'll warn you, I've barely slept, and this is my first caffeine of the day. I may need a minute before I can offer any sage advice."

My phone pinged, and I smiled, guessing who it was. Jackson and I had been messaging pretty steadily since we'd swapped numbers last week. Just flirty little texts back and forth, nothing deep or meaningful. I was determined to keep this strictly about sex. But I couldn't help the grin that overtook my face as I thought of him, and Tiff caught on immediately, as I'd known she would.

"And who has you so happy on a Saturday morning? That wouldn't be pretty boy, would it?"

"You know his name is Jackson."

"Uh-huh. And I'm sure it means nothing that he's messaging you at," she mimicked looking at a watch, even though her wrist was bare, "ass o'clock in the morning on a weekend. Are you sure *you* don't have a sexy naked man you could be attending to?"

"Okay, firstly, eight a.m. is a perfectly normal time for adult humans to be awake, thank you very much. And secondly, no, he's busy at the moment, but now that we're able to message, it's easier to set something up."

"Finally. I have better things to do than play matchmaker with you two."

"Like Diego?"

Her grin was wolfish. "Exactly."

We settled into a comfortable silence on the walk downtown, Tiff needing the time to let the coffee kick in. It wasn't until we reached the Mile that she spoke again. "So tell me, what are we shopping for today?"

We didn't usually require any particular reason for retail therapy. Most Saturdays, we just walked aimlessly and window shopped. But today, I was on a mission—no more boring underwear.

"Lingerie. I realized I own maybe one good set, and the rest are fine but hardly make me feel sexy."

"Oh! You don't know how long I've waited for this moment!" Tiff squeezed the air out of my lungs with a tight hug.

"Okay, okay! Let me go." I choked out a laugh with the air I had left before she loosened her grip and started pulling me along the shops. To where, I had no idea.

"Auds, I'm serious. I've wanted to take you here for years! Ooh, we're going to have so much fun today. Pretty boy won't know what hit 'im."

"Well, what are we waiting for then?"

———

WHEN I ENTERED the office on Monday, it was with a lingering lightheadedness and slight sting on my lips. After my little shopping trip on Saturday with Tiff, Jackson had ended up coming over, and it was the perfect opportunity to try one of my new purchases.

His reaction to it had more than justified the price, in my opinion.

I smiled, recalling it.

What really stayed with me were his eyes. They had ranged from warm and playful while we talked, devilish while I was riding him, and hazy with lust while he went down on me. They were so expressive; I felt them on me even now.

And while the sex had been amazing, what I enjoyed the most, what I hadn't even realized I'd forgotten, was feeling desired. The moments when he was overcome with want and made his pleasure known, loud and clear. I hadn't felt that in a long time.

Oh, and his hands. So strong and capable. He knew exactly what he was doing as he kept his touch teasing and light, knowing when I wanted more. When I wanted it rough. When I wanted him to grab, scrap, and mark me. And when he did, when he manhandled me and moved me and devoted himself to my pleasure, I still felt cared for and safe.

For the first time in a long time, I remembered what I enjoyed about sex, and it was so much more than orgasms. It was the play, the banter, the exploration. I wanted to squirrel him away from the rest of reality so that we could explore every single fantasy I'd ever had.

David's musical knock startled me out of my thoughts. "What's gotten into you today?"

I felt like the cat caught with the canary. "What? What do you mean?" I willed my face not to blush, but I could feel my temperature rising. David couldn't have known I'd just been picturing Jackson doing dirty, dirty things to me, but I still felt embarrassed.

"You're practically giddy. I've known you a long time, and I've never seen you this happy. Whatever it is, I'm glad. Or maybe I should say whoever it is."

"I'm not ... There's not ..." I blew out a laugh. It was a poor response. And did nothing to dissuade him. "How do you know it's not work?"

"As much as I would love to believe that, I think we both know work has never left you humming in the elevator."

"I was humming?"

"Yep."

I felt heat rise to my cheeks before burying my face in my hands, trying to hide the splitting smile that had erupted. "Can we please not talk about this?"

"It's alright, kiddo. I didn't mean to embarrass you. I'm just glad to see you happy."

"Thanks, David." When he didn't step away, I asked, "Was there anything else?"

"Yes. Are you free this morning? I have something I'd like to discuss with you."

I checked my calendar. "Yeah, all free. Everything ok?"

"Everything is fine. Just come by my office at nine, and I'll fill you in."

When he left, I buried my head in my hands again, laughing at how giddy I felt.

I felt like I was standing on a precipice of mirth, like laughter was caged within me, fighting to escape at any moment. Every time I opened my mouth, I was terrified it was about to burst forth. I could never remember feeling this lightheaded before. And now I knew everyone could see it as well. My face reddened deeper.

Was this normal? I couldn't remember being this way with Brad, but that had been so long ago, and we'd been in college when we'd met. I knew I wasn't developing feelings for Jackson because I'd only seen him the four times we'd slept together and the whole point of this arrangement was that it was strictly casual. No dates, no labels, nothing serious.

But it was true that I felt a little bit intoxicated by him. Infatuated if I really thought about it, but I locked that thought away to worry about some other time. At worst, it was a crush. A harmless, completely casual, not at all serious crush over an extremely handsome man, who just so happened to be the best sex I'd ever had. And who was also smart, funny, kind, interesting. Nope, not going there.

It was just the honeymoon phase. That happened with fuck buddies, right?

I felt a burning in my chest, not completely unpleasant, and the churn of butterflies flitting about my insides. Whatever this was, it didn't change the fact that I didn't want a relationship. Not now. Maybe not ever.

Ok, that was likely an exaggeration, but honestly, I just didn't want to think about it. All I wanted was some casual fun, and Jackson was on board with that. So why did it feel like my own body was betraying me?

The butterflies stuck around throughout my morning, a constant fluttering ache that kept Jackson close to mind, and it required effort to remain focused through my meetings. It didn't help, then, when Jackson texted me.

Jackson: I can't stop thinking about that sexy red bra. I don't know how I'll make it through filming today. I'm going to need to see it again.

Jackson: For science.

Jesus. He was going to be the death of me. For the first time in my life, I considered taking the rest of the afternoon off and heading over to his place. I'd never skipped out early before, and I could hardly believe I was even entertaining the idea. Surely I couldn't? Could I? The very concept thrilled me. But I couldn't. I was far too busy, and even if I did, Jackson was filming today.

But that didn't mean I couldn't give a little back. Maybe even … make things a little *harder* for him …

Before I could talk myself out of it, I messaged him.

Me: Luckily I saved a visual aid for research purposes. Hope it helps

I attached a photo I'd taken of myself in that particular pair. After our successful shopping trip over the weekend, I'd gone home and tried everything on, taking photos of a few and texting Tiff for her opinion on which one would be best for seeing Jackson that night. I hadn't deleted the photos afterward, and now I was glad for it.

I put my mobile down after pressing send, my giddiness skyrocketing. I'd never sent a man a suggestive photo of me before, and I felt like a teenager sneaking a guy into my room without my parent's knowledge. I laughed at myself. What the hell was Jackson doing to me?

"Audrey, can you come into my office?" David was standing in my doorway, and my smile faltered a little. This sounded ... well, not serious; he didn't have his serious face on. But it was certainly curious. For David to call me in first thing meant something. I hoped it had nothing to do with the launch.

This was silly. I'd known David for years now, so why was there a bubble of anxious anticipation swirling in my gut?

David waved me in when I approached. "Audrey, I want you to meet Winnie and Jet."

I looked over at two blond twenty-somethings, who were nervously smiling at me.

"Uh, hi. Nice to meet you. I'm Audrey."

The girl standing closest to me came forward and shook my hand vigorously. "It's so cool to meet you. I'm really looking forward to working together."

Wait, what?

I looked over at David, and he had a fixed smile on his face. If the blond babies hadn't been staring at me starry-eyed, I'd definitely have asked him what the hell he was trying to pull. But it would have to wait until later.

A nagging feeling stirred in me, and I knew before I asked, I was going to regret asking, "Working with me?"

"Yes, Winnie and Jet are our new interns, and I've assigned them to work with you on the MacMillan launch."

I swallowed down my frustration. Did David really think I had the time to be mentoring two complete newbies? I'd told him I could handle it on my own.

Between the four other client accounts I was managing and the seven customer accounts, I barely had time to get home before dark most days, and the added launch would leave me with less time than ever before.

And now I was expected to show these interns the ropes and how to do my job in between all of that? It would result in every task taking twice as long, and I just couldn't believe David thought this was a good idea. Why now?

Fully prepared to tell him to reassign them, the hopeful look on their faces made my resolve crumble. I still remembered what it had been like to start out. Hell, it was David himself who had been the one to show me most of what I knew once upon a time.

And now he was trusting me to do the same.

I swallowed my frustration. I didn't know where I'd find the time, but I would try and make this work.

Surely it wouldn't be too hard to find them something to busy themselves with. "Ok, great, I could use the help. It's really nice to have you two on board."

David looked relieved. "I'm going to get them set up, and I thought you could show them the ropes."

When I returned to my office, I ran over my schedule for the day, rearranging what I could so that I'd be able to spend some time with the interns.

It wasn't until after lunch that Winnie and Jet became my responsibility. It quickly became obvious that they weren't ready to be left on their own. Not that they weren't capable, they seemed smart and proficient, but they had no hands-on experience.

My original plan was to have them manage a few of my other accounts while I focused on the launch, but they couldn't go five minutes without asking me another question or deferring to me before making a decision like they were scared to have the wrong opinion.

But it was their first day, and they just seemed so eager and happy to be there. I couldn't bring myself to complain about it, even to myself. It would be like being mad at two puppies.

Still, for all their "help." I still had to do everything myself, just a lot slower since I walked them through it as I went.

At this rate, we could probably launch the rum in ... Oh, I don't know, a year?

16

AUDREY

"That was meant to be sexy, sorry." We were both laughing as we stepped out of the shower and dried off.

"That's ok; it was funny."

"Sex with me is funny?" He playfully snapped his towel at me, making me yelp.

"I meant fun, not funny."

"So kneeing me in the balls is fun, is it?"

I playfully slapped his shoulder. "It's not my fault you slipped!" Our combined laughter reverberated against the tiles. "Ok, not a great example. And to be honest, I've never had sex be fun before. I've never had so much fun having sex before."

I avoided his gaze while I finished drying off. It was more than I thought I should have said, considering this was just a casual fling. But I couldn't avoid looking at him when he tilted my chin up with a gentle hand and closed the distance between us. "It's the most fun I've had, too."

He looked so sincere, so tender, that my brain shorted out. I didn't really understand how I came to be standing here, pressed up against the sexiest man I'd ever met, who looked at me with more affection than I ever remembered seeing from Brad. I didn't really have any response, not one that contained words anyway, so instead, I threaded my hands into his damp silky hair, now curling slightly, and tried to convey everything I was feeling in a kiss.

When we pulled back, I asked, "I'm guessing the shower isn't the craziest place you've had sex."

"Not exactly. You?"

I wrinkled my nose, feeling more than a little vanilla. "Kind of? I'm not really an exhibitionist, and my ex wasn't very adventurous."

"Tell me this then, what was the best kiss you've ever had?"

Every kiss with you.

But it was too much to say, so I bit my lip and hoped it looked like I was thinking it over. "Ooh, tough one. Probably my first kiss because I snuck out of class to meet Jimmy by the cafeteria, and it was the most naughty thing I'd done to that point."

He feigned offense. "Wow. I don't even rate above Jimmy from school."

I smirk. "You're top five."

His eyes crinkled with humor, and my skin tingled at the sound. "Good to know. Best date?"

"Am I being interviewed right now?"

"I'm just curious. Google will pretty much tell you what you want to know about my love life, and I'm just evening the playing field."

"Fair. Hmm, well, it's going to sound weird, but when I turned twenty-one, Brad took me out to see the Bulls play because he was a huge fan, and I'd never been to a game before. Of course, he spent the entire night trying to educate me on the game and why the Bulls are the best, blah blah blah."

"Sounds like the perfect date so far," he deadpanned.

"Shh, I'm getting there. Now, don't get me wrong, I'm a Jordan fan. I get why the Bulls have the legacy they do, but Brad was driving me a little crazy, so I started going for the other team. And that was the night the Kings came back by thirty-five points, which pretty much made my night even if Brad wasn't happy."

"That's your best date? The Bulls were robbed that night."

"They were not robbed; they were cocky. They came in from a

two-game winning streak, pulled ahead early, then slacked off midway through the third quarter. They assumed they had it in the bag, and the Kings took advantage. They deserved that loss."

"Wow. All this time, I thought you had no flaws, but it turns out you're a terrible Bulls fan." I playfully slapped his bicep. "How did the date end?"

I grimaced at the memory. "The night went downhill pretty fast. After that, we spent date nights at home and only watched the games Brad already knew they'd won." It had been one of the first and last real dates Brad had taken me on, and yet I'd stayed with him for ten years. What did that say about me?

"He's an idiot. If it had been me, I would've taken you out every chance I had."

"Just not to a Bulls game."

"I'm not a masochist." He joked before kissing me and dropping my towel to the floor.

"So would I make the top five?" I asked between kisses.

His damp chest was flush against mine, and the scent of soap and something uniquely him filled my every breath. "Without a doubt."

I didn't register the change in our location until I felt the world tipping and the soft, giving embrace of my bed beneath me as Jackson lowered me.

I was starting to want him in my bed like this more frequently than the sporadic nights we currently had, and that scared the hell out of me.

———

"AUDREY KING'S OFFICE, how can I help you?" Jet had answered the phone on my desk with hardly a second thought, and I was torn between surprise and insult. I'd never had anyone answer my phone before, and I wasn't entirely sure I enjoyed it. I was perfectly capable of answering my own phone and having someone else do it made me feel slightly impotent.

Jet nodded at whoever was on the line, making notes on the pad in front of him, and I pasted on a smile when he hung up and turned to me. The last thing I wanted to do was make him feel unhelpful. Or that I was ungrateful.

Despite my reticence, having them around was actually nice; I just wished I had more for them to do.

"That was Julia, asking if you could move your meeting with them."

"Ok, did she say when she'd prefer to have it?"

"They want you to come over to the distillery this afternoon so you can agree on the launch plans."

On the one hand, I was glad they'd made a decision. I pitched them my two ideas a week ago, and they'd asked for time to mull it over. With the hopeful launch date being just eight weeks away, I was glad they hadn't taken too long to decide.

On the other hand, there went my afternoon. "Ok. That's ok. I think I can make that work." I looked over my calendar; I had three scheduled customer calls to confirm stock counts for reordering. Tapping my fingers on the desk, I wondered what my options were. Maybe I could call them from the road? No, I wouldn't be able to make notes if they wanted changes. Maybe I could just call during my lunch break?

I could just reach out to them first thing in the morning, but we had to send off the order confirmations to the clients tomorrow, and I was cutting it fine already by only giving myself the afternoon to get the numbers sorted.

"Hmm."

"I could go if you're too busy," Jet offered. My fingers stilled in the air.

"No, no, I just need to make some phone calls. Thank you, Jet."

"If you're talking about this month's reorders, I can take care of that. It's a piece of cake."

I chewed the inside of my cheek. It would save me some time, and it would also clear out my afternoon tomorrow.

"Ok."

"Really?" He seemed surprised.

"Of course, that would be great. Now, you'll need to prepare beforehand, go into the system and have last month's order up in case they want a repeat. If not, note down what they want to change, and update the amounts on the invoice before sending it. If you have any trouble, get David or one of the other account managers. But remember—"

"Don't send it until tomorrow. I got it."

Huh, I guess he had been paying attention.

"Ok." My nerves fluttered, but I pushed them down. I really didn't have a choice, and I needed to get on the road already. "Ok. And call me if there's anything. It doesn't matter how small. I'll have reception."

"Don't worry about it; I got this."

He better. And with that, I was out the door.

Jeff and Julia were waiting for me in their office. "As much as we love the idea of a flight tour, Audrey, we think it's a little small for what we were hoping." Jeff always launched straight into business as soon as the niceties were done with, and I'd come to appreciate that. Some clients loved to chatter, and while it was lovely to get to know them, I felt guilty for rushing them when we had a deadline to meet.

Julia jumped in. "Not that we want to go big! Lord knows we can't afford anything like that."

"Right. We want the line to stand for itself, but flights just seemed so ..."

"Boring?" I offered with a smile.

Julia heaved with relief. "Oh, thank god you're not mad. Yes! We've done so many here at the cellar door that it just seems so old hat, and we were really hoping to go with something more hip."

"Good for the 'gram, my son calls it." I bit down on the laugh that threatened to come out and nodded.

"Of course. That's completely understandable. It's still relatively 'hip' in the city, especially for rum, but" I held out a hand, "I understand you want to go with something a little different and a little bigger?"

They nodded.

When they offered nothing else, I continued. "So can I assume that you want to go with the cocktail event?"

"Well, that's what we wanted to talk to you about."

Oh, no. Please don't make me go back to the drawing board. The other ideas were either too expensive or too … well, boring.

"In the draft you sent us, you mentioned it would be like a mini degustation, with the food and cocktails paired … but the expenses you estimated didn't seem like enough for that to be possible."

Sweet relief filled me. "Yes. Actually, I'm glad you brought that up because it's a lot easier to explain in person. Now, degustation was the wrong word, but it was the closest I could come to 'multiple bite-sized meals in a row'." I chuckled. "What I'd really like to do is have the catering focus on local produce and produce a number of options that match the cocktails we decide on, and they'll be walked around and handed out to each guest."

"And everyone would be sitting or standing?"

"Sitting, but we'll arrange lots of options, like bar tables, couches, some armchairs, all in groups of three or four so people can come together, but it keeps the atmosphere more intimate. Especially because we'll limit the event to around fifty people."

"And the price?"

"Well, I based the estimates on some early quotes, so it may change. And for the food, it all depends on the cocktail list and what works best, what's in season, all of that. But once we set a budget, I can promise you we won't go over it."

They passed a look between them, but they were still smiling, so I took it as a good sign.

Jeff nodded and held out a hand to me. "Sounds like we have a plan."

My smile widened. "That's fantastic. I'll get to work immediately and keep you updated."

17

JACKSON

As I stumbled into my apartment, I idly wondered if I had enough ice to cover the number of bruises I was sporting.

Filming this week had been brutal, but today's action scenes, including a particularly acrobatic aerial sequence, had left me battered. Thankfully, I wasn't expected back on set for a few days, which left me just enough time to sleep off most of it.

The issue with rehearsing fight scenes for four straight hours before filming for another four meant that the moment you came to a standstill, your entire body wanted to find the nearest flat surface and remain there for as long as humanly possible.

Every muscle ached as I removed my jacket and draped it over the back of a chair. I'd hang it up properly tomorrow.

Collecting some ice in a towel, I briefly considered opening a beer, but I would probably be asleep before I finished it.

It wasn't until there was a knock at my door that I realized I'd made plans to see Audrey tonight. Shit.

We typically only saw each other late at night, fitting it in around our bizarre schedules, but honestly, I liked that about the situation. Audrey was someone who—so far—hadn't gotten annoyed by my unpredictable hours, and because of her own habit of working late, actually understood.

I couldn't exactly tell her to head home after she'd traveled over here at this time of night, but I could barely stand without swaying. How the hell was I going to have sex?

I opened the door half convinced I was going to apologize and send her home. She must have come straight from the office. Her hair was mussed, strands escaping her high bun in many directions, and her pants crinkled from wear.

But her eyes were bright and her smile wide, and she'd never looked more beautiful.

I was kicking myself for not having the energy to spend the night with her.

"Hi."

"Hi." A crinkle in her brow. "You forgot, didn't you?"

"No, I …" I sighed, my shoulders sagging. "Yes. I'm sorry. I feel like an ass."

"No, don't! It's fine."

"It's not." I was suddenly sure she was about to leave, and I no longer wanted her to. "At least let me make it up to you with a tea or something."

She stifled a laugh. "You think tea is going to make it up to me?"

"Hot chocolate?"

"Oh, now you're talking," she said suggestively.

I felt I was doing a pretty decent job hiding how awful I felt until Audrey moved in to kiss me against the kitchen island, her hand pushing against a particularly tender area of my chest, and I wasn't able to hide my wince. "Ugh"

Immediately she pulled back, concerned. "Are you ok?"

"Actually, no." I looked at her apologetically. "I'm sorry, I'm completely exhausted. We filmed a big fight scene today, and I'm a bit banged up. Then I forgot you were coming over, and I feel awful, but I just don't think I'm capable of anything tonight."

"You should have sent me home then," she said, softly chiding me before straightening up and asking, "Do you have a bath?"

"Yeah, why?"

"Because I know exactly what you need. Do you think you can stay awake for the next ten minutes?"

"Should I be worried?"

She laughed. "Don't you trust me?" She leaned in, careful not to lean against me, and kissed me lightly. "Just wait here; I'll be right back."

She stood and watched me with a smile, then disappeared in the direction of my bathroom.

I let my eyes drift, just for a moment, my head falling back onto the couch.

"Jace?"

"Mmm?"

"Oh. I almost feel bad about waking you."

"Was I asleep?"

"Yes, and I promise, if this weren't the best thing for those aching muscles, I wouldn't make you get up right now."

I groaned as she pulled me up off the couch and into the bathroom, where I was struck by the sight of my bathtub filled to the brim with bubbles. I couldn't help but laugh. The last time I had a bubble bath, I must have been nine years old. How did I even own bubble bath? Was it left over from the last tenant? Was it even ok to still use it? Did bubble bath go bad?

My thoughts were interrupted as Audrey began lifting my shirt, her fingers skirting over my skin. I wished I wasn't so damn tired.

"Not how I expected to be getting you naked tonight, but I'll take it." She moved on to my belt as I took the shirt from her hands, barely stifling the groan as I tugged it over my head and threw it to the floor.

It wasn't until I was stepping out of my pants and underwear that I heard Audrey's soft gasp. "Holy hell, Jace, this was just from today?"

The biggest bruise was splayed across my left side, a deep, angry red splotch that was going to make any sort of exercise an impossibility for at least a few days.

"Yeah, we got the timing wrong, and I got a foot to the ribs." Just another day in the office.

She shook her head with disbelief before pinching her nose. "Ok, get in the bath."

"Yes, ma'am." Her eyes immediately flew open and fixed me with a dark stare. God, she looked cute, all riled up. I lifted my hands in surrender and took a tentative step into the bubbles.

The water was on the right side of hot, but as I slid into it, all my muscles took a collective sigh. "Jesus, I've been missing out." My eyes slid shut, and I let my head sag back against the edge.

"Told you." She sounded smug.

I smiled. It suited her.

Her fingers brushed through my scalp, making something warm unfurl within me. "A massage would be better, but that's probably best left to the professionals."

"Mmmm." I rolled my head to the left and cracked an eye open to find her perched on the side of the bath. "Are you getting in?"

"Are you sure? I can go if you want."

That was the last thing I wanted. "No, stay."

She stood up and started to undress, avoiding my eyes while a shy smile played on her lips. I really didn't know what I found more intoxicating, the moments when she was confident or the moments she was shy. Both were sending my heart into a frenzy.

Then my mouth went dry as I saw the lingerie that had been hiding underneath her work clothes. Jesus, had she worn that to work?

I couldn't tear my eyes off her, even if I'd wanted to. "You're beautiful. You know that?"

She hid her face as she removed the last of her clothes, but the blush on her cheeks remained as she stepped nearer. She stood at the end of the bath where my head was and motioned me forwards.

I indulged in a long look at her naked body, mentally kicking myself for being so tired while simultaneously wondering how I got so lucky. I scooted forward to let her sit behind me, enjoying the feel of her warm thighs slotting around my waist and the feel of her soft breasts against my back. She encouraged me to lean into her, and my head fell back against her shoulder. I hummed pleasantly as her hand absently raked through my hair.

Honestly, I was quite happy where I was. I'd never felt more relaxed, minus the aching all over my body, and I couldn't remember any time I'd felt that way with the women I slept with. This was new territory for me.

Her breath ghosted across my neck. "Feel good?"

"Mmm." My breathing had become deep and drawn out, all movement and thoughts languid. I felt her responding chuckle rumble against my back.

"If you fall asleep on me, I might be stuck here forever."

I smiled. Having her around forever sounded fan-fucking-tastic if it meant more nights like this, but we had agreed to take this slow, so I just ran my hands down her calves where they were crossed at my waist. "You'll have to keep me awake then."

She dipped her head down and placed a few open kisses on my neck, speaking softly. "Ok then, tell me a story. How did you get into acting?"

I opened my eyes, recalling the answer fondly. I'd told this story a million times over when the show had become a hit.

But I never told them the whole truth, only a version of it. The real story was mine, and I liked knowing I wasn't giving all of myself away, even if I had suddenly gained a million followers on social media and was being photographed on red carpets.

And yet. I wanted to tell Audrey. Maybe it was how relaxed I felt, enveloped as I was by the bubbles and her body. Or maybe it was how safe I felt with her. I trusted her.

"Believe it or not, I was a shy kid, couldn't really figure out what I wanted to do, but tried a bit of everything. I loved sports but never really stood out or wanted to. When my baby sister Sarah was really young, Mom took a second job at night to help pay the bills since I was half a decade older, I helped out by babysitting." Audrey had begun tracing patterns on my forearm, and I moved to interlace our fingers together, hugging her hand to my chest.

Being a big brother was one of my proudest jobs, and it felt good to open up to Audrey about it. "Sarah liked reading, and she loved bedtime stories, so I started messing about with the voices as I read to her just to make her laugh. Her favorite was *The Twits*, do you know it?"

"No."

I twisted a little so that I could see her face, huffing as my body reminded me of how sore I was. The fond look in Audrey's eyes was almost overwhelming, so I leaned in to kiss her before I said something stupid. It was soft and sweet, and for a long moment, I forgot that she wasn't my girlfriend, we weren't dating, and I shouldn't be thinking about researching faraway resorts with in-room spas so we could do all the things I wanted to but couldn't right now.

I leaned my head back against her when our lips parted, my eyes trained on the ceiling. "I found I liked playing around at being someone else, so when I hit high school, I tried drama. Theater still gives me anxiety, but I like film and TV. And I'm good at it. I'm just not so hot on the press and attention."

"Well, now I feel bad."

"What for?"

"I, um, may have looked you up."

"May have, huh?" I pulled my hand out of her grasp to tickle her.

"Ok, ok, stop!" She giggled and wriggled her foot out of my grasp, water sloshing against the tub. "I felt terrible for not knowing who you were at the bar that first night, so I did some research."

"Not everything they say is true, you know. Most of the interviews we give are fluff pieces, and after a few hours, you get bored enough you just start talking nonsense."

"Why do I get the feeling you're preparing me for something awful?"

"No, it's nothing like that. I guess I just don't want you to think that's me, is all. It's all most people see."

She considered this. "I'm sorry."

"Why? It's not your fault. It just comes with the job."

"Still …" She sighed. "If it helps, I only ended up looking through some photos. You get topless a lot."

My laugh bounced against the tile. "You do one shirtless scene …"

"I don't think anyone is complaining. I'm certainly not."

"See something you liked?"

She chuckled to herself. "Actually, there was one that made me laugh; maybe you can explain it to me," Her phone was lying on the floor on top of her pants, and as she stretched out of the bath to get it, I started to wonder which one she was referring to.

Maybe it was the shoot where they had me on top of a children's rocking horse in jeans and a cowboy hat? It was for Vogue, but still … Sometimes I really did wonder about this job.

I watched as she opened her Instagram app, scrolled through, and saw what looked like a series of bar and restaurant accounts. I assumed she followed for work purposes, followed by an overwhelming amount of photos of dogs dressed in various outfits.

Fuck, she was adorable. I buried my smile into her neck.

Finally, she found what she was after. "Here it is! Ok, you have to tell me, who pissed you off here?"

When I saw the photo, I started laughing. Of course, it was that one. How could I forget? That damn photo the promo team had taken at the table read had been retweeted so many times I'd lost count. Usually with the hashtag #bedroomeyes.

I was surprised at her interpretation of it. "What makes you think I was angry with someone?"

She lifted a hand to trail a finger along my chin. "Your jaw gets kind of set when you're holding something back. Plus, it sort of looks like you want to kill whoever you're looking at."

Catching her hand with my own, I proceeded to kiss each fingertip. "That's Wes' fault." I twisted as best as I could in the tight space so I could kiss her. "He was messing around during the table read. He knew the camera crew was behind him, so he'd sent me a text telling me my pants were undone."

Her laughter echoed around me, and I sunk back into her, happier than I could remember feeling in a long, long time.

"Funny, you're the only person who has seen that photo and saw I was angry, except for Sarah."

"Actually, there was one thing I read about you." It sounded casual in a way that was anything but, and I waited for her to continue.

"That you have a habit of sleeping around."

I fought to keep my expression unchanged while she rushed on. "Not that that's a bad thing! In fact, it's what made me realize you were probably the perfect person to have this sort of arrangement with, you know?"

Ouch.

Audrey had just laid out my history, and while it was hardly a lie that I hadn't had any long-term romantic relationships in recent years—hell, it was something Sarah harped about at least once every time we saw each other—it hurt to hear it from Audrey.

Especially when she was holding it up as the exact reason she was interested in me.

Because, in her mind, we would never be anything more than sex.

The disappointment was palpable, but I hid it. I liked her a lot, and I wanted to be with her. And if the only way to have that was to keep it casual, then I'd take what I could get.

"So you've never had a serious girlfriend?" Audrey ventured when I still hadn't said anything.

"Not for a few years," I said, although it had probably been longer than that. "I've been too focused on my career. Even before starting on the show, it was a constant grind, each role or opportunity making the next one possible. And once we knew the show was a hit, it didn't stop. It's a bit of a double-edged sword—the more you build up your rep, the less worried you have to be about being offered work, but the more you're expected to do for the public." I threaded our fingers together and noted how well we fit, fighting the urge to say that to her. "It's hard to offer much to someone else in those circumstances."

"You must have dated a lot of beautiful women." I heard the insecurity behind her statement.

"Yes. In fact, I'm seeing a gorgeous senior account manager right now."

She snorted. "You know what I mean."

"Audrey, I don't know how to break it to you, but you're beautiful. Seriously."

"I know! Thank you. I guess I'm just not used to hearing it from someone else."

While I was glad she could acknowledge it herself, it made me wonder why she wasn't comfortable hearing it from others. Again, I wondered what the hell her idiot of an ex must have been thinking.

In fact, I was curious about several things regarding him, which was probably why I didn't stop myself from asking, "Do you ever regret getting married?"

"Sometimes." There was so much unsaid in that one word, and I wished she felt comfortable enough that she could tell me everything behind it.

Her tone was pensive when she spoke again. "Do you think all relationships are doomed?"

This time I turned to look at her. "That's dark."

Her brow creased, but she was mostly contemplative. "Is it? I guess my experience isn't really a good example." There it was again, that glimpse into her past that she wasn't ready to share with me. Ever since the night we had met at the bar when she'd mentioned that all she'd wanted to be "was enough," I'd wanted to know what it was that had brought her to this point.

A tilt of her head. "Or maybe I'm wondering what the secret is."

"The secret to relationships?"

"To making it last."

"I … don't think there is one."

"That's what I'm afraid of."

"Is that why you don't want anything serious?"

"Maybe …" She sighed.

"Do you think you'll ever get married again?"

"Um, I don't know, I hadn't really given it much thought. It seems so far off, I guess. But yeah, I think I would if I met the right person. But I definitely wouldn't bother with all the bells and whistles the second time around. Ugh, to think of all the money I could have saved if we hadn't bothered with guest favors," she groaned.

I found it easier to laugh with her than to deal with the block of ice that had just formed in my stomach.

Later, after Audrey had gone home, I laid in bed wondering how the hell I'd gone and fallen for such an incredible woman when the last thing she wanted was to date me.

18

AUDREY

The thing about Jackson's apartment was that it was obvious that the whole place had come pre-packaged, although it at least looked lived in. Jackson's room was the only place that looked exclusively like him, furnished in dark charcoals, navy, and a smattering of dirty clothes. The only other uniquely him piece in the place was the cluttered shelving unit that acted as the divider between the living and dining areas. What was probably once very minimally arranged knick-knacks was now a litter of books, scripts, show memorabilia, framed pictures of his family, and some selected fan gifts.

I was enjoying some well-earned post-orgasmic bliss, happily reading with my back propped up against Jace's headboard as he laid beside me, one hand drawing lazy patterns over my thigh.

"This is a great script," I said, still reading.

His head turned towards me. "You think so?"

I nodded. "Definitely. I know next to nothing about movies, except for the ones I like, but this is really clever and funny, and not really like any of the millions of movies I normally see coming out."

"Yeah, it's kind of perfect."

"I can see you as Parker."

His laughter made me inordinately happy, a sort of smug joy that I was able to bring that out of him. Placing a gentle kiss on my hip, he continued his ministrations on my leg. "Thank you. I'm having a hard time convincing anyone else."

"Really? Why?"

"It's not exactly what I'm known for right now, and the director straight up told me to my face that he couldn't picture me in the role. Said he was surprised someone on my current trajectory was even interested."

"Damn," I said, and he hummed dryly in agreement. I spared him a look, trying to read his expression. "You sound disappointed."

"I am." He rolled onto his back, rubbing a hand over his face. "I don't know. Now is the right time to capitalize on where the show is at in the ratings. One bad season and scripts like this," he said, gesturing to it, "definitely won't be coming my way anymore."

He punctuated this with a long, resigned sigh.

"And even if I manage to get the role somehow—and that's a big *if*—it's a risk. Taking on a movie like that will move my career in a totally different direction. If it flops, it could affect the show."

"And if it doesn't?"

"Then it doesn't. But it's always better to plan for the worst and be surprised."

"Wow, that's an obscure way of looking at it. And a rather depressing one."

"Welcome to showbiz."

"In Tiff's words, fuck that." I placed the script on the side table and maneuvered down the bed to lay beside him, bringing a hand up to cup his cheek. "Forget about all the other stuff, the critics and the producers and the audience—all that junk. It should be about what you want. And if this role doesn't work out, then you go for the next one. You're hard-working, dedicated, and passionate. They'd be stupid not to hire you."

I waited as he thought it over, his eyes searching mine in quiet contemplation. As the seconds passed, I wondered if I'd crossed a line, presumed something too personal for the kind of relationship we had. We hadn't known each other that long, but it felt like we were becoming friends, and I wouldn't have thought twice about talking to a friend like that.

He brushed a stray hair behind my ear. "You're incredible; you know that?"

Before I could respond, his fingers reached into the hair at my neck, pulling me in closer, and I sank into the caress of his lips on mine.

It was lazy and slow, a far cry from the first night we spent together, but just as enjoyable. If I let myself, I could picture this, us, whiling away the weekends curled up in each other.

What would it be like to have that?

To wake up next to him instead of always leaving?

"You're not so bad yourself," I said when we eventually separated. When I tucked myself into his side, I caught sight of my bag over his shoulder and remembered what I had brought with me tonight.

Would he think it was sweet or strange?

"Jackson?"

"Hmm?" His contented answer rumbled under my cheek.

"Pass me my bag?"

He stretched one arm out to get it, passing it to me. I let it fall to the floor once I pulled the small paperback out.

"What's this?" He asked.

Wanting to see his reaction, I sat up, and he followed suit, taking the offering when I held it out to him. "I hope it's not weird. I stumbled across it at second hand bookstore and thought of you."

He looked up from the thin, worn copy of Roahl Dahl's *The Twits*. The force of his smile took my breath away. "I haven't seen this in years. Thank you."

"You're welcome."

We settled back on the bed, bodies flush against each other but not in a rush to do anything except lie together. After a long moment, he spoke, changing the subject completely. "So, you told me how you met, but how long have you known Tiffany?"

"Years. She was my rock during the divorce, too. We both work long hours, and she works most nights, and she still managed to be at my place every weekend, with a terrible movie and enough chocolate to heal any heartbreak. I don't know where I'd be without her."

"She sounds like a great friend."

"She really is. I never had any siblings growing up, but she's the closest thing to a sister I have."

"Not to mention, she made this happen." He motioned between us.

"Something she loves to remind me of every chance she gets. I may never live it down."

"You say that like it's a bad thing."

"Not at all. It's a great thing." I trailed my hand down his incredible abs and wrapped it around the base of his dick, gently squeezing and stroking him slowly. "Spectacular, really."

"Spectacular?" His voice was low, rough. "Mmm, yeah, just like that."

God, he was delicious. Brushing my nose along the curve of his neck, I breathed in his scent, kissing my favorite spot at the hinge of his jaw, where I could whisper in his ear. I'd learned he really enjoyed that, and the hungry sounds it resulted in also happened to be one of my favorite things.

It was win/win, really.

"Tell me what you like." We'd slept together enough now that I didn't need to ask, but it had become a sort of game now. And I'd found the answers were always enjoyable.

His lip quirked up. "You, baby. Everything about you."

How was it that he could make me blush so furiously with a few words while I had his thickening cock in my hand; I didn't know.

Unfairly, he continued. "I like these lips." He tilted my chin up so he could kiss them, catching each lip between his and sucking a little before leaning back.

"And I really like your hands." He thrust up into my hand, and I squeezed harder, continuing my strokes. When I reached his tip, I twisted my wrist and thumbed over the liquid that was beginning to collect. My mouth watered at the sight of it.

"I like you," he said, and my heart fluttered at the sincerity of those words, an echo of my own thoughts.

Because I liked him.

A lot.

For more than just the sex.

I liked how much he loved his sister and how passionately he spoke about his work, how intently he listened when we talked and how genuinely he cared about my answers. How beautiful he could make me feel.

But I also knew I couldn't tell him any of this. We'd said it was casual. That's what we—what I wanted. What we'd agreed. And he'd said it himself; he'd only ever had short flings. Who knew if he even wanted anything more?

Besides, the last thing I needed was to rush into something. Not that Jackson was anything like Brad, but I mean, I still had work and the launch—I was still trying to juggle the interns as well—and yet. And yet. All of the noise in my head seemed to quieten when I was with him. And I found myself wanting more. Wanting to know what it might be like to go out on a date. To wake up next to him. To have this be more.

If that were even possible.

Would we even fit into each other's lives outside of the late nights and great sex?

"I like you, too," I finally said, feeling a sudden nervousness that I hadn't felt since our first night together.

"You know, in the few years since I moved in, this might be the most time I've spent in this apartment." His expression was fond but unreadable.

Oh.

Guilt trickled, cold in my veins. Because I was the reason.

Over the last few weeks, any time together had been spent inside, either at my place or his, and I suddenly wondered if there was somewhere else he was supposed to be. Somewhere he'd rather be.

"I hadn't thought of it like that. In the last year, I've spent so much time between the office and home; I'm not a very exciting date." I forced a casual laugh, or at least what I hoped passed as casual, despite the sinking feeling I had. "Does it bother you?"

"No. It's nice to enjoy something out of the public eye. Anytime I'm spotted with a woman, even a friend, it's posted and scrutinized."

There was something he wasn't saying, and I blinked, at a loss of how to respond. Because, like an idiot, I'd started wanting more without giving any thought to what that might actually mean.

And even if it didn't change how I felt about him, I didn't know that I was ready for all the extras that being with him might entail.

"That sounds awful. I wouldn't want that kind of attention on me, that's for sure."

"So I guess that rules out taking you to dinner," he joked, not meeting my eyes.

"I guess so." I brushed an imaginary piece of fluff off of the comforter. "But …"

"But?"

"How do you feel about take-out and cocktails?"

———

THE NEXT NIGHT FOUND JACKSON, Tiffany, and myself lounging in my living room, drinks in hand and an abandoned card game on the coffee table.

It was the first time since Jackson and I had met that we were doing something I would consider more couple than casual.

I had the distinct sense we were both avoiding a discussion on what we were or where this was going, and I was glad about that. Selfishly, I would rather live in ignorance than have to give this up. I liked what we had right now.

Conversation was easy, even when we weren't talking about anything at all, and he never seemed bothered when I talked about work or needed to vent after a particularly bad day. Time always seemed to disappear when we were together.

Although, that's how it had started with Brad.

Another reason I was glad to put off the talk with Jackson.

After dinner, we had half-heartedly tried to play a game called "Oh Hell," which we'd subsequently given up on, both because the rules were a bit confusing but mostly because Tiff and Jace had gotten embroiled in a discussion about their favorite science fiction films. I had nothing to add, so I sat quietly aside and enjoyed watching them banter.

I ignored the ache in my heart.

"Why is it so hard to believe I've never seen *Star Trek*? It's so old! I mean, I guess I've seen a bit of all of them at some point—original, next-gen, voyager, discovery ... Was there another one?" She topped up her martini. "Besides, *Lord of the Rings* is where it's at. Those elves can get it."

Jackson laughed. "You're a closet nerd, aren't you?"

"Honey, I haven't seen a closet in years. And if I'm a nerd, then I'm fucking proud of it."

"And yet you haven't seen *Star Trek*! I suppose you wouldn't have a favorite captain then."

Tiff pondered the question. "Maybe Picard? Whoever Patrick Stewart plays."

"That's the one."

"Although I would let Chris Pine do pretty much whatever he wants to me. Except choking. No offense if that's your thing." Tiff's tone was perfectly calm, like she was commenting on the weather.

I bit my lip to stop myself laughing, but it was a lost cause as soon as Jackson coughed on his drink. He recovered quickly, wiping off his shirt and looking between Tiff and me questioningly. "You're screwing with me, aren't you?"

I chuckled and shook my head. "'Fraid not." Of all the things Tiff liked or didn't like in bed, that was on the tame side of things. His head would probably explode if he knew the full list of kinks she had. Some of which I shared. Some of which Jackson himself had introduced me to.

I had always been fascinated by Tiff's stories of the things she'd tried. It had helped me get to know what I wanted to try and what I definitely, under no circumstances ever, would go anywhere near.

I turned to Tiff, who was no doubt itching to actually mess with him, but I pointed a finger at her and hoped like hell I could at least save him from the many dirty images she'd already put in my head. "Don't even think about it; you'll scare him."

She faked offense. "Oh, come on, he's a big boy. He can handle it!" I knew from the twist of her mouth and the playful look in her eye that she was up to something, but my reaction time wasn't fast enough to stop her from turning to Jackson and saying, "I mean, you did say he was a … *big* boy … didn't you?" She used her hands to indicate an appropriately "big" size, and my face flushed faster than the time it had taken her even to finish her statement.

Ground? Please swallow me whole now.

My attention was then caught by Jackson's belly laugh, and I took a deep breath. Ok, maybe this was ok. I mean, she wasn't wrong about his size, but Jesus, did she need to let it slip that I'd told her that?

"Damn, ok. I didn't actually know women talked about shit like that," He looked at Tiff. "Jealous?"

It was now Tiff's turn to bark with laughter, a short sharp sound that only ever came out when she was truly surprised by something funny. "Fuck, no, stud. But I'm proud of my little Audrey here. I just hope you know what you're doing with that thing."

I stood up from the couch. "Okay, that's enough about my sex life, thank you very much. If you both don't mind, I'm just going to get another drink." I could still hear their laughter as I retreated to the kitchen. Hearing them get along so well spread a warmth deep through my gut, settled and calm.

Fuck, I was so screwed.

19

JACKSON

It had been weeks since my conversation with Addison Michaels, and there was some buzz going around that he was ready to offer the role to someone, so when Terry called me, I hoped he had good news.

He didn't.

"Bad news, buddy. Apparently, Addison's got someone in mind for the part you wanted. Word's getting around that he's not taking auditions until he's spoken to his first choice."

Damnit. "That's ok, Terry. Thanks for letting me know. There'll be other roles."

"That's the spirit! Exactly. Want me to say yes to the teen series?"

I grimaced. I'd really hoped that getting the role in *Subversion* would take that choice out of my hands. "How soon do I need to give them an answer?"

"We probably don't want to wait much longer, but they're definitely keen to get you on board. Why? Are you trying to get them to up the offer?"

"Not exactly. It's not that I don't appreciate the gig, but do you think you could canvas for some other options? Ones more aligned with the Michael's role?"

"Of course! I've been hoping you'd say that. What changed, man?"

"Just got some good advice."

"I shouldn't be worried about my job, should I?" Terry asked jokingly.

"Definitely not."

"Leave it with me, J."

Disappointed, I returned to set. It wasn't like something else wouldn't come along, but damn, getting Parker would have been good. I knew I could bring something special to it, and while Addison hadn't exactly been responsive when I'd met him, he had seemed interested in my ideas. Unless that was just his way of letting me down easy. I wondered if he'd already known then who he wanted in it.

I hoped he didn't think I was going to let this part go without a fight.

———

SUNDAY, I found myself surrounded by more tulle and satin than I'd ever thought possible. It was two weeks away from my sister's big day, and apparently, now was the only time Sarah could find to schedule her last dress fitting.

Which meant, instead of our usual Sunday tradition of bacon and eggs, I was sipping terrible shop coffee and starving. Sarah had promised me she'd thank me by taking me out to brunch after. I agreed because not only was I the best big brother ever—a fact I told Sarah at least three times that morning—but also because I normally cooked.

"You're my only big brother; you're my only brother, period, so that's cheating. Also, you can't proclaim yourself to be the best. That's my job." Her voice was muffled by the thick curtain of the dressing room, but her sarcastic tone was loud and clear.

"Have you decided on where we're going for brunch yet?"

"No, I'll google it."

Her head popped out from behind the curtain, "Don't you know what's good around here? We're right by your apartment."

"I haven't really bothered to check anything out yet."

She rolled her eyes and disappeared again. "You've lived there for three years already. Stop acting like it's temporary. Just buy the place. At least then I'll know where to send your mail."

We'd had this conversation a few times since I'd moved back home for the show, but how could I? It was hard putting roots down anywhere because my next job could be anywhere. Yes, having a more permanent home where my family was would be great, but it was a big decision.

You'd barely believe I was the older sibling the way she acted sometimes, but I was grateful that Sarah did her best to keep me grounded.

"And what if my next job is in LA or Vancouver?"

"Then you can rent it, or Matt and I can housesit, I don't know. You can figure it out when it happens." The curtain pulled back, and she stepped out, the softness of the silk dress clashing with the scowl she directed towards me. "What is so wrong about making plans?"

It was the first time I'd seen the dress outside of some screenshots Sarah had texted me months ago. "Wow, Sarah ..."

She looked down, smoothing her hands over the material. "It's ok?"

"You look stunning."

She blinked rapidly, holding her tears at bay, and I felt a lump form in my throat. "Thanks, Jace." She turned to the mirror and let out a long breath. "I can't believe it's happening."

"Matt's a lucky man."

She turned back to me. "You deserve this, too, someday." I started to respond, but Sarah waved me off. "I know. You never pictured yourself as the marrying type."

And the thing was, she was right.

But lately, something had shifted.

In the past, if I gave marriage any thought, it was only to

dismiss it as a possibility for far down the road—something to consider once life felt more stable. Once I was in the right place to be the partner I wanted to be.

It wasn't so long ago that I had needed to take any odd job to pay my rent, including a particularly awful period where my parents had forced me to take money from them so I could continue auditioning. I owed them a lot, literally and figuratively, and I intended to pay back every cent with interest.

So how could I even start thinking about starting my own family?

Which was why it was easier to say I wasn't interested in marriage than have to answer why I was still single constantly.

Keep things simple. Nothing personal. Nothing lasting.

But with Audrey ...

"Actually ..."

"What?!" Her shout echoed in the small shop, sending some worried glances in our direction. Sarah smiled as the dressmaker came over to see if everything was alright, and then they both disappeared behind the curtain again so Sarah could get back into her regular clothes.

It wasn't until we were seated at a nearby cafe, waiting for our meals, that Sarah brought it up again. I was surprised it had taken her this long, to be honest.

"Ok, where is Jackson, and what have you done with him? Are you seriously thinking of getting married? Who is she? You haven't already eloped, have you?"

"Calm down. I don't mean right now. It's just something that I'm not necessarily opposed to anymore. I don't want a whole circus, but I get it, I think. Wanting it."

She brought her hands to her mouth, trying to contain her glee. "I think I might cry! Does this mean you've changed your mind about helping us put together the favors for the wedding?"

"Actually, I've heard you could save a lot by not bothering with favors."

"Did Mom tell you to say that? She's been going on and on about how tacky she thinks it is."

"She does? I thought it would be right up her alley. She loves all that traditional stuff."

"I know! That's what I said." She raised her cup, then stilled. "So, wait. If it wasn't Mom, then who? Since when do you know anything about weddings?"

Shit, she had me there.

Her eyes narrowed, suspicious. "What aren't you telling me?"

"Nothing. It was just something a friend told me."

"A *friend* friend?"

Moments like this reminded me of the age gap between us. "If you're asking me whether I'm seeing someone, then the answer is yes." Not exactly the whole truth, but now was hardly the time to explain to Sarah what was going on with Audrey and me. Mostly because I barely knew myself.

"Are you sleeping with a married woman?" She sounded so scandalized that I stifled a laugh.

"No, fuck no. Geez, Sarah, think a little better of me."

Her relief was evident. "No, I do. That's what shocked me. Ok, so what then? A wedding planner? A celebrant? A singer who does weddings on the side? I haven't been keeping up with your Twitter mentions."

"It's none of those things. Forget I said anything."

"Yeah, no chance. Come on, tell me about her."

"It's … I'm trying not to jinx it. She's special."

She was silent for so long I almost wondered if she hadn't heard me, then she blinked and said, "Huh."

"Go on."

"What?"

"Say it."

"I've never seen you like this before. You really like her, don't you?"

"I really do. I'm just not sure how she feels."

"You're in so much trouble."

"Oh, I know. I definitely know."

"So when do I get to meet this miracle woman who is amazing enough to change my brother's mind about relationships?"

"Ok, calm down. You don't have to act like my wanting a relationship is some miracle, and secondly, you are not meeting her."

"Firstly, yes it is, and second, good luck stopping me."

"Sarah," I said, firm.

"Jackson," she mimicked.

I huffed a sigh, knowing there was no winning.

While Sarah wasn't the type to actually stalk someone, there would be no getting her off my case until I relented. And ok, maybe I actually liked the idea of having them meet. Sarah was my closest friend, and family was important to me, and Audrey was quickly becoming someone I could see myself being with long term.

No matter how often I told myself it wasn't going to be anything more, that Audrey only wanted something casual and it wasn't likely going to last, I couldn't help the way I felt. I was falling for her. I couldn't stop it.

I was going crazy trying to work out what was going on between us. I liked Audrey more than I had liked someone in a really long time, so yes, sue me for wanting to introduce the two most important women in my life to each other.

And I hoped that if they met and liked each other, it would help Audrey see that we could work as something more.

Two birds, one stone.

Or possibly, a complete and utter disaster.

"Fine. How about next weekend? Our usual Sunday brunch at my place."

"Wow, really? You barely even put up a fight there. She really has got you wrapped around her finger."

"Oh, look, our food's here, eat up."

"Subtle, Jace." she chuckled. "Now, I really can't wait to meet her."

20

JACKSON

The light that crept into the room between half-drawn shades woke me. I wondered for a dazed moment why I'd never had this issue before, then realized it was because I'd rolled away from my usual spot on the bed, the reason for which was curled up next to me.

I'd had Audrey in my bed many times now but never like this.

Any nights we'd spent together had ended long before morning, one of us heading home to sleep in our own bed, something I'd be grateful for when we first met. I rarely let anyone stay at my place in the past.

But with Audrey, I found it hard not to want more of her. More of her time, more of her body, more of her mind.

And ever since that night where we'd done nothing more than talk in a bath full of bubbles, I'd wanted to wake up next to her.

Last night had given me hope that she wanted the same thing since all it had taken was a gentle kiss and a quiet "stay with me" to convince her.

I propped myself on one elbow to get a better look at her just because I could.

She faced me, curled on her side, still asleep, burrowed under the covers. It was adorable.

She was even more beautiful like this, if that was possible. Her hair was in disarray against the pillow, and my fingers ached to run through it, to sort out the tangles and smooth it down, but it would likely wake her, so I settled with gently moving a wayward strand away from her face. There was a small wrinkle embossed across her cheek where the pillowcase had marked her during the night.

I couldn't hold myself back. The soft expression of her face and that damn little crease called out to me, and I leaned down to kiss it.

Her smile formed beneath my lips when I moved to capture them with my own.

"Mmm, morning," she said between lazy kisses.

But I wasn't interested in talking.

We moved slowly, more instinct than action, skin on skin and warmth and closeness, intimate in a way I couldn't quite name. Our kisses were messy, just languid slides of lips against lips, cheeks, skin.

Audrey shifted onto her stomach, reaching and pulling until I was blanketed over her, arching and rolling her ass against my dick, the only part of me more awake than the rest.

It was a slow slide between her thighs, and when she hitched her hips just right, I was fucking the hot, wet warmth of her, and fuck, it was incredible. We were touching, everywhere we could, head to toe, in and out and around each other. My entire existence was focused on her.

How we fit together, how close we were. How close I wanted to be.

And she was wet, so wet, slicking me up between her thighs. It was tight and hot, wet and velvet smooth. The way she curled into and around me, her hands pulling me closer, arching into me. It made me protective, possessive of her.

"Everything you do feels amazing," Audrey said as she moved with me, rolling steady, our bodies finding a rhythm. When I brushed against her clit, she pushed back, asking for, wanting more. "Wish we could stay like this."

"Yes, stay here. Stay with me" I felt incoherent, words breathed out against the slope of her shoulder.

Audrey was the same, quick breaths that were soft moans half lost into the pillow, interlaced with pleas of "I'm so close" and "Hold me" and "I want you."

My forearms shook with the effort of holding myself up. "You have me." Forever.

"Oh, right there, yes."

"Fu—" Whatever I was about to say was lost as we came together, every inch of us pressed tightly together.

The sun was more demanding by the time we finally pulled ourselves from the bed, bone-weary and sated from pleasure.

Her stomach growled. "Hungry?" I asked.

"Starving." Her lips curled into a wide smile. "I could run down to the bakery on the corner, grab us something?"

"Ah. About that." I tried to sound casual when I was anything but. "Would you like to stay and have brunch with Sarah and me? She'd really like to meet you."

I'd really like you to stay.

Caught off guard, she chewed on her lip as she slipped back into her underwear.

"Ok." She finally said. "Do you think she'll like me?"

"Of course. Probably more than she likes me." Audrey rewarded me with a bright laugh and a relaxed shift in her shoulders.

"Is there anything I need to know before I meet her?"

I'd just finished pulling a pair of jeans on, t-shirt in hand, but I drop it onto the bed in preference of taking her face in my hands and kissing her, languid and deep.

When I came up for air, I stayed close, touching my forehead to hers. "Just be you."

It was the right thing to say because she relaxed in my arms, a happy little sigh escaping her, and I clamp my lips shut before I said something ridiculous like, "be mine," or "I love you."

The buzzer goes, alerting us to Sarah's arrival.

"Are you sure about this? I could sneak you out," I jokingly said, relieved when she pushed me out of the bedroom so she could finish getting dressed.

I stepped outside the apartment before Sarah reached the door because it had just occurred to me that I hadn't really told her that Audrey and I weren't officially dating, and if Sarah goes into full sister mode, we might not be talking after today either.

Sarah's face contorted into confusion when she spotted me. "What are you doing hovering outside your door like a weirdo?"

I kept my voice quiet. "Ok, I need to ask you to do something, and you need to be cool about it."

"What did you do?"

I was aware that we were loitering outside my doorway where any of my neighbors could walk by and hear us, but I was also not about to have this conversation inside my apartment where Audrey was, so I sped through it as quickly as I could. "I really like this woman, and I love you, but I need you to try not to give her a hard time—"

"Why would I—"

"Because you're looking out for me. And I appreciate that; I do. But she didn't know you were coming over until about five minutes ago, and this is still very new, and I haven't told her that I want more yet."

Sarah's lips formed a hard line, and she blew a stern breath out of her nose. "Dear God, you're such an idiot." And then she stormed past me to the apartment.

Well, this should be fun.

"Oh, hi." I closed the door to find Sarah walking up to Audrey, who was sitting nervously at the kitchen island.

Sarah bounded over to Audrey and reached her hand out, "I'm Sarah, Jackson's little sister."

They shook. "Audrey. Nice to meet you."

"You, too." I watched with apprehension as Sarah casually took up the stool next to Audrey. "So, how did you two meet?"

I made my way into the kitchen, busying myself with brewing a fresh pot, and interrupted to save Audrey from answering. "Anyone want coffee?"

But Audrey didn't need saving. "A friend of mine runs The Basement bar downtown and recognized him when he came in one night. Messaged me to get there and then basically set us up."

"You must have been surprised to get there to find a celebrity," Sarah said. I cleared my throat in warning, which Sarah ignored. So much for not giving her a hard time.

Audrey reddened. "Actually, I didn't know who he was."

Sarah laughed gleefully. "Oh, my god! I like you so much better already."

I set coffee in front of both of them. "Be nice," I directed to Sarah, who rolled her eyes and turned back to Audrey. Don't scare her off was what I wanted to say but couldn't.

"So you've never watched the show?"

"No, I keep meaning to, but I never have the time."

"Ok, we have to fix that right now!"

"Sarah—"

"Aren't you meant to be making breakfast right now? Come on, Audrey."

Audrey apologetically shrugged at me before heading to the living room where Sarah was already fiddling with the TV to set up the first episode.

I gathered the ingredients for brunch from the fridge and started listening to what Sarah and Audrey were saying.

"OMG, I totally forgot this terrible haircut you had! What the hell were they thinking anyway?" Sarah called over the TV.

"They thought it was more futuristic," I called back.

Sarah snorted, but her response was quieter, so I could only assume she'd directed it to Audrey and not me, even though I could still hear them from the kitchen. "They changed it before season two because he wasn't attractive enough."

As I prepared the bacon and eggs, I overheard Sarah adding her own commentary throughout the episode, but since every other sentence was drowned out with Audrey's vibrant laughter, I guessed she didn't mind the interruptions too much.

I caught a glimpse of them when I was laying out some plates and cutlery on the table, and they looked like old friends, half facing the TV and half each other, talking and laughing together as they commented on the episode.

And I knew there was no turning back for me. What I felt for Audrey was more than just attraction. I wanted her in my life.

There was a flash on the screen, and I groaned as I caught sight of myself. That really was a terrible haircut.

Once breakfast was ready, I called them back, and together we placed everything on the table, Sarah and Audrey settling into seats across from each other.

"So Jackson mentioned you're getting married soon?" Audrey asked.

"Next month, I can't believe it."

"That soon! I'm surprised you're so calm. I was a mess of nerves."

"You're married?" I have to give it to Sarah; she really was selling this whole "I know nothing about you" routine.

"Divorced."

"Oh, I'm sorry."

"Please don't be. It was ..." A shadow passed over her eyes, and I wanted to find that no good ex of hers and hurt him, even if I didn't know the details of what happened between them.

Audrey continued. "It was for the best. Actually, that's the reason I was at the bar that night. I was celebrating one year of freedom." Audrey smiled ruefully before looking up at Sarah in apology. "Shit, sorry. I don't mean that marriage is something to be free of, just mine. Yours will be wonderful, I'm sure."

Sarah waved her off, completely unbothered. "Mom and Dad freaked out when Matt initially proposed and ended up inviting all their divorced friends over to," she air quoted, "'tell us that marriage isn't some fairytale'. I thought it was hilarious, but Matt still can't look at a gravy boat without feeling sick." She noticed Audrey's confused response. "Don't ask."

They veered into a conversation about table settings and floral arrangements while we ate, while I was content to enjoy how well this was going.

I should have known better.

"So …" Sarah started innocently, and I was at least grateful that Audrey hadn't shown any discomfort with Sarah's blunt style of questioning so far this morning. "What was it like getting divorced?"

"What was it like?" Audrey and I spoke at the same time. "Sarah …"

"Sorry, no offense." Sarah had the decency to shy away from my disappointed glare. "It's just I've never met anyone who did it so young. All Mom and Dad's friends were in their sixties with kids and all that. Was it hard?"

Audrey's hand found my knee under the table, and I was at least thankful that she wasn't offended by my sister's overly nosy nature. I placed my hand over hers and gently squeezed.

"Well, it wasn't easy." Audrey's eyes were downcast, and I didn't expect her to continue. "But I was lucky that Brad didn't want to drag it out. He set the terms when he left, and that was that."

I wasn't an angry person by nature, but I definitely wanted to punch this guy in the face.

"Do you ever speak to him?" Sarah asked, and I knew this would be the last question I'd allow. It was obvious this wasn't something Audrey was comfortable talking about, and despite my own strong curiosity, it was absolutely not Sarah's place to dig into it.

"No." It was said with a coldness I'd never heard from Audrey.

"I wonder what Matt and I will do if we divorce?" Sarah sounded shockingly calm and almost curious about the idea, and I was extremely glad Mom and Dad weren't here to hear it. Mom would probably faint.

"I don't think you need to worry about that, at least not for a long time." I decided a change of subject was at hand. "Did I tell you I missed out on the role in *Subversion*? Terry called me last week."

Both of them whipped their attention to me so fast. I thought I was seeing double for a second. "What?!" They said in unison.

"Apparently, Addison Michael's has someone specific in mind, so I'm out." I shrugged. "They might have been chasing this actor the entire time and just put out interest as a ploy to get him to agree."

"Well, that's bullshit." Audrey dryly replied.

Sarah pointed in her direction, "Yeah. What she said." Then she placed one hand on my arm, "I'm sorry, Jace. There'll be other stuff."

"And there's nothing you can do?" Audrey asked.

"That's what I have to work out. I'm not about to walk away if there's something I can do. Until the contract is signed, I still have a chance; you just have to know who to talk to, so the next step is getting a hold of Addison and convincing him."

An hour later, Audrey excused herself to collect her things, saying she needed to get home and shower, and although I wanted to convince her to stay the rest of the day with me, I walked her out.

"Your sister is really great. It's obvious how much she cares about you. Makes me wish I had siblings. I mean, apart from Tiffany."

"I hope that wasn't too much. Sarah can be a little …" I searched for the word, "overprotective."

"She's looking out for you. It's sweet." Her gaze dropped, nervous. "I had a really nice time this morning."

"So did I. We should wake up together more often."

"I'd like that."

And before I could say anything more, Audrey kissed me goodbye and walked down the street.

I let it go for the moment. After this morning, I'd seen how easily Audrey and my lives fit together and seeing her and Sarah get along so well only convinced me further that we were perfect for each other. Audrey might not be ready for something serious, but she hadn't run screaming, so that had to be a good sign, right?

Sarah looked smug when I returned. "Mom and Dad are going to love her."

I still hadn't shaken my annoyance at her over her nosiness earlier and so busied myself with clearing the table. Once the sink was full of dirty dishes, I threw the dishtowel at Sarah. "It's your turn to dry up."

She caught the towel and playfully whacked me on the should with it, "Jace and Audrey, sitting in a tree-"

"You're twenty-three, not twelve," I grumbled.

"F-U-C-" I put a hand over her mouth, and she dissolved into giggles. I returned to the sink, turning off the tap and passing her plates as I cleaned them.

"I'm really happy for you, Jace." Her tone was soft and warm. "I don't think I've ever seen you so happy, except about work. She must be really special."

21

AUDREY

I was in trouble.

Now that Jackson and I had started staying the night, I was finding it difficult to stop myself from wanting to wake up with him.

Frankly, it was getting difficult to want to do anything other than see him, which was a problem. Because it was beginning to affect the one thing I had promised myself I would put before everything else.

My work.

After snoozing my alarm this morning, I'd allowed myself the luxury of a lie-in. Not that we did much sleeping. I couldn't remember the last time I'd come into work late, but I decided that the two orgasms I'd had that morning more than made up for whatever guilt I felt.

So, of course, something had gone wrong.

It turned out I'd picked the worst possible morning to not be in the office because no one had been around to talk down an irate delivery driver from dumping a truckload of stock at our doorstep this morning.

Apparently, one of our customers had made last-minute changes to their inventory order, but the client hadn't been told in time and didn't actually have the stock to meet the new request. In retaliation, the restaurant decided they didn't want any of the order and were refusing to take the stock off the delivery guy's hands or pay the transport fee. The client refused to take the stock back because everyone had forgotten they were adults today.

In short, it was a nightmare.

By the time I had sorted it out, hours had gone by, but the delivery driver had been paid, I'd convinced the customer to take the available stock, and I'd even managed to get the client to accept a discounted rate, once it had been discovered that their figures were the issue.

And while I was grateful that the crisis had been averted, it had only become a crisis because I'd chosen to play hooky this morning instead of being here. I would have to be more careful in the future.

To my reluctant surprise, Winnie and Jet had been extremely helpful. Having them there to field calls for me while I mediated was a small blessing.

As a thank you, I'd let them take a long lunch while I tried to rearrange my afternoon.

Lately, Winnie and Jet had been pressing to do more with the launch, but I had trouble handing off my work to someone else. This was my baby. My way of showing David I could do this.

Anthony, one of the junior account managers, ducked into my office around one p.m. while I was reading over the contract for the event space I wanted for the launch. It was a charming little spot that once had a life as a chop shop for motorbikes and scooters. It had since been bought and converted into a useable function space, complete with bathrooms and a kitchen. Thankfully, the new owners hadn't replaced the bright red roller door that spanned an entire wall or covered up the exquisite, exposed brick that made up the remaining walls.

The contract was standard, but the owner was pushing back on allowing us to use our own caterers since they had some sort of arrangement with another company I hadn't planned on using. I expected them to make us pay extra for the "inconvenience," but I was confident I could negotiate a reasonable compromise.

I waved Anthony over to a chair in my office. "What's up?"

"I was wondering if I can borrow the interns next week."

A flare of protectiveness came over me. "What for?"

"My parents are flying into town tonight, and between them and the new baby, Michelle needs some help." I'd heard a lot about his parents from his wife, Michelle, and I suspected she mostly needed Anthony to run interference for her while she cared for their four-month-old.

I smiled. "Of course. What will you need them to do?"

"I have a list of clients to meet with, mostly routine check-ins to see if they have any concerns, and a meeting with the distributor to follow up on some delivery delays."

"Ok, I think we can make that work. They're on their way back from a visit now. I'll send them to your office when they get here."

"Thanks, Audrey."

"You're welcome. And good luck next week."

"Thanks, I'll need it."

When he left, I pulled out my phone, messaging Jackson that I would be working late tonight. Maybe he could come over tomorrow instead? With Winnie and Jet occupied by Anthony's work, I'd need to take back some of the jobs I'd given them, and I still needed to decide on a caterer and lock in this contract with the venue. I had had an idea this morning about the cocktail list that I was really excited about, and I hoped I could sort it out before the end of the day.

His response came back after a few moments.

Jackson: Ditching me already? Found another sex god to take my place?

Me: Just for tonight, he's busy tomorrow

Jackson: Lucky me. And will I get to see the red set again?

Me: I might have something better in mind

Jackson: Tease

Me: Takes one to know one

Jackson: Touche

Jackson: Let me know how late you work. I'm on set for a possible reshoot tonight that might run over. If we're both up at the same time, you can make it up to me

I was still smiling to myself as I called Tiff.

She answered after a single ring. "Is everything ok?"

"Yes, everything's fine. Why?"

"You never call me during work hours."

I laughed. "Well, that's probably because I'm never calling you about something work-related. Are you busy right now?"

"Only pulling my hair out trying to draw up the shift schedule for the next month. Please save me."

"Are you at home? I can meet you."

"The bar. I'm pulling a double, so I had to come in early."

"Oh, if you're working, we can—"

"Not for another hour. Come over. We can expense some bar snacks to your work tab because I'm assuming you haven't eaten lunch yet." She was right, unfortunately.

"Great. Be there in ten."

She poured me a drink when I walked in. "Tiff, you know I don't drink while I'm working."

"It's two in the afternoon. It's practically the weekend; live a little." It was a line she'd tried on me multiple times, and it never worked, but that didn't stopp her from trying. She pushed it towards me as I took a seat at the bar. "Just take a sip. It's a spin on a sazerac I'm testing out, and I need an objective taste tester."

"Ha, like I'm going to be objective."

"You'll be honest, and it's the next best thing." She nudged it closer to me, and I felt my resistance crumbling. "Please," she whined, drawing the word out with a twang of her mother's southern drawl.

I sighed and shook my head, smiling. "Fine. But just a sip. It's technically what I wanted to talk to you about anyway."

She gave me a quizzical look while I raised the glass to have a taste. The dark golden liquid looked and smelled fine enough, nothing out of the ordinary for a sazerac from memory. But as soon as it touched my tongue, I was overwhelmed with a strong combination of bitterness and heat, and my face conveyed my displeasure immediately. I struggled to swallow what I'd tasted while putting the offensive drink back on the bar.

Tiff hummed in thought and pulled the drink back towards her, eyeing it. "Yeah, that's what I thought. I shouldn't have added the chili oil."

I struggled to rid of the taste from my mouth, and she passed me a glass of water, which I drained in seconds. "You knew it was bad, and yet you still made me try it?"

"What?! I needed a second opinion!"

"Jesus, Tiff, warn me next time."

Her laugh floated through the empty room. "And where would be the fun in that?" She leaned back against the counter, facing me. "So, what did you want to talk to me about?"

"I want to hire you for the launch. All of the caterers I've talked to can supply us with wait and bar staff, but none of them are capable of crafting a cocktail list."

"Not unless you want the standard martini, cosmo, old fashioned BS."

"Exactly. And the whole point of this event is to make the rum the hero and have the cocktails showcase how special it is. Not just—"

"Throw it into some tired old recipes."

"Yes. Thank you. I knew you'd get it."

"Sure."

"Really?"

"Audrey, come on. Of course! I love you, first of all, and secondly, I actually have a few new recipes I've been trying out." She threw the remainder of the offensive sazerac the drain nearest to her, "I promise this one won't be on the list."

"Well, thank God for that. And thank you. I'm just hoping we can afford you."

"You can't, but I'll make an exception for my best friend. So it's a drinks and nibbles thing, yeah?" I nodded. "Well, just off the top of my head, I'm thinking an aperitif to start, light and fresh, maybe with one of their other spirits to showcase the rest of their range. Then a series of four cocktails, each tailored to a specific flavor profile, and lastly, a rich little digestif, maybe a shot of some kind, but we won't call it a shot. I can make up some wanky name for it, and we can serve it in those tiny ceramic tea cups the Japanese use for matcha ceremonies, match in with the terracotta theme." Somewhere in there, she'd gotten her phone out and started furiously making notes, nodding to herself while I sat, staring at her in awe.

I shouldn't have been surprised. Tiff was a genius when it came to alcohol. There was a reason she'd won the city's Best Bartender award the last three years in a row.

"Have I told you I love you lately?"

She looked up from her phone to wink at me. "Never hurts to hear it again." Setting her phone down, she asked, "So what's going on with pretty boy? Things still going well?"

"I met his sister the other day."

She hesitated briefly, but her expression didn't offer any clues as to what she thought of that. "And how did that go?"

"Well! I really like her. You would, too, I think. She's got a catty sense of humor."

"That's good. Big step, meeting the family."

And this was the point I was stuck on. In theory, I would have thought the same thing. Being introduced to friends and family seemed like a natural next step—if we were dating. Which we weren't. Or maybe we were. I knew what I wanted, but I still had no idea how Jackson felt.

"Do you think it means something? That I met her? We haven't really talked about it."

"Do you want it to mean something?"

Yes. "Maybe?"

It was more than I'd been able to admit out loud, clinging desperately to the lie that if I kept my feelings to myself, it would make them easier to forget. But this was Tiff. She was the one who held me together when Brad left. Who has had my back since we met. Who knew me better than anyone.

She was the last person I wanted to hide from. "I think I'm falling for him."

If Tiff was surprised, I couldn't tell. Maybe she already suspected. "You don't sound too happy about that."

I wasn't.

I wanted to be. I wanted to be over the moon about it. And there were times where I could just about burst with how much I was feeling, but there was always a dark cloud attached. Like I was waiting for the other shoe to drop. Or reality to kick in.

My only real experience with love had been Brad, whose particular brand of cynicism had made me question every opinion I had until I didn't trust my instincts anymore. Until I'd relied on him.

It always started with an innocent, "are you sure?" Or a "trust me." And I had. For a while, it had been nice. I felt looked after, like he had my best interests at heart.

But when I had stopped wanting to follow him, he got angry. Then he left. And I spent a year relearning who I was and what I wanted.

I wasn't about to give that up again.

———

SOMEDAYS, I wanted to quit this wonderful job. Not enough to actually do it, but just enough that I would daydream about storming into David's office and loudly announcing it.

To be fair, it wasn't David who was making me miserable. It was this damn venue owner who just would not come to the table on this damn catering issue. He'd gone back and forth about agreeing to let us use our own at least three times since last Friday, and I wanted to scream. And it was only a Tuesday. It was going to be a hell of a long week.

I needed a holiday. Or a back rub.

I settled for some fresh air and a coffee from the shop down the street. It didn't help. I knew I'd have to be back on the phone with the guy as soon as I got back in the office, but it was better than nothing.

On my way back, my phone buzzed, and it did more to allay my mood than the coffee ever could. Jackson was quickly becoming my own happiness drug, which was as exciting as it was daunting.

I just couldn't seem to get enough of him. And for some

unknown reason, he felt the same way about me. For however long this lasted, I was going to make the most of it.

It was relatively early by my standards when he knocked on my door that night. I had opened a bottle of wine as soon as I'd come home from work, utterly drained after going another round with the venue douche, as I'd come to call him, and I was near the end of my first glass when Jackson arrived.

It had only been two days since I'd last seen him, but damn, was he a sight for sore eyes.

And when he offered me that back rub I needed, I wondered how devastated I would be if—when—this all fell apart.

22

JACKSON

Never say nothing happens on a Tuesday.

It was instinct now to check the number before answering my cell, even more so when it was an unknown number, but sometimes Bryson or Naomi had an assistant call if something was urgent. I wasn't about to save everyone's number on my phone, so I took the chance it was work-related and picked up.

"Jackson Ward."

"Jackson, Addison Michaels."

My thoughts short-circuited. Since I'd heard the news about the role, I'd been pestering Terry with ideas for how to get another audience with Addison. I'd reached out to anyone I thought might help, although most had said good luck in the kind of tone that did not instill confidence.

I tried not to sound too surprised. "Mr. Michaels, it's good to hear from you."

"Addison, please. I'm sure you know why I'm calling."

Most likely to tell me to back off, but now that I had him on the phone, I wasn't going to miss the opportunity for one more pitch. "I heard you'd decided on someone for Parker."

"I had. They didn't work out, so I'm taking a chance on

someone else. We would have formalized it sooner but working with the studio has been a circus. Still, we're on track now, I hope. Filming is slated to start in the summer, so I'll need an answer fairly soon."

Well, that confirmed it. Straight from Addison's mouth, the part was gone.

"Of course."

"I must say, it's been difficult to make a decision until now. There's been a lot of interest in this role in particular. But I'm sure you were aware of that."

"Yes, it's been a badly kept secret."

"As most things are in this industry."

After another beat, I had the strange feeling he was waiting for me to say something like it was my line, but we were reading off two different scripts.

Addison slowly exhaled. "Jackson, why do you think I've called you?"

I decided to drop the charade. "Well, considering you've cast the role I wanted, I'm not really sure."

Another sighed, and I could almost picture him pinching his nose in frustration. He likely thought me a complete idiot, and to be honest, right now, I would probably agree with him.

"I have cast the role of Parker. With you. That is if you're still interested."

"Absolutely." I sounded as eager as I felt, and I did not give a damn.

"Good. It'll be a three-month shoot, mostly on location, but with some studio work in New York. Now that we've spoken, I'll start to work out the details with your agent."

"Not a problem." At some point, I should probably check that the scheduling wouldn't conflict with the show, but for now, I was way too excited to think about silly little details. Terry could work them out anyway.

Shit, I had better call Terry. And Sarah. And Audrey.

"I'll be honest, Jackson, I'm not one hundred percent convinced yet that you are Parker, but your insight into the character shows me you're trying to understand him. It's important to me to work with people who are invested in the material."

"Thank you."

He continued, voice firm. "I want you to know I'm not interested in stunt casting. This hasn't anything to do with putting a hyper-masculine actor into a non-typical role. The truth of it is, you're one of the only people to recognize that his journey has nothing to do with power or confidence or breaking away from his submissive needs. This is a story about trust and betrayal and how we can be pushed to act against our interests in the act of self-preservation."

"I appreciate that."

After telling Terry the good news, I texted Sarah, who congratulated me and agreed we'd celebrate at brunch on the weekend—although she very unsubtly added that I was welcome to postpone if I was going to be too busy "celebrating" with Audrey.

And I did plan on celebrating with Audrey, although I wasn't about to get into that with Sarah.

The plan, as far as there was any sort of plan considering I didn't know where the hell to start and was just making this up as I went along, was to do something special. Something outside of our normal dates, if you could call them that. Dinner would be a good start.

Unfortunately, I was ill-prepared to know where we could go that would offer us some semblance of privacy, but I was hoping Wes or Liv might have some options. Liv would likely be the better choice.

I came to set early to get in some time to practice with the bow, so It was fortuitous that Naomi said she'd seen Liv entering the gym.

Borrowing the gear from Felix, I made my way there, but as I entered, it was obvious no one else was expecting me here this early because I found Olivia and Bryson kissing against a stack of foam blocks lining the wall.

Stunned, a choked sound escaped me, and they tore apart.

Forced to awkwardly back out of the room, I grasped the bow

and arrows in a death grip until I remembered I was meant to be gentle with them and loosened my hold.

As I was debating my next move, Bryson exited the room, brushing past me with a curt nod and nothing else, although I suspected that a conversation would come later.

Tentatively, I stepped back into the gym and found Liv waiting, hesitant.

"So ..." I had no idea how to end this sentence. I wanted to lighten the mood with a joke, but I genuinely couldn't think of one. It would be easy enough to pretend I hadn't seen them. My surprise aside, it wasn't uncommon to come across in our line of work. And I could hardly judge two consenting adults from doing whatever they wanted to do.

Liv, I should have known, was not one for holding back. "Yes, we're together, and no, we're not telling anyone. Please don't say anything." She pleaded.

"How long have you two ..."

"About six months."

"Wow, I had no idea."

She laughed. "That was kind of the point."

"Right. Yeah, of course."

She started pacing. "Shit. After Wes saw us the other week, I told Bryson we needed to be more careful. Can you just promise me you won't tell anyone else?"

I step into her way, doing my best to calm her. "Liv, I promise I won't say anything. To anyone. It's none of my business." Her lips curled into a small, relieved smile while I was still processing the image of her and Bryson together. "I'm just surprised. I didn't think you two even got along."

She twisted a strand of hair around her finger. "We just fit together; I don't know how else to explain it. He gets me. And it made me realize what I wanted in a relationship. I wanted someone who was in the industry. That's why I was dating actors all the time, but it wasn't working, and honestly, I couldn't figure out why for the longest time. I kept thinking it was just that we were apart all the time. Then after we dated, I realized it wasn't enough. Just being around didn't solve everything. It helped, but it was too much and not enough. I wanted someone on the same level as me work-wise." She stopped herself, reaching out to me. "Not that you're not ... I just wanted someone who could talk to me for hours about direction beats and dialogue and staging. I want to be a director someday, and I thought dating one would be a disaster. You know how most of them are."

I couldn't help an amused chuckle. I knew exactly how most of them were.

"And I thought hell would freeze over before I dated Bryson, but things just happened, and now I can't imagine being with anyone else."

"I'm happy for you."

"And what about you?" Liv asked. "You've been awfully chipper recently. Wes mentioned you might be seeing someone yourself."

"I am. She's pretty amazing."

"Would I know her?"

"No, she's not an actress or anything."

"Not your usual type, then." Liv joked.

"No," I said, and the expression on my face must say enough because Liv replied, "Does she know how you feel?"

"She will." And I remembered why I was looking for Liv in the first place. "Actually, I was hoping you could help with that. I want to do something special. Do you know any good restaurants where we might not get spotted?"

"You think Bryson and I get to go out on dates?"

"Good point."

"We just make the most of what we have right now. A few weeks ago, I came over to find he'd moved all the furniture around in his lounge so we could have a picnic. It was probably the sweetest thing anyone has ever done for me. Maybe you could try something like that. The thing is, Jackson, most people want the same thing in relationships,"

"And what's that?"

"Someone who cares." Her eyes shifted to the door Bryson had left through earlier. "The rest you just figure out together."

"Thanks, Liv."

We shared a hug before Liv excused herself, and I made use of the gym's privacy to call Audrey, a plan forming.

Dialing Audrey's number was exciting beyond just my good news because I'd decided it was time to acknowledge what we'd both been avoiding.

"Hey, you."

Her voice was like a shot of whiskey on a cold night, comfort and warmth, and I was helpless to fight off the effect she had on me.

"Morning, beautiful. I wanted to know if you're free for dinner tonight."

"Is this leading up to a joke about skipping the main and getting straight to dessert? Because I've heard that one before."

I was giddy at the sound of her laughter, and I steadied myself with a deep breath, redirecting my nervous energy into the foot that was currently tapping on the floor. "It isn't, but I'll remember that for next time. Can you get to mine by eight?"

23

JACKSON

I left the lot as soon as I was able that evening, in a rush to gather ingredients, even though I hadn't decided on what to cook. I wanted something impressive, but I hadn't left myself with a lot of time, not if I also wanted to shower and change, which wasn't a question.

In the end, I decided to throw together a pasta, one of my dad's favorite recipes, and focused on dressing my apartment up a bit. On a whim, I'd picked up some tulips at the grocers, and they now sat pride of place on the table in an old canister I'd found at the back of the pantry.

I'd even managed to locate some tea lights in the back of the bathroom cupboard. I really should take the time to explore my apartment more.

Thankfully, all my effort wouldn't go to waste. Audrey had reconfirmed earlier that she was still coming since she'd postponed two other times this last week for work. It was hard to see her slaving away without being able to help. I knew how much the launch meant to her, and if there was some way I could ...

Huh. There was a thought.

I opened up Instagram on my phone and took a quick shot of

the bottle of MacMillan rum Audrey had given me. Due to the show's younger fanbase, I tended not to share much in terms of alcohol, but this was for a good cause.

Adding a praise emoji and a drink responsibly hashtag, I threw it up on my stories. It'll only be up for twenty-four hours, but I was sure that would be enough, and I liked being able to show support for Audrey's work.

Pocketing my phone, I looked over my haphazard attempt at a romantic setup. I hoped it played as more romantic than silly.

Luckily, it was too late to second guess it because the buzzer went, signaling Audrey was on her way up.

Fingers crossed, I didn't fuck this all the way up.

She was a vision when I opened the door, silencing my thoughts and damn near stopping my heart.

A black silk skirt hugged the soft curve of her waist to her thighs, the material skimming her mid-calf. On top, a soft black t-shirt was knotted at the small of her waist, its short sleeves showing off the galaxy of freckles that dotted her milky skin.

I was so enamored; it took me a minute to realize the print on her shirt was the show's logo.

"What do you think? Too fan-girly?" she said, motioning to the shirt.

And all I was able to do was shake my head in response. The overwhelming need to have this woman overrode my every other thought.

Nothing was cooked yet; maybe we *could* just skip straight to dessert for a while.

She stepped in and kissed my cheek. "Hi, handsome." Her hair, loosely curled today, tickled my nose before she pulled back, the smell of her shampoo lingering in its wake. "Mmm." She appraised me, one hand molding to my bicep, the heat of her hand searing through the thin material of my shirt. "You look good tonight."

I slid a hand to her neck, caressing the line of her jaw with my thumb. "You look good every night." Then I leaned in to capture those perfect pink lips with mine.

Her hands slipped around my neck, and I felt her weight shift as the door closed behind her. She pushed forward, closer, her nails lightly scratching my scalp, causing heat to race through me, and I gripped her hips closer.

Then she kissed along my jaw. "I've been thinking about you all day. I even wore something extra special."

Ever since our first night together, Audrey had been getting progressively more confident in herself, in her sexuality. I didn't know what I did to deserve her, but I was damn thankful that it was me she wanted to share this with.

Just as she was nibbling on my ear and arching into me, I remembered that I wanted tonight to be more than just sex, and reluctantly, oh so reluctantly, I pulled away.

"Come on. I'm just about to make us dinner."

"Oh? You were serious?" I took her hand and guided her around the sofa to the dining table. "Wow." The word was quiet, merely a breath. It gave nothing away, and I was dying to know what she was thinking, but also a little scared of it, too.

"What is all this?" she asked, still facing the table, no doubt taking in the flowers, candles, everything.

"I got some good news today and thought we could celebrate."

"Jace ..." her voice hopeful, yet tentative. "This is incredible." Her hold tightened in mine, and the nerves settled within me.

"Don't speak too soon. You haven't tried my cooking yet."

When in doubt, push on and hope for the best. I moved into the kitchen, and Audrey settled down on a stool, eager to watch me work.

Ok, maybe my nerves weren't completely gone. "I was just about to start dinner. I hope you like carbonara. It's not as good as my dad's, but it's close, and I even managed to find proper guanciale, which is the only way to really have it."

Her smile widened, a little too pleased with my rambling. "Sounds delicious."

"Would you like some wine? I've got some bottles put away in that cabinet by the TV if you want to pick something. I have no idea if they are any good; most of them were gifts."

"Benefits of being a celebrity?"

"There are perks. What can I say?"

She hopped off the stool and started looking through the cabinet. I genuinely hoped that there was something decent, considering I'd never learned anything about wine and couldn't remember the last time I looked in there.

"Oh, wow, you have a bottle of Grange in here. Did someone really gift you this?"

"Huh? Oh, yeah, I can't remember who I got that from. Is it meant to be good?"

"Is it ..." She looked at me like I'd grown a second head. "Jace, this bottle is worth over $1000. I damn well hope it's good."

I shrugged. "Only one way to find out."

There was an incredulous snort before she carefully put the bottle back, finding something more suitable. "Ok, firstly, no. We're not popping a bottle of Grange for no reason. That is the kind of wine you save for your twentieth wedding anniversary, not a random Tuesday night." She returned, placing a bottle of rosé on the counter. "Secondly, you don't pair a red that strong with a cream-based pasta. It would completely overpower the food."

I forgot the food and pulled her into my arms, turned on by her wine knowledge. "Ok, well, firstly, that was hot." I paused to kiss her. "Secondly, I think a random Tuesday night is the perfect excuse for any kind of wine. And thirdly, you're very sexy when you're wine pairing."

She playfully swatted my chest but didn't make a move to go anywhere. "You mentioned."

I allowed myself one more kiss before I reluctantly turned back to the counter, cooking the guanciale. "Do you have to know that for work?"

"Not anymore. Years ago, I worked as a sommelier at this Michelin star farm-to-table restaurant near the loop. The pay sucked, and the owner was an ass, but I loved learning more about wines and food."

"How did you get from that to what you're doing now?"

"I told you how I worked at Empire before Bespoke, right?" I nodded, and she continued, "Well, the wine rep who sold to the restaurant worked there. He made it sound really interesting, lots of stories about traveling around, meeting and learning from the winemakers themselves, and being able to market the wines for these passionate makers to bars and restaurants around the country. It sounded like an adventure. One I wanted in on."

While I mixed the egg yolks and cheeses in preparation, she maneuvered behind me to pull out a large serving bowl from the cupboard. I watched as she filled it with water and then added ice. When I cocked a brow in question, she replied, "It cools the wine quickly," while placing the wine in the ice bath.

Damn, she was impressive. "That's where you met David, wasn't it?" I asked, piecing together snippets from other conversations we'd had. This was the most she'd talked about her past, and I didn't want her to stop.

"Yep. He helped me work my way up from research grunt to senior regional sales manager. I wouldn't be half as good at my job if it weren't for his help."

"Sounds like a great boss."

Her grin widened. "He really is. I still can't believe he asked me to go with him to Bespoke, but I'm so thankful he did." Now that the ingredients were ready, I started to boil the water for the pasta, and I took advantage of the fact that I didn't have anything pressing to do right now to touch her again.

I moved away from the stove to where she'd been leaning and watching me and crowded her against the counter, her body fitting against mine perfectly.

She stretched up for a kiss, but I wanted to hear more about her life. I ducked playfully away from her lips and asked, "What made you want to go with him?"

Her chest rose and fell with a sigh. "I learned so much working at Empire, but they cared more about money and markups and profit than the people or wine itself. I'd literally hear my co-workers creating bullshit lies just to add an extra zero to the bottle price. It was soul-sucking." Her hands found their way into my hair as she spoke, absentmindedly scratching my scalp, sending tremors through me. "David felt the same. The whole point of Bespoke is that we focus on something authentic—celebrating local creators and local businesses. He said it didn't matter that I'd never sold spirits before, and I trusted him to know what he was doing."

I was completely captivated.

The water boiled, pulling me away, but the great thing about carbonara was how quick it was to throw together.

While I pulled together the pasta, Audrey opened the now chilled wine and poured us both a glass. Having never been much of a wine drinker, I was skeptical but trusted her judgment. If pressed, I would pick a red over anything else, but I was surprised to find I enjoyed it. It was crisp, clean, and a little sweet.

Audrey took the wine, complete with its ice bath, to the table, then came back to get the glasses while I served dinner, and when her eyes lit up at the sight of the meal, I knew without a doubt that I wanted to be the person to evoke that lightness in her for as long as I could.

Because Olivia was right, when you found someone who made you feel the way I felt when I was with Audrey, you couldn't imagine being with anyone else.

24

AUDREY

As I'd hoped, the wine paired excellently with the pasta, smooth enough to compliment the sharpness of the parmesan but with a soft sweetness that offset the smoky flavor of the meat. I'd never had guanciale before, but I already knew that all other pastas had been ruined for me. Maybe all other food.

And wasn't that surprise number two of the evening.

To say I hadn't expected a home-cooked meal would have been a massive understatement. To say I hadn't expected a full-blown candlelight dinner would have been … the crowning prince of understatements. Or something like that. I had officially lost all ability to think straight when I spotted the makeshift vase of tulips on the table.

Brad had never once given me flowers in ten years. And I guess, technically, Jackson hadn't given me any either, but the fact that he'd gone to the effort of getting them, of arranging the table and cooking me dinner … It was the most romantic thing that had ever happened to me.

It had become laughingly obvious that this relationship had moved decidedly on from casual to serious and that I wasn't alone in feeling, and wanting, more.

Damnit, I could hear Tiff laughing from here.

As we ate, I was completely overwhelmed with how sweet Jackson was. That he had done all of this for me. And so I sat there, studying him like he was the answer to the big mystery of my life. Maybe he was.

Jackson was able to look wise beyond his years. It was those eyes—endless pools of shimmering sapphire. And yet, when he smiled, really smiled, he was youth eternal, boyish. It hadn't surprised me to learn that his fans were split between two camps; those who favored the broody, muscular, scruffy him and those that preferred the clean-shaven, mirthful, playful him. Honestly, I didn't know how anyone picked between them. He was both. And more.

The words I wanted to say were so heavy in my mouth that I was sure they would tumble into a pile on the table if I let them.

This whole thing had started because I took a crazy chance. What was one more?

"I think I'm—"

Jackson spoke at the same time. "Come to Sarah's wedding with me."

I latched on to the statement, relieved to have a pause in my own admission. "Wait, really?"

"Yes. I want you there. I ..." His jaw momentarily clenched before he shook it off, making a decision. "I'm crazy about you; you have to know that."

While I had begun to suspect, to hope, hearing it was like an adrenaline shot to my heart. So much so that I didn't know whether to laugh or dance or crawl into his lap and kiss him until we were both breathless. Probably a combination of all three.

"I feel the same way. I've never felt like this before." And I didn't mean to, I really didn't, but that same worried edge bled into my voice, the same one Tiff had heard the other day, and Jackson, sweet, observant Jackson, heard it, too.

"Audrey?"

Ugh. Why was this so damn hard?

I didn't want to hurt him. I didn't know if I was any more ready for a relationship than when we'd first met, but I also didn't want to walk away. And I had no idea how to navigate that.

I was torn. I liked him. I more than liked him. I thought about him all the time. Either remembering what we'd done together or imagining the things I wanted us to do. And ok, this whole thing had started with sex and was meant to only be about sex, but I couldn't deny how easy he was to talk to or how relaxed I felt when I was with him.

But I didn't know if it was enough.

"It's just …" It killed me to see the disappointment in his eyes, but I needed to be honest with him. "I want you. I want to be with you. I just … I can't lose myself again."

I'd become a ghost when I was with Brad, or maybe it was more accurate to say I was a shadow of myself. I still worked, ate, slept, but it was out of habit. If we went out, it was always together. Brad's friends became my friends, and my friends—aka Tiff—were tolerated on occasion. We watched the things Brad liked to watch and did the things Brad liked to do. No matter my interest.

After he'd left, I'd felt stripped of all the little markers of what I'd come to know of myself. It was like having to find my personality again. My voice.

And now that I had it, you'd have to pry it from my cold dead hands before I gave it up again.

Not that Jackson was like that. At least, not from what I'd seen so far.

But how did I know that being part of an "us" wouldn't rob me of me?

He pushed away from the table and came close, laying a gentle hand on mine where it had been toying with the material of my skirt. I twisted my hand so that our hands were linked and met his eyes, his deep blues stormy with concern.

"What if it's just lust? What if there's nothing more than sex between us?"

"Do you really believe that?"

"No, of course not." And damn, if his kindness didn't make me want to disappear into him right now. "Although the sex is pretty good." I hoped a joke would help shift the thick cloud of emotion in the air, although the delivery fell flat.

To his credit, Jackson managed a small smile, but he didn't let the topic go. He really was too good. "What's wrong? Come on, talk to me."

I let out a reluctant laugh, the force of the conflicting emotions within me forcing it from my lungs. "I can't promise you I'll be very good at this."

"And you think I can?" he joked before looking at me very seriously, considering his next words. "I know you don't like talking about what happened with your ex, but you know you can talk to me. I want to hear it."

"I know. I want to tell you. I'm so sick of being afraid of opening up again. I just, I know that sounds ridiculous—"

"Hey," he stopped me. "It doesn't. At all. I don't need you to be anything, or anyone, other than yourself."

He brought our hands up to his lips, kissing my knuckles. My lip curled into a responding smile before I could stop it. He just had this way of making me feel safe and cared for.

I realized he was waiting, giving me the time to think this over, and wow, had anyone ever really done that for me before? Just ... trusted me to work things over in my mind instead of demanding an answer?

Damn, he really was wonderful. And gentle. And thoughtful. Goosebumps rippled across my shoulder, hip, arm, and stomach like a series of fireworks setting across my skin.

I was so head over heels for this man.

And with an imperceptible shift, the sinking in my gut rose, bubbling to the surface as happiness and filling my chest with a joy I didn't think I could contain. The fears weren't gone, but I was practiced enough to put them aside for now.

"Ok," I said, and I couldn't even begin to school my face into something other than outright joy right now. "I'll date you, but I have a couple of conditions."

I was relieved to see his expression lighten. "Conditions? I'm sensing a theme with you and these arrangements." I poked his ribs. "Ok, ok. What are these conditions?"

"I still want to be able to come over late at night for sex."

"Oh, is that all?" He laughed.

"And I want to still have time by myself. I don't suddenly want to spend all our time together. Sometimes I want to go out with Tiff. Or have a night in alone."

"Anything else?"

"And I'm not ready for the public yet, is that ok?"

"How public are we talking? Because as nice as my apartment is, it would be nice to go out sometime."

"Of course! I was talking more like events and things. Not that I'm expecting you to take me on the red carpet or anything. Or that that's even a thing you would want to do," I was rambling. "I honestly don't know what dating an actor even entails, but anything with press kind of scares me a little."

He chuckled, and I buried my face in my hands, trying to shake off my embarrassment, "I'm being ridiculous, aren't I?"

He reached over, caressing my cheek with his thumb before leaning in, lips meeting mine softly, slowly, just for a moment before he pulled back, smiling. "A little, but it's adorable."

My groan was diluted by the smile that overtook my face. I leaned in to kiss his cheek softly. "And yes, I'll be your date for Sarah's wedding."

Did I feel like I was on that part of a rollercoaster where you're slowly chugging upwards, heart beating rapidly with the knowledge that in just a moment, the world would fall away beneath you? Sure.

But maybe I wanted to be a little crazy. A little reckless. Maybe I wanted to not think about what could go wrong, or even what could go right, but instead, just put on a beautiful dress and go to the wedding of the sister of the guy I was falling for.

"Wait. What's the dress code? Should I bring a gift? Which hotel is it again?"

Dinner now forgotten, Jackson stood up, hand still in mine, and moved us over to the couch as he spoke. "It's at the Athletic hotel. I thought we could go up Friday night and get some time together before the wedding. For everything else, I think the invite is on the counter, or I can just give Sarah your number and have her text you everything you want to know."

He laid down first, pulling me until I was sprawled on top of him, and despite the slightly awkward positioning, it was the most comfortable I'd felt all day.

I let out a deep breath, which became a sigh as he brushed the hair away from my neck to start kissing there. I turned my head to give him more access.

He continued between kisses, his voice rough. "There was something else I wanted to do tonight."

"Oh?" I was quickly losing focus, and I knew I was close to letting him have whatever he wanted.

"Mmm."

Fingers dipped under my shirt, stretching the material until the knot came undone, his hands now free to explore underneath.

His exploration continued down, rounding my hips and cupping my ass.

Knowing what he would find there, I bit back a smirk, anticipating the moment he felt it and having the pleasure of seeing the exact moment he did. Confusion, then curiosity flashed across his face, his fingers now working deftly to remove my skirt so he could get a better look.

"You weren't wrong about wearing something special, damn." His fingers traced along the edge of the lace against my hip, following it down to where the small string of pearls began. I had never worn open underwear before and never even knew that they existed, but once I'd seen them online, well, it was the fastest I'd ever purchased anything. And boy, was it worth it for how sexy I felt right now. "Is this what you wear to work every day?"

"Are you kidding me? They're great, but I hardly think I'd get any work done."

"Too distracting?"

"Too uncomfortable." I laughed. "If I'm going to get this launch right, I need all my wits about me. I can't be spending ten hours running to the bathroom every few minutes to unpick a pearl wedgie."

His head tipped back as he laughed. "Point taken. How is the launch coming?"

"Good, I think. I've never been more stressed about anything before, but I wouldn't give it up, you know? It feels so good to be in charge of my own life finally. And I want to make David proud. I really want this to go well."

"It's going to be great."

"Thanks. I just want it to be special. Did I tell you that one of the founders used to be a carpenter? He made all kinds of furniture and one-off pieces, then got commissioned to start making oak barrels for a local whiskey distillery. He made more on those barrels than he did on his other pieces but still kept up the side stuff because he loved it so much. Then his friend, the one making whiskey, was talking to him about getting into the whiskey business and mentioned that they needed to sell the barrels after they aged the liquor because the law states you can only age whiskey in new oak, right? Well, Jeff sees an opportunity. He buys back his own barrels after they've used them, at a pretty good rate, and starts making rum instead, using the second-hand barrels to age the rum, and he basically makes a profit twice over."

"Once on the barrels, then on the rum. Smart man."

"Isn't he! It's why I love what we do so much. Being able to support local businesses, but more than that, being able to celebrate them, the people behind them, and their love for what they do … It's so much more fulfilling than just making money."

"You're really cute when you're protecting the little man."

I buried my smile into his chest, leaning into the warmth of his arms, stupidly content just to stay here forever.

"So I had an interesting call today. From Addison Michaels." I couldn't see his face, but he sounded happy, so I could only assume it was good news.

"That's the writer of the movie you wanted, right?"

"And director. He, uh, he called to offer me the role."

"Holy shit. Please tell me you said yes."

"No, actually, I turned him down."

"What?" I narrowed my eyes. "Jerk."

"Sorry, I couldn't help myself." He laughed.

"Why the hell are you just telling me now?" I asked playfully.

"I had more important things to talk to you about," He said, pinning me with a look so earnest and hopeful that my chest ached.

25

JACKSON

The hotel was incredible, full of rich deep colors, an over-abundance of lounges, drapes, and the kind of stuffiness that was both reminiscent of its gentleman's club roots while also being completely fabricated.

I spotted someone vaguely familiar across the lobby before recognizing Matt's parents. Most of our family lived in the area, but I knew a lot of Matt's extended family lived out of state and were traveling up for the wedding. Matt's dad gave me a friendly nod but thankfully didn't engage me beyond that. I had hoped for it just to be Audrey and me tonight. Let the circus begin tomorrow.

The clerk tapped away at the keyboard. "Ah yes, here we are, Mr. Ward. We have you booked for two nights, yes?"

"That's right."

"Lovely. The suite is all ready for you. I'll just need a card for the incidentals." I passed over my card, and Audrey whispered, "Did he say suite?"

"Surprise," I replied, kissing her cheek.

Once all the details were taken care of at the front desk, we were shown to the elevator and told that our bags had already been taken to the room ahead of us.

The room wasn't sprawling by any means, but it was inviting and charming in its character. There was a short drop down some steps into a sitting area from the doorway, or what amounted to one with two large armchairs situated in front of a fireplace. A second fireplace sat farther along the same wall to the left in front of the bed. Our suitcases had been placed by the wardrobe near the bathroom, my suit bag hanging on the door.

Audrey stood by the window, which looked out over Millennium Park. "What a view."

I stepped close, my hands sliding around her waist, and she placed her hands atop mine. Her body felt tightly coiled, like a live wire. I had been noticing it more and more lately. I hugged her closer.

She made a sound of remorse. "Sorry, I'm a little stressed about work. This launch is getting close, and I feel like I won't be able to relax until it's over."

"Hey, it's ok, I can help. Maybe I can talk to the show's PR, and we could—"

"No." She cut me off, then softened. "No, that's ok. I've got it."

"Of course you do." I kissed the tender skin below her ear, running my nose along the sleek line of her neck. I was pleased to feel her relax a little in my arms. "You're a very capable woman."

"So, what is the agenda for tomorrow?" she asked, changing the subject. "I'm guessing you'll be busy with groomsman duties?"

"A little, but we'll still have the morning together. I have to be dressed and in Scott's room by lunchtime. Then Sarah and Matt are doing a first look over at Lurie Gardens, then back for the ceremony. After that, it's the usual food, drinks, and dancing."

"So …"

"So?"

"We have the whole night to ourselves … anything you'd like to do?"

"Mmm. The whole night, huh?" She twisted around and threaded her fingers through my belt loops. "I can think of a couple of ideas."

———

I FINISHED STRAIGHTENING MY TIE, then fixed the cuffs of my shirt under my tux jacket. The fit was perfect.

"What do you think? Do I look alright?" I asked, walking out of the bathroom to where Audrey lounged on the bed in her pajamas.

"Oh." I didn't miss the way her eyes widened.

"Good oh?"

"Very, very good." Then she was standing in front of me, eyes glued to the suit. "So good I want to tear it off you."

I hummed, the beginnings of arousal stirring within me. "You're making it difficult to leave right now."

"You're making it difficult not to ruin that tux." She lightly trailed her fingertips along my lapels, hunger burning in her eyes. It was obvious she was holding back by the way she bit her lip.

I, however, was under no obligation to restrain myself, grabbing two handfuls of her ass and giving a good squeeze. "Hold that thought. If I stay any longer, I might not leave."

Her giggle followed me out as I left the room.

Neither Sarah nor Matt had wanted a large wedding, and that had extended to the bridal party as well. I was one of three groomsmen, including Matt's best friend Lucas and his older brother Scott, who was the best man. I hadn't had many chances to meet either of them before, so I wasn't prepared when Lucas wrapped me up in a hug as soon as I walked into Scott's hotel room, where we'd agreed to meet prior to the ceremony.

"The third amigo arrives!" Lucas cheered, hustling me into the room.

Matt hovered by the window, jacket off and beer in hand, and he met me in the middle for a one-armed hug. Scott materialized from my right to hand me a drink, which I took before taking a seat on one of the lounge chairs. Lucas dropped onto the sofa next to me and held his beer out so we could toast. He was the one I knew the least since I'd met Scott a few times through family occasions, but he seemed nice enough. After we clinked bottles, Matt took a long swig and seemed to relax a little until the photographer stepped into the room.

I felt for Matt, who looked stiff and uncomfortable as the center of attention, but I was fairly sure most of the reason was nerves. Having had a lot of practice getting comfortable in front of a lens, I sat back and chatted with the other two while we waited for the signal to move downstairs.

His vows were typed on a piece of paper he'd folded and unfolded a half dozen times until Scott took it from him and promised to give it back at the right moment.

When the time came, we were whisked downstairs to the Games Room; a large open bar area complete with games tables, where we were united with the girls, and we all collectively awed at Sarah in her finery.

I'd seen the dress before, but with all the finishing touches, Sarah looked radiant.

We spent the better part of the next hour taking posed shots together. Although, Sarah was quick to tell us not to post anything on social media until after the ceremony because she didn't want to risk any of the guests seeing the dress early. Apparently, there was a specific hashtag she wanted us to use.

Afterward, any chance I had to go back to the room while Sarah and Matt were off on official wedding duties disappeared as more and more family members arrived.

It seemed the entirety of our family had managed to make their way into the city for the wedding, making it difficult to keep track of the time.

Before I knew it, Scott was leading Lucas and me up to the eighth floor for the ceremony.

The ballroom was stunning, with beautifully rich wooden flooring, gold speckled beams across the ceiling, and three massive chandeliers lining the walkway. In front of the windows at the end of the room, a freestanding fireplace marked the spot where the bride and groom would stand. An incredible array of flowers, rich in reds and pinks, adorned the mantlepiece. A spread of fake candles sat where a fire might have been and lined the aisle, their battery-operated lights flickering shadows against the floor.

Looking across the gathering crowd, I caught sight of my parents and waved. Mom was already clutching a handkerchief as she took her seat near the front of the room.

The photographer trailed Matt as he slowly made his way up the aisle, shaking hands and hugging his dad before taking his place. It was almost time.

"How are you doing?" Scott asked, concerned.

Matt looked like he was about to pass out. "I can't believe she actually agreed to marry me. I thought I would feel more relaxed right now."

I gave him a reassuring pat on the shoulder. "You're both lucky. There's nothing to be nervous about."

"Thanks, J."

I scanned the rows of chairs and just caught Audrey's eye near the back as the music started up.

Matt's slow exhale nearby caught my attention. "This is it," he said, mostly to himself, and Scott gave him a supportive nudge. "You've got this, Matt."

Matt nodded but didn't look any less nervous. I wondered how I might feel in his position—standing, waiting for the love of my life to walk towards me so we could spend the rest of our lives together.

I'd always considered weddings as an unfortunate requirement of getting married. Yes, I wanted to have someone to love and commit myself to, but the whole song and dance around it? It never appealed to me.

But standing here in front of my entire family, seeing the mix of nerves and excitement on Matt's face as he waited with anticipation for my sister to walk in and announce in front of everyone how she wanted to spend the rest of her life loving him, 'till death do they part ... Well, I finally got it.

I could finally picture it.

Yes, it was a song and dance, but not the kind where you were awkwardly stepping on someone's toes. It was the Gene Kelly,

"Singing in the Rain," about to burst out of my skin, I was so happy
kind.

It was what you did when you found someone to love and love
you back, someone who filled you with so much happiness that you
had to throw a party for all the people you knew just to share it
around.

Someone who made me a bubble bath after a long day. Who
would commiserate the roles I lost and celebrate the ones I won.
Someone who looked as sexy in sweats as she did dressed up. Who
made me laugh and could enjoy my company, even when we
weren't doing anything at all.

Someone like Audrey.

And with a suddenness I should have found frightening, I knew I
loved her. Was in love with her.

And later, while Matt read out his vows, I could picture myself
in his place, staring into those iridescent hazel eyes, bright and
shimmering like the night sky, trying to put into words how much I
wanted to spend the rest of my life deserving her.

Once the ceremony had finished, most of the room was
dismissed into the adjacent ballroom for the reception while the
bridal party and immediate family stuck around to take photos.

I was keen to get back to Audrey, grateful that we'd be sitting
together. I didn't even want to imagine Audrey stuck at a table with
what amounted to the far reaches of our family tree.

Just before I could detach myself from the main event, Mom
wrapped me up in a big hug, largely crumpling my jacket, but at
least most of the photos were taken now. "Darling, you look so
handsome!"

"Thanks, Mom. You look really lovely, too."

"The girl who did my makeup made my eyebrows too dark, but
I like how she did my hair." Considering how short it was, I wasn't
aware that she'd done anything different to it, but I wasn't about to
say that to her.

"Jackson." My dad's voice came up behind me as he joined us.

"Dad." My greeting was lost in his shoulder as he wrapped me
in a tight hug.

A few claps on my back and he pulled back. "How is work?"

"Great. We're in the middle of filming right now. It's going well." He looked good; hair a little greyer than it had been the last time I saw him, but bright with pride.

Mom brushed at whatever fluff she could find on my jacket. "Sarah said your girlfriend is lovely." Of course, she had.

"I think so."

"When do we get to meet her?"

"Tonight, hopefully. If I can find her among everyone."

"I'm just checking! You haven't introduced us to anyone in years. I was starting to think you were ashamed of us."

"Never." I gave her another hug, tighter than before. "I just never met anyone good enough before."

Mom looked gleeful. Uh oh. "Oh, now, I can't wait to meet her!"

26

JACKSON

I was itching to see Audrey, to touch her, even though it had only been a few hours.

Making my way into the ballroom where the reception was being held, I found Audrey sitting at our assigned table, chatting away to Lucas' date, who was seated next to her.

Audrey, Lucas, and his date were in deep conversation. Lucas was gesturing passionately, and Audrey's head tilted back to laugh the way she always did when she found something really funny. Her back was to me as I entered the ballroom, so it wasn't until I was pulling my chair out from the table that she noticed me.

"Oh, hello, stranger." She stood to hug me, and now that I could see her in full, I was struck by how incredibly gorgeous she looked tonight.

"Wow," I said, realizing I'd always be floored by this woman. "You look especially beautiful tonight."

She blushed from the compliment. "You don't look so bad yourself, but you already knew that."

I smiled against her lips as I kissed her. "Do I? It's always nice to hear it again."

"Aren't you two adorable!" Lucas' girlfriend Marie said. She introduced herself as we sat down. She was lively and never short of interesting conversation, and it turned out she was the sous chef at one of the restaurants Audrey sold to. "I knew she looked familiar; I just assumed she was famous because of who she's dating," Marie said, gesturing to me.

Lucas, now ecstatic that he could post as many photos as he liked, took a few selfies of us and promised to tag me in them.

We chatted idly throughout the meal and listened in earnest during the speeches. It wasn't until after dinner that Mom and Dad made a beeline to our table as I knew they would. Far be it from me to date someone that my mother hadn't met—sorry, interrogated.

"Mom, Dad, this is Audrey."

Mom reached out first, crushing Audrey in a tight hug. "Lovely to meet you. Jackson's told us absolutely nothing." Cue the disappointed look in my direction.

And here I had been worried about them ganging up on Audrey.

"Actually, that's my fault. I've been a little nervous about meeting everyone," Audrey offered.

"Nonsense, from what Sarah's told me, you've got nothing to worry about." Mom said. Then in a conspiratorial whisper, she added, "I hear I have you to thank for getting rid of the horrible favors."

"Please don't start on that again, Deb," Dad said, offering a hand to Audrey. "Hi, I'm Robert, the financier of this whole shebang."

It was now Mom's turn to scoff. "Bob, if I have to hear you go on about how much you paid for this wedding one more time ..."

Dad was nonplussed. "You said yourself, Deborah, it's not like Jace is getting married anytime soon."

So, this was going well.

I risked a glance at Audrey, hoping she wasn't as mortified as I felt right now, and felt immense relief when her lips pursed in amusement.

Mom, who was on fire tonight, unhelpfully added, "Well, you

never know, Rob. Audrey would be a fantastic addition to the family.
Right, Jace?"

Warning bells were flashing in my head. Abort! Abort! They'd
only met for five minutes, and already my mother was planning our
wedding. How the hell had we gotten on to this?

"It might be a bit early for that. I only just finished paying for
my divorce." Audrey laughed nervously.

"I'm not surprised, dear. It's how I know Robert will never leave
me. He could never afford it." I choked on a shocked laugh. Dad
just shook his head, like he'd heard that joke before.

I attempted to change the subject. "Speaking of, how nice was
the ceremony?"

Mom completely ignored me to speak to Audrey. "Oh, Audrey, I
should give you the name of the lawyer my friend Susan just used.
She made a mint in the split. Granted, her ex was a horrible man."

"Asshole tax is what it is. She should have gotten double. Man
has the worst backswing I've ever seen."

Even Dad was getting in on this? I really had to get a hold of
this conversation. "Have you said hi to Aunt Viv and Uncle Al yet? I
saw he wore his lucky pink socks again."

"Jackson, stop interrupting while I'm trying to talk to your
girlfriend. It's very rude." Mom turned to Audrey and proceeded to
ask her a series of questions about her job, apartment, and hobbies,
while Dad turned to me with the same, "you know your mother,"
look he'd perfected over their thirty-plus years of marriage.

We both came back into the conversation when Mom lightly
slapped Dad's arm while talking to Audrey. "Oh, you don't know
the half of it. His mother hated me."

"Only because I told her to," Dad joked.

Audrey thankfully laughed, and I wondered if she was ever
going to stop being perfect. I loved my parents to death, but they
were, like Sarah and myself, confident in their oddness, and it
sometimes took people off guard. After seeing Sarah and Audrey
click so well over brunch, I should have known = I had nothing to
worry about.

"But that was before I started meditating." Mom said, and I

realized I'd lost the thread of conversation. In the corner of my eye, I caught Dad pinching the bridge of his nose.

"Oh, really? How did you get into that?" Audrey genuinely looked interested, which was good because this would definitely end up being a long conversation.

"Well, I've been having some pain in my wrists, which my naturopath believes could be linked to a lack of—"

Dad sighed. "Honey, Audrey doesn't want to hear about your old age pains." He turned to Audrey. "She has pain everywhere. In her hips, her knees …"

"And you're the pain in my neck." Mom laughingly smacked his arm. "Now, shush, I'm trying to talk to Audrey. Why don't you and Jace go entertain your brother before he embarrasses himself on the dance floor."

I looked over to see my uncle trying to do what looked like an interpretive dance while the bridesmaids looked on in stunned silence. Sarah was laughing her ass off, but he had managed to scare almost everyone else off the dance floor, so it wasn't the worst idea for Dad and me to intervene.

As soon as I stepped onto the dance floor, Sarah sidled up to me. "Having a good night?" Her eyes were twinkling so bright; my heart might have burst. I always wanted to see her this happy.

Sarah cocked her chin in the direction of Mom and Audrey. "They look like they're getting on well. Mom will be knitting her a Christmas stocking next."

Oh, God, she absolutely would.

My next question came as much as a surprise to me as it did to Sarah. "How did you know Matt was the one?"

Sarah smiled wide enough that her eyes practically closed with glee, and she launched into my arms with a squeal. If anyone asked, I'd tell them it was the champagne.

"Ok, ok." I chuckled in her ear and let her down again. "Also, remind me to pay you back for whatever you told mom."

Sarah's only response was a self-satisfied laugh.

A few dances later and Dad finally managed to convince Mom

to give Audrey a break. I was thrilled when Audrey made her way over to join me on the dance floor.

"Tired yet, or do you think I can steal a dance?" she asked as the music changed to a swinging Sinatra tune.

I grabbed Audrey's hand and spun her around on the spot before catching her hips and closing the distance between us. The dance floor was fairly packed, now that all the important parts of the night had concluded. Everyone was free to let loose, and they were certainly taking the opportunity. In the corner of my eye, I could see Greg's grandmother dancing with my cousin. For eighty-one, she still had some moves.

Sarah winked at me when she caught us dancing, and I couldn't remember being so happy.

It was past midnight when we both finally lumbered back into our room, more tired than tipsy. Audrey flopped onto the bed immediately, groaning as she stretched out. I began undressing, still having enough of my wits to hang my jacket up before sitting on the edge of the bed to remove my shoes. The sheets rustled next to me, and I glanced over to find Audrey on her side, head propped up on her elbow while she watched me.

Standing, I faced her and made a show of the next few steps. Tie and cufflinks off and placed on the side table, I slowed to undo my shirt buttons one at a time. Catching her eye, I asked, "Enjoying the view?"

Her heated gaze lingered for a moment. "That might be the hottest thing I've ever seen."

And oh, the things I would do with her right now if I had the energy. "Would you be disappointed if I said I was too tired for sex?"

She sagged with relief. "Oh, thank God, I don't think I could move a muscle. Might be a bit weird."

I chuckled. "Good to know."

I watched as she squirmed on the bed, trying without any luck to reach the zip on the back of the dress. "Do you want a hand there? Not that this isn't entertaining," I asked, amused.

"Please." Her hand flopped back down on the bed like a

petulant child. I liked seeing her like this. It felt like I was seeing a side of her that not many did. It felt natural and familiar, like a worn sweater. Comforting.

I helped her out of her dress, which found itself discarded on the floor near her shoes. Left only in her underwear, she quickly crawled under the covers and burrowed in.

God, I loved this woman.

There were many things I would remember about tonight, but I knew without a doubt when I looked back, this was the memory I'd cherish.

I finished undressing, then folded and placed my suit pants on the side table.

"Did you have fun tonight?" I asked, hopeful.

Her smile was half-hidden by the pillow but obvious in her voice. "Definitely. Your family is great."

"Mom didn't scare you off?"

Her eyes opened, serious. "Of course not, she's wonderful. I can see where you and Sarah get your good humor."

"And our good looks." I pulled back the covers and slid in next to her. She shuffled closer, laying her head over my chest, and tangled our legs together. "I'm really glad you came today. It was nice having someone to share this with."

She hummed sleepily in agreement. As softly as I could, so I didn't wake her, I stroked along her spine. I knew without a doubt I wanted this every night. She felt so right in my arms.

Now that she'd met my parents, I wanted to take her home, show her where I grew up. Enjoy more Sundays with her and Sarah. Hell, maybe Matt could come, and we could double date at some of the so-called amazing brunch places that I lived near but never bothered to go to. I wanted to support Audrey's launch, maybe even talk to Wes or Liv and get some good social media support for the brand. I'd have to mention it to Audrey, see what she thought.

And just as I felt sleep tugging at me, I had a single consistent thought. I was completely and utterly head over heels for Audrey Adams.

27

AUDREY

A few days later, Tiff sat beside me at Chicago's foremost annual non-media affiliated culinary awards. Apparently, all of that was important, but I was just here for Tiff. It was her fourth time being nominated in the bartending category, but the first I'd been able to attend.

It wasn't exactly what I had been expecting.

The restaurant it was held in hadn't been transformed so much as mildly dressed up. A small stage had been erected along one wall, and on it stood a speaker's podium and a trestle table piled high with fancy bronze awards. Several gentlemen in three-piece suits stood up there, one hosting and the other guarding the statues before passing them out as each winner approached the stage.

Most of the audience wasn't paying any attention as they were focused more on drinking and networking with each other, taking breaks only to clap at the appropriate points.

Tiff rhythmically tapped her nails on the table while impatiently watching for a waitress. Her shrewd eyes passed over me. "You seem awfully chipper. I'm assuming the wedding went well. Or else you got laid. Either way, spill. I need details."

"Um, yes?"

"Yes to what?"

"Both," I answered smugly.

"And how was it meeting the Ward clan?"

"Surprisingly fun. His mom is hilarious." It had been easy to see where Sarah and Jackson got their liveliness from, and the clear devotion of his parents made me ache. In one evening, Deb had made me feel more welcomed than my parents ever had.

My smile slipped, and I shook off the melancholy. This was Tiff's night. "Now, tell me again why this major awards night is being held on a Wednesday?"

"It's to stop everyone from getting shitfaced," Tiff said, matter-of-factly.

I snorted. "Does it ever work?"

"Hell, no. Everyone here works in, manages, or owns a bar or restaurant. We like our liquor."

"Well, I'm not about to go wild. I have work in the morning."

"Like you haven't gone to work hungover before."

"That was one time. Also, it was your fault."

"I wasn't the one who opened the second bottle of wine."

"Yes, you were!"

"Fine, maybe I was." She flagged down one of the waitresses who was handing out drinks and took two glasses of bubbly off the tray. Then two more. "Now, let's get shitfaced."

We were another two drinks in when Tiff spotted someone over my shoulder and grimaced. "Ugh, this is always such a sausage fest."

The someone she spotted walked over to the table; it was a man in a badly fitted black suit. "Tiffany Young, what a surprise. It's a pity that Graham Stonier isn't the chair of the awards committee anymore. You probably could have slept your way to a fourth win."

"Eat a dick, Steve."

He sneered. "So glad we have such a charming diversity nominee." Thankfully, he walked away before I could get any ideas about hurting him.

Tiff rolled her eyes. "I want to call him a dick, but that would be an insult to dicks. That guy ruins all genitalia." She pondered. "Hey, what's a body part that's non-binary but equally hateful?"

I came up empty. "Bellybuttons? I don't know that they're hated, but they can be pretty weird looking."

Her face contorted. "Oh, God, have you ever seen one when it was pushed out on a pregnant lady? So gross."

I was incredulous. "Seriously? You just told me you googled rosebud the other day."

"Don't kink shame. I didn't say I liked it, just that I was curious."

"And?"

She shrugged. "Each to their own. But I mean ... some stuff is just meant to stay inside your body."

The sound I made was half-groan, half-laugh. "Oh, God, that's too much information."

"Another drink?" She was already flagging the waitress again.

"Is that even a question?"

Unfortunately, the waitress told us that she'd have to come back with another tray of drinks in five minutes, and I was about to offer to go to the bar instead when I saw the last person I expected.

I was thankful I wasn't doing anything more than sitting down and breathing, although the latter was taking some considerable effort at this moment.

I felt my heart pounding against my ribs like an angry neighbor. "Shit. Brad."

Tiff started. "What? Where?"

"Behind you. Fuck, I think he's walking over here."

Tiff looked over, and I could tell when she saw him because she straightened in her chair, angling herself in front of me like a shield.

"Is that his date?" she asked.

"Looks like it."

And then there he was, my ex-husband, standing in this poorly lighted restaurant, politely smiling like this wasn't awkward as fuck.

"Audrey. Tiffany."

"Brad."

A harsh-looking woman in a little black dress hung off his arm, and she looked vaguely familiar, but I couldn't place it.

When neither Tiffany nor I greeted her, she shifted her weight on her heels and bared her teeth in a fake smile. "Nice to see you again, Audrey."

The face hadn't done it, but boy, had her nasal, blunt voice brought the memories flooding back. Even in my rare moments of missing work at Empire, I hadn't for a second missed the condescension and cattiness from this particular co-worker. I forced a smile in her direction. "You, too, Natalie."

"Who the hell let you in here." Trust Tiff to say what I was thinking without any shame whatsoever. I was so glad she was my friend.

Natalie didn't seem rattled. "My company sponsors the awards, and Brad is my date."

"How have you been, Audrey?" Brad asked.

"Fine."

"Still working with David?"

"Yes, actually, and it's going really well."

Natalie piped up. "A little rumor is going around that you're trying to launch a new rum by a local distillery. How quaint. Probably for the best that you're handling smaller accounts. You wouldn't want to overtax your abilities."

"Listen, you b—"

Natalie continued, ignoring Tiff's outburst. "The MacMillan account, I heard. Bit small for our tastes, but who knew, maybe if they expand, we could make them an offer."

I would not engage. I would not engage. "Do what you want, Natalie."

"Well, this has been delightful. Excuse me while I speak to more important people. Darling," She turned to Brad, "Don't be much longer." And with that, she was off. Hopefully, someone spilled a drink on her, and she melted, but I wasn't about to hold my breath.

"You look stressed."

It was so familiar and yet so ridiculous I almost laughed. "Jesus, Brad, seriously?"

"What? I'm worried about you."

Tiff snorted next to me but said nothing when I knocked her

knee with my hand under the table. "You don't have to worry about me anymore, Brad. That's the great thing about divorce."

"You should be taking care of yourself."

Grinding my teeth, I turned to Tiff. "Can you get us a drink?"

"Sure. I'll get a waiter over here." I placed a hand on her arm to stop her.

"I meant from the bar," I said, imploring her to give Brad and me some space.

"You sure?"

"Yeah."

She eyed Brad warily for a long moment, then stood up and walked toward the bar.

"She hasn't changed, I see." Brad filled the spot Tiffany left, and I fought against my gut reaction to shift my chair away from him.

He had never been Tiff's biggest fan, but he'd obviously stopped caring about upsetting me by saying anything about it.

With a resolve I wouldn't have had a few months ago, I let his comment remain untouched and moved on. "I didn't realize you were seeing anyone."

"I wasn't expecting to. It just happened."

"How long?"

"Almost a year. We're pretty focussed on our careers, but we're making it work."

"Wow." I hadn't meant to say it, but it had hardly been more than a year since the divorce, which meant Brad hadn't wasted any time. I was torn between wanting to know just how short of a period he'd waited before jumping back into a relationship and wishing I could already forget the small amount he'd told me.

"And you?" Brad asked.

I resented the question immediately. Brad wanted to compete. He wanted to prove to me he had moved on. That of the two of us, he had his shit together. I'd spent years hearing him "support" me by always questioning my choices and trying to get me to "find my purpose" as long as that purpose was one he deemed acceptable.

And yes, I was seeing someone, but he didn't care about that. This was just another way he could one-up me in life. Oh, you've been dating someone for a few weeks? Well, Natalie and I are about to move in together. He hadn't changed.

"I'm happy," I finally said.

"I'll take that as a no then." I felt my jaw clench, but I reminded myself I didn't want to engage. It was what he wanted, and I had promised myself I wouldn't fall into his traps anymore. I'd left it all behind.

So why could he still get to me like this?

"I'd be careful with that startup, too. Sixty percent of new businesses fail in the first year. And trust me, you couldn't handle that."

"You don't know anything about me anymore, Brad. Surprisingly, I'm able to function without you."

He scoffed, unconvinced. "You don't know what you want. Never did. You always preferred someone telling you what to do. Anytime it got hard, it was always 'Brad what do you think?' And 'Brad what should I do?'"

He didn't seem to notice my frustration, or perhaps he always noticed and never cared. He continued. "You should find someone, Audrey. If you're determined to accept the life you have and nothing more, you could at least make sure you're not alone. And that doesn't mean spending all of your time at that bar, getting drunk."

My focus was locked onto my plate as I fiddled with the cutlery and blinked back tears. I couldn't believe him. I knew we hadn't exactly left things in a great place, but to still hold a grudge after this long? To still want to hurt me like this?

His chair was forcibly pulled out from the table by Tiffany. "Ok, asshole, time to go back to your ice princess."

He scoffed and stood. "You're still as charming as I remember you, Tiffany. Goodnight, Audrey. Think about what I said."

I refused to look at him as he walked away.

Tiff plopped down on the seat and placed a gentle hand on my shoulder. "You ok?"

I let out a shaky breath and nodded. I didn't trust myself to speak, and luckily Tiffany didn't push beyond a supportive grip on my shoulder and a whispered "asshole" that managed to make me smile.

Tiff's award was the one after this if the program was correct, and I was relieved when she told me that we were leaving afterward no matter how it went.

In what seemed like mere seconds, she stood and accepted the award with the same casual confidence with which she did everything, and blissfully, there were no speeches. Just a simple handshake, photo op, and then she was grabbing my arm, and we hightailed it out of there.

"I can't believe that dick. I wish he really was dead."

"You don't mean that. That's a horrible thing to say."

Tiff just rolled her eyes. "Can I at least wish him some serious bodily harm? And what about that witch he was with? I wanted to throw a drink on her to see if she'd melt."

My throat was thick with emotion, but at this, I choked out a laugh, dropping my head to her shoulder and hugging her arm as the taxi took us home.

She turned her head and dropped a kiss into my hair. "You're better than him, Auds."

I was too emotional to smile, so I weakly nodded and said, "Thanks, Tiff. I love you, too."

I was silent the rest of the way home, and it wasn't until I was curled up on my bed in the dark that I let myself cry.

All I wanted to do was bury myself under a blanket and forget the world existed. Forget that tonight had happened.

But I also really didn't want to be alone.

When he answered the phone, he sounded so relaxed I immediately regretted bothering him. "Hey, gorgeous, how did it go? I'm guessing Tiff won again."

"Do you think you could come over?" My voice sounded as fragile as I felt.

His concern was immediate. "What happened? Are you ok?"

"Not really. Can you ..." I drifted off, not even sure what I wanted to ask. I just wanted him here already, to be wrapped up in his arms and reminded that everything was alright.

"I'll be there as soon as I can."

In the time it took for him to arrive, I'd run out of tears and was now pacing by the kettle as it boiled. I debated telling Jackson to go home, embarrassed that I'd worried him over what was essentially silly baggage left over from a relationship I was glad to be rid of.

There was a reason I hadn't wanted to talk about it before now. What if he heard it and decided I wasn't worth the trouble?

I really, really liked him. More than I remembered liking Brad at this stage. More than I remember liking Brad at any stage, and wasn't that a scary thought. That I married someone who I never felt like this for.

The knock on the door came, and I realized that as much as I'd rather avoid this conversation, I owed Jackson the truth. If he really wanted to see where this relationship went, he should know what he was getting himself into.

He wrapped me in his arms the moment I opened the door, the surety in his hold loosening the tightness in my chest. My eyes prickled with new tears.

"Hey," I offered weakly, blinking them back as I clung to him, burying myself in his warmth.

When we finally broke apart, there was a dark patch on his shirt where I'd cried, and he set me on the couch while he finished making the tea I had abandoned when he knocked.

He settled in beside me, close enough to touch but letting me decide what I wanted. I shuffled closer, needing the contact to calm me.

"I saw Brad tonight," I started, watching the steam rise from the mug in my hands. Jackson was a calm presence beside me, and I breathed it in, letting it seep into my lungs before I continued. "I wasn't expecting him to be there. He just showed up with someone." I left out the details about Natalie because that wasn't the part I was having issues with. "He hasn't changed, but I don't know, I thought —I felt—like I had, and yet … he was still able to get to me as easily as he used to."

Jackson's hand was gentle. "Tell me about him."

"Do you really want to know?" I finally turned to face him.

"Yes. I want to know everything about you." And the sincerity in his voice damn near made me want to cry again.

I closed my eyes. Started from the beginning. "We met in college. Brad was studying economics while I did business. We met at a party and just sort of fell into a relationship. I liked that he had his own life, his own friends outside of me, and I had mine. After we graduated, we moved in together without really deciding to, and then one day, we realized we'd been dating for five years, and it was probably time to get married."

I continued, "At first, it felt like I had someone in my corner, a cheerleader. He was always looking ahead, seeing all the things I could be doing and motivating me to go after them, even if I didn't feel ready. And it helped. It was nice to have someone see something positive in me for a change. With my parents, it was always about what more I could have done like nothing I did was enough. Brad celebrated with me and kept telling me about the next thing I could do."

Jackson's thumb brushed my arm, reassuring, and I smiled into it, grateful that he was here.

"But then it became too much. I started wanting my own things, and Brad would find ways of making me question it, or he'd make little dismissive remarks so that it didn't seem like something good anymore. It got to the point where I felt I always needed his approval before I did anything. I stopped even having an opinion on anything after a while, just deferred to him."

The muscles in Jackson's arm flexed, but he said nothing. "He didn't understand why I wanted to leave Empire, didn't understand why I wasn't angling for a promotion. Always asked me what was the point of working so hard if it wasn't going to personally benefit me. For him, everything had to be building towards a goal." I paused to take a sip of my tea, my mouth dry.

"I just, it got to a point where I wasn't happy with him anymore, but I didn't want to be alone. We had so much history together; how could I give that up? Marriage is about work, so I kept trying to work at it." All that effort, and for what? A man who was able to walk away without a second thought. "But Brad wasn't satisfied.

Kept saying I was giving up on myself. On us. That I was wasting my life."

"Fucking asshole," Jackson said with a force that took me by surprise, holding me closer to him.

A rough chuckle escaped me. "That's what Tiff said."

"So that's why you said what you did at the bar that night? About being enough?"

"You remember that?"

"Yes. And I shouldn't need to tell you this, but you are enough, Audrey. You're incredible. Smart, sexy, compassionate. A million other things, and probably more that I haven't even begun to know yet. No one can take that from you or diminish it because it's you. It's who you are." He punctuated his words with a searing kiss, which I returned eagerly, pouring into it everything I felt but was too scared to say.

"You're good at this."

"You make it easy to be."

28

AUDREY

Returning to work the next day, I felt lighter, a weight lifted with the knowledge that Jackson now knew my history and hadn't run screaming.

Waking up with him curled up behind me in bed this morning had been wonderful. I'd forgotten how much I missed these intimate moments with someone. And while I would rather have spent the entire day keeping him in my bed, I had far too much on my plate to take a day off.

This rum wasn't about to launch itself.

The event was under a month away, and most things were on track. The venue was locked in, Tiff had planned a great cocktail list, one that even Jeff and Julie were excited about, and the caterer had finally confirmed this morning. I still had to talk with the furniture hire company to lock in the bar tables and chairs, and there was also the lighting, the bar staff ... Ok, maybe there was still a fair bit more to do.

Jackson's sneaky little promo hadn't hurt either; it managed to drum up enough buzz that tickets had already sold out. I'd thanked him because it was sweet, really, but it hadn't stopped the nagging doubt that plagued me. Now I'd never know if I could have managed the same without his help.

I was still searching for something extra to make the launch special. The previous day, I came up with the idea of bringing pieces of the distillery to the venue so the guests could learn about the history behind the brand and the backstory of how the rum came to be. I set a reminder for myself to call Jeff about it later this afternoon.

"Audrey, are you sure there's nothing more we could help with? Maybe Jet and I could take over some of your client visits? I was looking at the plans for the launch and thought maybe I could manage the catering and hire contracts? I have a minor in event management and actually ran a lot of our school events, so it really wouldn't be a problem." Winnie and Jet were settled in their usual seats in my office, and both now looked at me, hopeful.

I blinked, frozen in contemplation.

On the one hand, I knew they were bored and needed more to do. I'd been trying, really I had, but I'd already handed over all of the easier stuff. Anything else meant shadowing them as they followed up with customers, spoke with our vendors, and completed the mountains of paperwork which kept the inventory and shipping on track, which would leave me almost no time to focus on the launch.

There was the rub, wasn't it? If I spent the time to train them, I would be free to really focus, but I would have to stop working to train them ... Not for the first time, I was angry at David for putting me in this position.

That wasn't fair. I was angry at myself.

I knew I was messing this up. I wasn't being a good leader. I had a list a mile long of calls to make to get the launch ready, and all I could think was, I wish I could talk to Jackson right now. Maybe run away to a beach somewhere and have marathon sex until I forgot what day of the week it was.

Not that I needed a getaway to do that. I actually had no idea what today was; I was that scattered.

Winnie was looking at me expectantly, and I let out a long

breath. I needed their help, but I was torn in wanting it. Letting go and delegating was hard for me, and I'd never had to do it before. I was finding it a lot harder than I expected.

"Thanks, Winnie, I really appreciate that. Let me look over the workload and see what I can do."

She jumped up suddenly and clapped, something I didn't realize anyone other than children did anymore, and nope, I wasn't going to think about how old that made me feel. "That would be great! It's just we see how hard you're working, and we'd love to help more. That's what we're here for, you know?"

I nodded and smiled, guilt sinking into my stomach. I suddenly wished she had a better mentor. I couldn't imagine I was doing much for them right now. I'd have to speak with David and maybe have them reassigned to someone else.

And when had I started feeling like I couldn't do this? Just a few weeks ago, I'd been on top of the world, feeling like I could master anything.

Now I was barely holding on by a thread.

I needed some air. And some time to think.

I stood. "I'm going to do a coffee run. Can I get either of you something?" I was starting to realize I wasn't boss material, but this, I could do.

"Dirty chai," Jet replied.

"And a half-strength, no fat latte for me, thanks, Audrey."

I fought the urge to laugh. Tiff would absolutely hate this coffee order. I grabbed my coat. "Back in ten."

Outside, the fresh air helped me breathe easier, but it didn't do anything to shift the sinking feeling in my stomach.

Winnie had a point. I'd seen the event experience on her resume and was admittedly impressed. She could probably run the entire launch herself. And didn't that thought just make me a little nauseous? I struggled to imagine passing off the reins to her. Even the idea of having her take control of the catering work set me on edge.

This was my launch. My opportunity to prove myself. To the MacMillan's. To David. To myself.

A year ago, I wouldn't have believed I could do it. Then Brad left, and I scraped together every bit of confidence I had to pull myself together to show that I didn't need him to be ok. I didn't need anyone.

I could do this.

A text from Tiff served as a welcome distraction, albeit a confused one when it just read, "you 2 are so cute!!!" It took another ten seconds for the photos to come through, multiple photos from Sarah's wedding that Jackson had been tagged in on Instagram. The first, a selfie of us with Lucas and Marie, another of Jackson and I chatting animatedly to each other at the reception, and the last of us kissing on the dance floor.

Apart from the selfie, I couldn't even remember these photos being taken.

Before I could respond, Tiff added, "I deserve the matchmaking CROWN." No one—least of all me—could deny her bragging rights for bringing Jace and me together, but it was her support and her acceptance of Jackson that filled me with happiness.

I saved all the photos on my phone, told Tiff that it was beginner's luck and that no one liked a braggart. She sent back an emoji of a hand flipping me off.

Back at the office, I delivered the coffees then excused myself, leaving Winnie and Jet to finish some paperwork. I might not be prepared to delegate any of the launch, but I could at least find them something to do.

I remembered how they'd assisted Anthony the other week and decided that I'd been hogging our help far too much. David's initial point had been for them to assist the whole team, surely. And if they were busy managing their own, albeit smaller accounts, I would be able to work on the launch without disruption.

After an hour of running around, I'd spoken to half of the other account managers—the half that were in the office anyway—and sent Winnie and Jet off to get acquainted with their new workload, leaving my office blissfully empty again.

Of course, that wasn't going to last.

"Knock knock," David said by way of actually knocking, "Are you free?"

There were about ten different things I needed to be doing at that moment, but I could probably spare five minutes for whatever David needed to see me about. "Sure, take a seat."

"No can do, kiddo. Grab your coat. I'm taking you to lunch."

"I'm too busy for lunch."

He smiled. "I know. That's why we're going."

He wasn't going to take no for an answer, so I stood and grabbed the coat off the back of my chair, along with my purse. David would never let me pay for lunch, but it felt rude to go without it anyway. His smile widened as I followed him to the elevator. "I have to check in on a customer anyway, so you can still feel like you're working while we eat."

We took David's car downtown, and as soon I saw the Tavolino sign, I shot David a wry look. "A customer, huh?"

David chuckled as I followed him into the trattoria.

Strangely, I hadn't visited the restaurant much, but anytime I did, I was always disappointed I didn't make more of an effort. The small space was filled with very traditional styling; red and white chequered tablecloths, a wood-fired stove, even a semi-open kitchen, so you could hear snippets of frustrated Italian from the chefs as they cooked.

Nicky, David's husband, immediately gravitated into the dining room as if some magnetic force had propelled him. His hands came up to David's face as they kissed, and I melted at their easy display of affection. Twenty years together and still so in love. It gave me hope.

Technically, Nicky was one of our customers, but I knew we weren't there for work. David tried to go there for lunch most days. "Perks of being the boss," he'd said when I asked, but I knew it was really because he missed Nicky. He was just a giant marshmallow underneath that beard.

We got seated, and I quickly realized that this wasn't going to be a simple, friendly chat. No, it was going to be a friendly, "I wanted to check in with you because I'm your boss" chat.

Which meant David was worried about something.

This was a common tactic David used when we worked at Empire. Back when I was still trying to work out what I was doing. We'd had a fair few when my marriage collapsed as well.

So it was natural for me to start wondering where I'd gone wrong for him to want to have one now. I guiltily thought back over the last few months, how distracted I'd become since I'd met Jackson, all those days I left while it was still daylight outside, instead of staying back and getting more done.

No wonder David wanted to check in with me.

"So, I wanted to check with you, see how you're doing."

"I'm good. Busy with the launch."

"Anything else going on?"

"I don't know what you mean."

"You don't have to look so worried, Audrey. I've noticed a change in you, a good one, and I want you to know you should cherish that, whatever it is. You seem happier lately."

He paused, but I stayed silent, so he continued, "How are the plans for the launch coming along?"

"Fine."

"Fine. No issues you want to raise, no problems I can help with?"

"Nope."

"And Winnie and Jet are working out?"

"Mm-hmm," I said, stuffing my mouth as an excuse not to have to say anymore, then groaned in delight. The food was amazing. I really needed to come more often.

"You're actually getting some help, aren't you? That was the reason I brought them in in the first place. Because if they have time to help, I want you to use them."

"They're already busy with everyone else's work. Besides, I have it all under control."

I could see this frustrated him, his greying eyebrows dipping in frustration, but he let it go. "Work isn't everything, Audrey. You need to learn to relax."

I was firm. "I'll relax after the launch has been a success."

Nicky brought over our meals and left after kissing David's cheek. Damnit, they were as heart-warming as one of those Christmas ads with little kids and puppies. It was impossible to be angry in the face of that cuteness.

David continued. "You work harder than almost anyone I know, myself included somedays, but life is important and love even more so. Whatever it is that has you smiling lately is a good thing. I wouldn't want you to let something good go by, and you shouldn't be worried that it's going to turn out the same as with Brad."

"I ..." I swallowed against the lump in my throat. "Thanks, David."

Despite his kind words, I still felt a sinking in my gut. He might think I was working too much, but I knew better. As far as he knew, I'd been non-stop on this launch, but all I could remember were the hours I'd spent texting Jackson or daydreaming about seeing him or leaving early to see him.

Ok, five p.m. wasn't exactly early, but it was for me.

For all that David said, I knew it was not the whole truth. The reality was that I'd been steadily letting this thing with Jackson take up more space in my life after I'd promised myself I wouldn't let anything distract me from getting this launch right.

I hated the idea that something was going to have to give.

29

JACKSON

"It's been weeks, Terry. Why haven't they made a decision yet?" It was a rare day off, and I was currently pacing the length of my couch while I waited for Terry to explain why the contract renewal discussions with the network were taking so long.

"It'll be fine, don't worry about it. This is what you have me for."

I paused mid-stride, raking a hand through my hair. "I'd feel better knowing that things were leaning in our direction. I want you to take something to them. Wes, Liv, and I were agreed on it. In exchange for the raise, we will all sign on for an additional two seasons, plus agree to a certain percentage of additional marketing appearances to boost promotion for the show, this season included."

It was something Wes, Liv, and I had started to discuss after Audrey's comments to me a while back, and it felt like the best compromise for us to make. We were going to have to do a set amount of press anyway, but if we set the terms in the contract, we'd know exactly how much in advance, and that was something we could work with.

"Not a bad offer. They've been pushing for the promos in

particular. Are you sure you want me to take it to them? You could still get the raise without it."

"I'm sure. Let them know I'm about to record a live guest spot with the fancast, 'The Pantheon' to hype up the new season."

"Any more surprises you have for me?"

"No."

"Good. While I appreciate your enthusiasm, J, maybe next time you talk to me about this first."

"Yeah, Terry. I will. Good luck with the network."

"Won't need it. We've got this."

I hoped so. I was never one to count my chickens, but the additional money would go a long way toward paying back my parents, as well as allowing me to start saving for the future.

A future that seemed a hell of a lot closer than it had a few months ago.

All this time, I knew I wanted to get my shit together enough that I would have something to offer when the right person came along, but outside of a stable job and security, both of which were a relative impossibility as an actor, I'd never given any thought as to how my life might have to change to make it work with the right person.

My life right now wasn't exactly ideal for building a strong relationship. I worked all the time, and before we even finished filming the season, I'd be starting the press circuit, not to mention award season, then when we did finally finish filming, I'd be flying to New York for three months to film *Subversion*. Rinse, then repeat.

I could hardly ask Audrey to put up with all that. And what? Wait until things settled down to start a life together?

She deserved better.

Considering what she'd gone through with her ex—and I wished there was a way to erase the doubts he'd sown—it was all the more amazing how compassionate she was. That her kindness and strength had survived years of putting herself aside for someone else.

I wanted to help her celebrate that, show her all the things I saw when I looked at her, protect her from ever doubting herself again, give her something stable to rely on.

Audrey messaged me good luck as I arrived, saying she couldn't wait to listen to it later. I send back a thank you and spent at least two minutes arguing with myself over whether I should add a kiss emoji before I realized I was being ridiculous and left it off.

Then I sent it because if being in love made me ridiculous, then so be it.

Two friends ran the podcast out of their apartment along the Green Line, and I'd timed it, so I was knocking on their door five minutes early.

Sabine answered the door, Hunter a half step behind her, and their mutual excitement was evident in their expressions.

I shook Hunter's hand while Sabine directed me over to a round dining table where they'd set up three mics, along with headphones for each of us and the laptop they were recording with.

"Thanks again for reaching out. We're really excited to have someone from the show."

"Of course, I'm definitely a fan of the podcast. The recap you did on last season's finale was hilarious."

"Wow, thanks! That means a lot," Hunter said with a smile.

"Yeah," Sabine added, "I mean, we just started it for ourselves, a way to geek out over different mythology as well as talk about the show, and people liked it enough for us to keep going."

"Now your mic is already wired up and ready to go, but can I get you some water before we start?"

"Thanks, that'd be great."

Hunter returned with a glass for us both, and we all made ourselves comfortable around the table. I slid the headphones on and did a quick sound test to make sure everything was in order before Sabine gave the signal that we were live.

"Jackson! We can't tell you how thrilled we are that you're here," Sabine added once they had run through their intro.

Hunter nodded. Though we were only recording audio, I suspected it was a hard habit to break. "We're both huge fans."

"Hopefully, this means we can get more of the cast on here some time."

I chuckled. "I'll be sure to put in a good word."

"So, let's jump right in and talk about season three. Obviously, the biggest change is Ares switching sides and becoming one of the good guys, although we can only wonder how long that will last, given his track record."

"I'm pretty excited to see Wes get his ass kicked this season."

"Aren't we all," I joked. "He's a crafty god, that one. You can pretty much always bet that he has a plan, especially when things aren't going his way."

"That must be interesting to play against?" Sabine asked.

"It is. And Ryder doesn't trust him at all, so there's a lot of animosity between them. Still, they recognize a usefulness in each other against The Three."

"Those are the dream gods, this season's big bad, right?" Hunter clarified.

I nodded. "Yes."

Hunter was particularly enthusiastic about this, following up with several more questions. I offered a few more details about the show, being careful with what I shared before they began diving into my personal life.

"As a Chicago native, you must love being able to film on location."

"Absolutely. It's been a real gift being able to film in my hometown. I know everyone complains about the weather, but I actually missed it when I was in LA."

"Don't lie to us now," Hunter said wryly.

"No, it's true!" I admitted, laughing.

"And I hear congratulations are in order for your sister, who just got married."

We hadn't discussed what topics were off-limits, but I was always selective when talking about my family. I put on my polite and professional mask, prepared to redirect the conversation if they tried to get too personal. "Oh, thank you. Yes. It was a great night."

"Speaking of, I know we don't normally get into this sort of thing, but you're here, so we couldn't help ourselves. Some photos have been floating around recently. It seems you have a new girl on your arm."

Hunter made a teasing sound. "Yes, I don't know if you've seen the comment sections of your social media lately, but there's a lot of speculation as to who she is. No one can figure it out. A new co-star, perhaps?"

"Nothing like that, no." There was a beat of silence where they waited for me to elaborate, but I didn't.

"Well, I know that there are a lot of heartbroken fans out there, but I for one think you two make a beautiful couple. Is it serious?"

Apprehension rose within me.

I'd been in this situation countless times before. Made a joke, waved it off, moved on. But this wasn't some one-night stand. This was Audrey. I'd love nothing more than to tell everyone how much she meant to me, but shit, we hadn't even discussed this yet—telling people. Being in public.

And she'd said before how much she wouldn't like to be in the spotlight. The last thing I would ever want was for my career to hurt her.

Plus, I knew how much the network liked to play up my bachelor status. They'd forgiven previous rumors about my love life because they got to lean into the rakish playboy aspect of my character. It sold the show. And right now, the whole reason I was even doing this damn interview was to keep selling the show.

So I made a choice.

"Have you ever known me to be in a serious relationship?" I joked.

Hunter laughed. "You've got us there."

"So you don't have someone special in your life right now?"

And with a practiced smile and a tightening in my throat, I said, "No one."

30

AUDREY

The sun was warm but not overbearing as I made myself comfortable on the park bench, juggling my take-away coffee as I brought up the podcast app on my phone. I was excited to support Jackson both as a recent fan of his show and as his girlfriend.

Technically, I was on my lunch break. I could have stayed in the office, but it was an uncharacteristically beautiful day outside, and it seemed like the perfect mirror for my joyful mood.

It made me phenomenally proud that he had come up with a way to negotiate for his contract renewal, especially when he'd said it was something I'd said that had helped him think of it.

He kept finding ways of making me feel capable, bringing light to parts of myself I'd learned to shove in a corner and forget. I could barely believe how lucky I was to have found him. To feel the way I did about him. And while I was still too scared to say it, I could feel that four-letter word pressed against my heart, the truth of it sitting on the tip of my tongue.

I was still floating a little on air. Somewhere in the back of my mind, I knew I should probably talk to Jackson about the photos that had been posted of us on social media, but he would have mentioned it if I needed to be worried, so I hadn't given it much thought yet.

What preoccupied me was wonder at the incredible situation I'd found myself in.

I listened as they started with some fun banter about the show, laughing when they made a dig about Wes, remembering his casual cockiness that second night I saw Jackson at The Basement. I knew Jace was close with the cast, and suddenly, the thought of meeting his friends filled me with excitement. Seeing more of his life, and being a part of it going forward, was something I wanted.

It was obvious the hosts had a great love for the show and the lore, and it was wonderful to hear Jackson indulge in his own enjoyment of it. He'd mentioned to me once that engaging with the show's fans over the little details was one of his favorite things. Most people wrote it off as too low-brow or acted like he should be embarrassed because the target demographic was teenage girls, but he genuinely liked the campiness and said that the cast had a lot of fun playing in the world of the show. I was glad that he had the chance to express that side of himself on the podcast.

When they bought up Sarah's wedding, I could hear the change in his voice and could practically see the way his jaw must have twitched like it always did when he was holding his emotions back.

My pulse stuttered when they asked about me, and even though it was unlikely, the idea that Jackson might mention me, even if just in a vague way, was exciting. But that excitement curdled when he answered, making it known in two words that there wasn't anyone special in his life.

Tearing my headphones out of my ears, I robotically took a sip of my coffee, but its bitterness only made me feel worse, so I threw it in a nearby bin. Now that I was on my feet, my restlessness pushed me to walk through the park, unsuccessfully hoping to forget what I'd just heard.

When I remembered that one of the hosts mentioned the fan comments on the photos, I opened Instagram and brought up Jackson's profile, finding the images in question. There was a war between my fingers and my gut—I knew I was going to regret reading these; no good could come from it. But I had to. Otherwise, I'd always wonder.

I read through the comments section, scrolling through hundreds of them, not being able to stop myself, even as my eyes got cloudy and my throat tightened in sorrow and anger.

VIEW ALL 4,149 COMMENTS:
> I … do not care for her outfit …
> That angle is doing her no favors
> Dam he looking handsome as always
> Beautiful couple
> She is so cute
> That should be me
> Who is this woman with my husband?
> I thought he dated models? She looks so plain
> its a choice that's for sure
> That dress looks cheap af
> Yeah, it's clear what she's after. J you can do so much better!
> Whoever that girl is is lucky as hell
> I hate whoever that is lol
> i feel sorry for her she's just flavor of the month

DESPITE THE WARM DAY, a chill ran through me, hurt prickling my insides like a lance.

Damn.

Jackson hadn't been wrong; some people were brutal. And while it certainly hurt to read, I was more put out by Jackson's answer. He'd been the one to say he wanted us to be something more, inviting me to meet his entire family at Sarah's wedding. There were photos of us together. So how would he explain pretending I wasn't someone important in his life?

Returning to work, I found myself typing a message to see if he was free later so we could talk. He responded quickly, saying he'd be home and that he was looking forward to seeing me. When I couldn't bring myself to say the same, I just sent a thumbs up. It definitely made me feel worse.

I wanted to laugh at how naïve I'd been. I'd thought being in public would be more about being photographed if we went to an event together or having my co-workers knowing about my personal life; I hadn't ever expected this.

But Jackson had warned me, hadn't he?

Weeks ago, he'd mentioned that this was what the women he slept with faced.

That's what he meant when he joked just now about not being known for being in a serious relationship.

Because if he was seen with someone, they were just a fling.

But that wasn't what he'd called me.

No one, he'd said.

I was disappointed, I realized. I had wanted him to acknowledge what we had.

And yet ... the thought of it being *official* ... of what that might mean for my life and my work. Jackson had already proved with one photo that his influence could sell out an event I was hosting, and that was before anyone could connect us.

Once people knew ... How would I ever really know what successes were mine alone or if they happened because I was "Jackson Ward's girlfriend"?

Even if loving him was worth it, was I even ready for that?

The launch was close now, and I had a lot to focus on. It really wasn't a good time to be doing anything other than working. I had feelings for him; there was no question about that in my mind. But I had been slipping incrementally out of my routine for weeks now, and the guilt I had about choosing him over my other responsibilities was starting to build into something I found difficult to ignore.

Jet entered my office with a tentative knock.

"Yes?" I asked, not looking away from my computer.

"Um, I just wanted to double-check something. Your email said to pay the invoice to Wilsons."

"Yes."

"But we already sent that through yesterday."

"Oh. We did?"

He nodded. "Did you maybe mean the invoice to Wildflower?"

I flushed, my thoughts erratic. Had that been what I'd meant? "Uh, yeah."

Jet looked visibly relieved. "Great. I'll go do that now."

Once he'd left, I dropped my head into my hands. What the hell was going on with me? I needed to get a grip. Jackson and I had already agreed to chat after work, so why couldn't I concentrate?

I took a couple of deep breaths while I rubbed at my temple, a dull ache blooming behind my right eye. Another knock came, this one more decisive than Jet's. Opening my eyes, I found David looking concerned. "You ok, kiddo?"

"Of course, why?"

"Well, you don't look so good. And I'm going to assume that you didn't mean to email me our inventory list and ask if I'd like to consider expanding on my order this quarter."

Shit. "Sorry. I'll fix it."

"Not what I'm worried about, Audrey." The intensity of his focus made my head throb. "I think you should go home."

This cut through my rampant efforts to redirect the email. "What?"

"You don't need to tell me what's going on, but I think it's obvious that whatever it is is a distraction for you right now, and I think it's a good idea if you go home and deal with it before you do something we can't fix. You can come back fresh in the morning, and we'll talk about it then."

"But David—"

"No, I'm sorry, I'm not going to be able to take no for an answer today."

After he unceremoniously pushed me out the door, I made my way to Tiff's apartment, my thoughts a jumbled mess. I knew I should talk to Jackson, but I was delaying the inevitable.

Thankfully, she was home.

"Fuck, Auds. What happened?" she said as soon as she saw me.

Clearly, I looked as bad as I felt.

"I'm going to assume this has something to do with Jackson?" she added when I still hadn't said anything.

And if Tiff was using his real name, she knew how serious this was.

I nodded silently, then stumbled my way through all of it: the podcast, Jackson's dismissal, the fans, David sending me home. By now, she'd corralled me to the couch, listening patiently as I let the words tumble out, pulling me into a tight hug once I'd finished.

"You know me, Tiff. I don't come in late or skip work or make stupid little mistakes like I did today. Ever since I met Jackson, I've been different." There was so much going on in my mind, like two debate teams speaking over one another. It made it hard to get the right words out. "I mean, he's amazing, and I really, really care about him," I do. So much. "But this has all gone so fast, and I feel like it's taking over everything."

"You're just feeling overwhelmed right now. It'll be fine. Once the launch is over, and you can breathe a little, it won't look so bad."

"I think I need to break up with him."

Tiff was incredulous. "You're serious."

I groaned, a bubble of condensed frustration making its way to the surface. "I can't see how we make this work right now, and I'm not going to give up everything I've worked for."

Tiff answered, slow and calm, "Audrey, that's the stress talking. You need to talk to Jackson about this, tell him how you're feeling. Work through it. Isn't that what relationships are all about?"

And she was right. I knew she was right. But it hardly helped. The crux of the damn thing was that I loved Jackson, but I missed what my life was like before I met him. Ok, not all of it, obviously, but the sense of self I'd found. To be my own person, on my own terms.

But when I thought about not having him in my life; his humor, his sweetness, his steady reassurance, and support … It felt like cutting out my own heart.

I was monumentally fucked.

"Oh, Auds," Tiff said, and she sounded as despairing as I felt. "Promise me you'll at least try."

———

I WAITED until I was on the El before I told Jackson I was on my way.

The trip didn't give me enough time to collect my thoughts. I still felt as lost as I had at Tiff's, but I was at least calmer than before. I had no idea what to expect when I talked to Jackson, but I felt each brick being laid down around my heart with every approaching stop.

The first thing I wanted to cover was the podcast and the "no one" comment.

Either Jackson lied. Or worse, he hadn't.

The best way to approach it was probably quick. Like a band-aid, wasn't that the phrase?

He was as gorgeous as ever when he opened his door, casually dressed in sweats and a tee. I imagined him spending the afternoon reading scripts on the couch, and it made me want to forget everything and just curl up in his arms.

Suddenly, I had a strong preference to avoid this conversation.

On instinct, or perhaps because it might be the last time I got to do it, I hugged him, reveling in the feel of him, his familiar smell, the comfort of his arms. More than anything, I wanted for it to be yesterday when there wasn't anything hanging over my head.

"Can I sit?" The question was unnecessary. I was already moving towards the couch, and I didn't expect him to say no, but the thick fog of the inevitable was starting to choke me, and I needed to say something.

When he took the seat next to me, I turned and rested my feet in his lap. It was a position we'd been in many times. His hands came to rest on my calves, and the gesture pulled at my heart, taunting me. *See how sweet he is?* My heart seemed to cry. *Don't hurt him.*

Clearing my throat, I said, "I wanted to talk to you about the interview today."

Quick. Just like a band-aid.

Jackson, understanding exactly which part of the interview I was referring to, gently squeezed my leg. "I'm sorry about that. They put me on the spot, and since we haven't talked about going public, I thought that was the best way to cut off the questions until I saw you. I know that's not an excuse, but I wanted you to know that I do see us as something serious."

"Ok." And it was. "I … that makes sense." And it did. "I have to admit I was a little disappointed, but you're right, we hadn't talked about going public, and after I saw some of the comments that they were talking about, I guess I'm glad no one knows who I am yet."

His frown deepened. "I'm also sorry about that. You don't deserve any of what they're saying, anonymous or not, and I plan on getting the PR team to make sure that anything hateful is deleted."

"Thank you. I appreciate that."

I slipped my gaze away from his, flexing my foot against his thigh, and watched as he thumbed along the seam of my pants.

"I wanted to if that helps." When I responded with a questioning look, he elaborated. "Tell them how I felt about you. I know we haven't been together very long, and it's a big step, but I wanted to call you my girlfriend today. To tell everyone how much you mean to me."

He was quiet, studying me while I continued to avoid looking directly at him. Scared that if I met his eyes, I would crumble. Into what, I wasn't sure yet.

"But only if that's something you want, too."

"I …" And I startled myself when I realized I had no idea what I wanted to say. I honestly couldn't decide between bringing it up or letting it go, and it made me so endlessly disappointed in myself. Because I didn't trust myself to know what I wanted.

Brad's voice rang in my ears. I really wished I'd let Tiff punch him.

Before the next words came out of his mouth, I could feel the change in the atmosphere, like a super sense, warning me about what was about to happen. But I had no way of stopping it.

"Audrey, I know it might be quick, but no, I know how I feel about you, and I don't care if it's too soon ..." The tenderness in his tone felt abrasive against the storm swirling inside me. "I love you."

Earlier today, it had taken two words to break through my rose-colored haze.

It took three to break my heart.

31

JACKSON

Her eyes drifted closed in the seconds that followed, and I prayed they would open and release me from the fear that was slowly creeping over me.

Then they met mine, and my breath caught in my throat.

It wasn't so much that she didn't immediately say it back. It wasn't exactly what I was hoping for, but on its own, I could accept it. I could even understand it. It was still early.

It was the look of shock and fear in her eyes that hurt.

"Audrey?"

She swung her legs off my lap and onto the floor, turning away from me, her voice icy. "I heard you."

The resulting silence was not comforting me. Something was wrong, but I was scared to ask.

Panic struck me as Audrey stood up from the couch, her face strained. "I really wish you hadn't said that."

My heart dropped.

She swore softly to herself.

"If you don't feel the same ..." I started but was barely able to finish the thought, let alone the sentence. Had I imagined this thing between us?

"No! I …" She caught herself. "Jackson, I really care about you. You have to know that. But this has just all gone so fast, and I don't know how to do this right now."

She wasn't making sense. "I don't understand."

She didn't answer.

I was at a loss. I wanted to say the right thing, but I wasn't sure what that even was. "Audrey," and it came out like a question. Like a plea.

She was quiet as I watched a myriad of emotions cross her face, her lips twitching with unsaid words. Eventually, after a long exhale, she whispered, "I think I better go."

I reach out, pleased this time when she didn't shy away. "Please stay. We should talk about this."

Taking a seat, I was hopeful when she did the same, but it waned when she couldn't quite meet my eye. When she didn't say anything after a minute, I tentatively unwound her hands where they were tightly clenched on her lap and clasped one between my own.

This broke her silence. "I'm not … I can't …" She pinched her nose with her free hand, clearly pained at not being able to find the words.

It was equally frustrating that she couldn't tell me what was going on in her head.

I couldn't understand what had changed, and she wouldn't explain it. I wanted to make it right, to fix it. I just needed her to tell me what I could do to help us get past this. Why was this so hard? Yesterday, everything had been easy, and now it was complicated.

I was scrambling to figure out what was going on. "Is this about the podcast? Do you want me to tell everyone how I feel about you? Because I'll do that. I can get on Twitter right now and tell everyone how much you mean to me." *Help me fix this.*

"No," she said, pulling her hands out of my grasp, and my jaw clenched as my annoyance built. *Talk to me,* I wanted to scream.

"I don't want that. I …" She cut herself off again with a frustrated groan, and I couldn't take it anymore.

"Audrey. Talk to me." My voice was firm. "What do you want?"
I felt like a broken record.

"You know what I want?" Her voice cracked, but there was no
mistaking the fire behind it. "I want not to be having this
conversation. I want not to have to choose between you and my
work. I want to go back to how it was before. I want it to be easier."
She shook her head. "We should have just kept it casual. Good thing
you covered yourself in that interview. It'll be easier this way."

My pulse stuttered, caught between thrumming in anger and
halting in panic. Where was this coming from?

I made a move toward her and couldn't hide the look of hurt
when she shied away from me and took a step back out of my
reach. Frustrated, I dragged a hand through my hair. "Is that what
this is about? The damn interview? I told you. I was protecting
you."

"I never asked you to do that! I can take care of myself."

"I never said you couldn't!"

If she heard me, I couldn't tell. She started to pace. "And what
about the post about the rum? Was that to protect me?"

"What?" It took me a moment to think back, understand what
she was referring to. "I did that to support you. I thought you'd be
happy."

"You didn't even ask me."

I stiffened. "I didn't think I needed to."

"It's not that …" She deflated somewhat, pausing mid-stride. "I
don't need you to fix my problems for me, Jackson. I can handle it.
Why doesn't anyone get that?"

"I know you don't need me to, but I want to."

"Well, I don't want that."

I paused, knowing I might not like the answer, but determined
to ask anyway. "What do you want?"

"Not this."

It was a gut punch.

I finally moved off the couch, needing some distance, though I
couldn't bring myself to move farther than a few steps from where
she was. Where had this all gone so wrong?

There were a million things I wanted to say. I wanted to tell her that I also wanted those things. That this was what had kept me from starting anything serious since I'd started acting. That I also had no idea how it would work, but that didn't stop me from wanting to be with her.

"I'm sorry," Audrey said, still seated, her head hanging down as she focused on her lap. "I'm not explaining myself right."

Releasing a heavy breath, I took a seat on the coffee table so I could face her, but I didn't reach out, and neither did she. We were going around in circles. Or speaking two different languages. It was exhausting. "No, you're not." I sounded as flat as I felt.

"Can we just ... Maybe we need to take a break." She gave me a pleading look and caught her bottom lip with her teeth. Seeing her like this was almost as painful as the idea of letting her walk away.

"No. That isn't what I want. I want to work this out. I love you."

Her whole face fell at those words. "Stop saying that."

A pit opened in my stomach, and I realized I'd been an idiot. She didn't feel the same, and I'd just thrown my heart out to be crushed.

"Do you love me?" Because I needed to hear her say it. Because if what she felt for me was anything close to what I felt for her, we could work this out.

In the seconds before she answered, I was hyper-aware of the space between us. She hadn't shifted away from me, and I found myself leaning toward her to close the gap.

Her voice was quiet. "I don't know what you want me to say."

I thought hearing no would be the worst answer, but I was wrong. This was.

"Ok ..." I stalled, trying to wrap my head around this situation. It was frustrating to be without words, so used to being full of them, even when they were someone else's.

The bottom was dropping out of my world, and there was nothing I could do about it.

She winced. "Jace, I ..."

I tried to ignore the sharp pinch in my chest at her apologetic tone. I knew what it sounded like, but I didn't really want to believe it. I couldn't. There was no way there wasn't love there. I knew that. But for some reason, Audrey couldn't acknowledge it. Or maybe she refused to.

"You say it like it's so easy," she said.

The moment stretched out, and I focused on the feeling of her soft skin, her hand in mine. When had she reached out for my hand?

Everything felt wrong. All I wanted was to gather her up in my arms, tell her everything was ok. That we'd be ok.

"It is easy. I know exactly how I feel." The implication was that she didn't.

She pulled her hand, hard, out of my grip. "That's not fair. I know how I feel. But this is … a lot, Jackson. Don't you get that?"

"Of course, I do. You think that I don't understand that?"

"You don't understand. You can't. It doesn't matter how I feel if I don't feel like myself. I want this to be real,"

I cut in, my fraying nerves not allowing me to sit silent. "It is real."

"You think so, but it isn't. You don't know what a real relationship is. You've never been in one."

White-hot anger flashed under my skin, and I was shocked by the intensity of it. But more than anger, it was fear. I could feel everything between us slipping away, trapped under our feet as we barked and bit at each other like this.

Insults seeped into my mind, words I knew would hit their target and hurt her just as acutely as she'd hurt me. A small part of me wanted to retaliate, wanted to cut into her the same way.

Maybe the most messed up part was that I agreed with her. I hadn't been in a relationship before. That wasn't to say she was right, but … she had a point. It was something I'd worried about and thought I had done a pretty good job of hiding from her. Clearly, I was wrong.

Which made this all the more frustrating. She knew me better than anyone, yet here she was, telling me she didn't know how she felt about me, throwing this back in my face.

How did I get it all so wrong?

I finally spit out, "It's not like your last relationship sets the gold standard." If I had been thinking at all, I would never have let those words past my lips, but I wasn't thinking. I was angry. I was furious.

Audrey's head shot up, and her expression was as pained as I'd ever seen it. Guilt and anger were all I could see, and there was a perverse sort of pleasure at knowing I'd landed a blow. That I wasn't the only one hurting right now.

Because I knew this was the end, and right now, I was standing by and watching it happen in real-time, like a spectator at an accident.

We stood at an impasse, neither of us speaking for a long time.

Then with a broken voice, she said, "You're right."

I said nothing as I watched the door shut behind her.

32

AUDREY

W hen I returned to work the next day, all thoughts of Jackson were locked away, hidden to preserve my sanity. There would be time to fall apart later. It was the only way I was going to make it through without crying.

I felt raw, exposed, un-contained. Like my broken heart was beating outside of my chest for everyone to see. Emotions pouring in and out of me like a battle of the tides.

There wasn't even time right now to question whether I'd done the right thing by walking out. More than anything, I felt horrible about everything I'd said, knowing I hurt Jackson with careless deflections.

My first hint that something was off was finding my office empty. I'd grown used to seeing Winnie and Jet squatting in here, waiting eagerly for the jobs I gave them.

I dropped my coat and bag on my desk and was on my way to David's office when I found the two missing interns sitting with him in the conference room. More surprising to me was that the MacMillan's were seated across from them.

Shock rushed through me, rooting me in place.

The MacMillan's never traveled to the city. Ever.

What the hell did it mean that they were here now, and why the hell were they laughing with Winnie and Jet like old school chums?

And why was I just standing out here like an idiot?

I walked into the room without another thought. "Hi, sorry, did we have a meeting?"

"Audrey, fantastic! Sit down. We've got great news."

Jeff corrected her. "Actually, it was terrible news that we're hoping is good news."

Julie patted his arm. "It's all going to work out, Jeff."

"Absolutely, Audrey will make sure of it." David smiled at me.

I looked around warily, "Anyone want to fill me in?"

I was surprised when Winnie took over. "We received a call yesterday after you'd left. The hire company double-booked half of our order for the launch and couldn't provide us with all the chairs and tables we needed. Jet," she gestured, "saw your notes on using some pieces of furniture that Jeff had made in the past as showpieces at the event, and I thought, why not use it to replace the half of the furniture we don't have!"

"And we love the idea, Audrey" Julia was so happy; it was almost painful not to be able to return it.

Even Jeff looked pleased. "Made a few calls to some friends on the way up here after David mentioned it, and we'll have more than enough on loan for the night to fix your issue."

Your issue.

My issue, they meant.

The one that the damn interns fixed.

Because I was too busy imploding my relationship to be here.

I fixated on my breathing so I wouldn't show the MacMillan's how guilty I felt.

Winnie spoke up again. "I also managed to negotiate a refund of the full amount while getting the hire company to agree to loan them the remainder of the order. I got the idea from that mess you sorted last month with the delivery truck."

"What a great idea." I agreed.

David was smiling at me, but I couldn't quite get my face to fit itself into the same expression. I was in shock.

I was completely embarrassed and left so off-kilter after the breakup that I felt one hair's breadth away from completely losing it. Each shallow breath only served to get my heart racing faster, fueling my frustration.

A dull weight had settled at my temple, heavy over my eyelids, and I couldn't ignore the knowledge that it was solely my own doing. With some effort, I could rid myself of it instead of embracing it childishly, wrapping the hurt and frustration around like a shield.

David was eyeing me with concern but kept his tone light. "Ah, Jeff, Julie, why don't you finalize the details with Winnie and Jet here while I update Audrey in my office."

"Of course."

I barely stopped myself from slamming David's door shut behind me. It still closed loudly enough that I was sure they heard it in the conference room, but hopefully, they didn't think too much of it.

"What's going on?" Even to myself, it sounded shrill.

"Audrey, I think you should sit down."

My body was buzzing with impotent anxiety. "I don't want to sit down, David. I want you to tell me what is going on. Why am I only finding out now that there was an issue yesterday? And why was a decision allowed to be made by the two interns, who, may I remind you, have only worked here a few weeks, instead of me, your most senior account manager?"

David slid into his seat, the very picture of calm.

I was trying, really I was, not to blow up in his face. But it was a very close thing. Instead, I gripped the back of a chair and blew out a hot breath. "And what if they hadn't been able to get Jeff's customers to lend us the furniture? What if they'd antagonized the hire company against helping us out in the future? I have to work with these people, David. I don't appreciate being undermined by some toddlers who just so happened to get a degree."

His voice was stern, and I could tell I was close to pushing my luck. "Audrey, calm down."

I forced myself to take a deep breath, pushing through the ache in my chest but made no move to sit.

Leaning his elbows on his desk, David continued, more softly now, "Audrey, do you know why I sent you home yesterday?"

I balked, remembering. "Because I was distracted." Because I'd forgotten myself.

"Because you were so distracted, you sent the hire company the wrong information, which resulted in us needing to find a solution."

Oh.

"Exactly." The caring tone of his voice did nothing to soothe my frayed nerves. "Luckily, someone caught it and called to confirm. Winnie wanted to check in with you, but I told them not to bother you with it. I made sure they didn't make any decisions without my ok, and I thought you'd be happy that they'd fixed the issue without worrying you. It saved you additional stress, and it all worked out in the end."

I should have been glad that he didn't look angry, but it barely helped. I was angry. I'd fucked up. Months and months of late nights and stress and taking it all on myself, and in a single moment, I'd almost ruined it.

Just like I'd ruined things with Jackson.

"David, I'm so sorry."

"Audrey, it's ok."

"No, it's not. I let you down. I promised you I could handle it, and I couldn't."

He thought this over, drumming his fingers on the table before changing tact. "You know, Winnie and Jet came to me because they felt they weren't helping out enough with the launch. Which you'll remember we discussed recently."

I averted my eyes to the floor, feeling appropriately chastised.

"They knew how heavy your workload was and saw an opportunity to lighten it, and I encouraged them to step up. Take on more responsibilities. And yesterday, that meant making a call without consulting you. I believe you owe them some gratitude."

And all I could think was, what was the point of all those late nights? All the time and energy that I poured into this, when at the end of the day, I'd abandoned my work for my relationship.

Thank god Winnie and Jet had been here.

God, what David must think of me right now. How disappointed he must be in me.

And the interns, I'd been so shitty to them since they started, hoarding my workload and pushing them off to the junior managers.

Had I even thanked them? Not just today, but ever? Surely I must have, but for some reason, I couldn't remember a single time. Fuck.

And they tried so hard. Always doing any job given to them with a smile on their faces. Willing to learn and eager for me to teach them, but I'd been so preoccupied doing everything myself. Preoccupied with Jackson.

My guilt multiplied. Honestly, David should just take the launch off of me until I got my shit together.

All the air deflated out of me, and I crashed down into one of the chairs across from David's desk. "You really think I've been doing too much?"

"Yes. It's all I've been trying to tell you for the last six months. Slow down, relax, use the team. Why do you think I hired Winnie and Jet in the first place? But you refused to let anyone help you."

"Because I knew I could do it myself."

"Audrey." And oh, he sounded so disappointed. "Why did you come to work with me when I started this place?"

This was easy to answer. "Because I believed in your idea. I believed in you, and I wanted to work for you."

"Why?"

"Because ..." Realization hit me, and I sighed. "Because you're the best boss I ever had. You always trusted me to do my job and gave me opportunities no one else had."

He didn't reply, only tilted his head with a knowing look in that mother hen sort of way that should have frustrated me but instead made me smile back at him until I rolled my eyes. "Okay, okay, you've made your point."

"I suspect that isn't the only reason you're upset. Can I ask what is happening with that man of yours, or would you rather not talk about it?"

"There's nothing to talk about. It's over."

And oh, God, the look of empathy on his face really sharpened the knife.

"You always give 110 percent, kiddo. I've seen it with my own eyes. I don't know if you're even able to give any less. When you want something, really feel passionate, you throw yourself into it. Why do you think I wanted you for Bespoke? You have a spark in you, Audrey, and when you decide to shine that light on something, you're blinding. You need to try and find more balance—lord knows you work yourself to the bone, but please, don't dull that spark. Not for me, not for him, not even for yourself. You're something special, and if I had to guess, it's part of why he loves you."

David walked around his desk to hand me a tissue, and it was only then that I realized I'd started crying. Perfect.

He perched on the edge of his desk. "What about working here is different than working at Empire?"

I was surprised by the change of subject, sniffling as I thought of my answer. "Because it doesn't feel like I'm just grinding away for nothing. I have purpose here."

"You might not feel like you're slaving away for someone else, but I think you're still going. You're just doing it to yourself now." David's lip curled into a concerned smile. "You need to have something else, Audrey. Something for you. If this all failed tomorrow, I'd still have Nicky, and that would be enough for me. I would hope you had something just as special to keep you going."

That thought stopped me in my tracks. I did have something. Someone. And yesterday, I'd walked away from it.

"I won't tell you work isn't important. I would never have started this place otherwise. But it's not your identity, Audrey, any more than your partner or life outside is. And it's also not solely up to you. And when there were other people involved, you need to trust them to help."

Trust. So elusive, so fragile.

David had mine. I'd followed him here from Empire because I trusted him implicitly. And I understood now that he had that same trust in me.

Winnie and Jet had earned it, despite all my efforts.

And Jackson. Who'd listened and waited and allowed me into his life, his home, his family. Who'd leaned into his—frankly misguided—rep of a womanizer to keep me out of the public eye for a little bit longer. Who had a career he cared about but always made time to ask about mine, who sought out ways he could help, no matter how small.

Who'd trusted me with his feelings. And I'd been too scared to trust him with mine.

Who saw the person I was and loved her.

Not who I could be. Not who I thought I was. Not who he could make me.

Just me.

Fuck.

Jackson hadn't been the one missing work; that had been me. He'd never minded if I couldn't text for a few hours or had to work late; I had.

"But how do you make it work?"

"Together usually helps."

It didn't matter if David was referring to work or love; it was true for both, I realized.

I was going to have to fix this.

Drying my eyes, I felt oddly renewed. Now that the cloud of melancholy had lifted, determination set in. I might not be able to fix everything with Jackson—or even have the faintest clue how to—but I could at least do the right thing by Jeff and Julie.

I stood in one clean movement, collected myself, and said, "Shall we?" before heading back into the conference room, my head clearer and my steps sure.

"Alright," I started as soon as I opened the door. "It seems we have some work to do in the next two weeks. Jeff, I'm going to need you to provide us a list of all the people you've spoken with about the furniture—Jet, you work with him to collect the names of the pieces and their phone numbers and get on the phone to our delivery partner and arrange for transport to the venue on the day." Jet was already furiously taking notes as I spoke.

"Winnie, I want you to continue to manage the hire company. Great job, by the way, and start working more closely with the caterer and bar staff to make sure that everyone is aligned. Do you feel you're comfortable with that?" Winnie nodded enthusiastically, her smile splitting her face.

"Julie, it's going to be a busy two weeks finalizing the launch, so I'll have to limit any trips to you, but I'd like to come by tomorrow to collect a sample set of stock for the launch so that we can test the cocktails. I also think it would be a good idea for you both to come in next week for a tasting before the launch, of course, or I can discuss bringing the mixologist to you if that isn't feasible."

Julie gave me a warm smile. "Jeff and I can definitely make something work for next week, Audrey." Although Jeff looked a little less convinced about that, he made no move to contradict her and was still smiling in my direction.

I gave a short, sharp nod. "Ok, I think that's it for now, but we'll make sure to keep you updated on our progress as we get closer. Before you leave today, I'd like to finalize the invoice, but after that, you're free to head back to the distillery."

"First, I think we should at least enjoy some of these pastries my husband made." David said, motioning to the tray of treats before us, then, raising his coffee mug, he added, "And toast to a successful launch."

And even though my heart was broken, I felt maybe everything could still work out alright.

33

JACKSON

I was tired. That's all I could think as I rolled over in bed late Saturday morning. Usually, I would have been at the gym, but I couldn't bring myself to go. After a week of working non-stop to distract myself, I'd been left exhausted and flat.

I'd woken in the morning to the same empty bed. The same quiet apartment. Apart from one obvious thing, very little had changed in my life, yet it felt like everything had. The space I used to be happy to have to myself now felt too large.

It was missing one specific piece.

Years of being content to wake up alone after meaningless affairs now felt hollow as I remembered the joy of having someone to wake up to, someone to cook breakfast for.

I wanted to hear her laugh, light and airy. Pull her close and wrap my arms around her. I wanted all the moments outside of sex —the conversations, the kisses, the quiet.

But what could I do?

I'd laid out how I felt, and Audrey had left.

Maybe it was better this way. Clearly, the way I'd handled the interview and our fight were proof enough that I had no idea how to be in a relationship. Audrey had been right about that.

I could have saved us both a lot of pain if I'd never gone back to the bar and let her get on with her life.

I didn't even blame her for leaving; I'd called her no one, then threw her failed marriage in her face. Of all the things I could have said, that might have been the worst one.

Even Terry had questioned me afterward, and Sarah had been on my case as well, only making me feel worse.

And the comments … I'd already stopped myself a few times from setting them straight, telling them how amazing Audrey was, but that would mean dragging her further into this mess, and that was the last thing I wanted.

As much as I missed her, I wasn't going to reach out. I knew I couldn't take the rejection. My pride stood in the way of that, at least.

When my phone rang, I answered without checking the caller ID, not allowing any hope that it was Audrey on the other side.

"Your offer worked, my man! I'm looking at your contract right now. Two more seasons and an extra zero for both of us. Great thinking with that podcast, by the way."

Glad that he couldn't see my wince, I said, "Thanks, Terry, that's great news." And in truth, I was pleased about it, but it was difficult to find the energy to get excited.

"You ok, J?"

I waved him off. "Yeah, don't worry about it." A thought occurred. "Hey, will tomorrow work for me to sign those? I've got something to do today."

"Of course. Call me tomorrow. We'll tee something up."

After my conversation with Terry, I messaged Sarah.

Me: Are you still at mom and dad's today?
Sarah: Yeah
Me: Tell them I'm on my way.

As I stretched out the last knots in my back, my mind cleared.

It would be a good thing. They'd talk some sense into me.

The train ride was shorter than I remembered. Sarah was waiting for me at the station, and although the drive back to our parent's house was short, she still managed to grill me.

"Wow, Jace, you look like shit."

"Thanks, I feel like shit." I kept my eyes on the passing buildings. "Audrey and I broke up."

"Oh, Jace. I'm sorry."

"Thanks. I'll be fine. I think. I just …"

Sarah stole a look in my direction at a red light. "Feel like your heart's been ripped out and thrown into a blender?"

It was a morbid joke, but it still made me smile. "Yeah."

"Aw, your first heartbreak."

"Little soon to be rubbing it in, Sarah."

Sarah looked appropriately sheepish. "Sorry."

"It's ok."

We spent the next twenty minutes rehashing the breakup. When I'd finished, we'd arrived at our parent's house. "Did I completely fuck up?" I asked as I unlocked the front door.

Sarah led us to the kitchen and pulled out the tin of homemade cookies that Mom always managed to have on hand for emergencies. "No! You said yourself that you hadn't talked about how to handle the press. You went with your gut, and that's the best you could have done. You don't know that it would have worked out any better if you'd decidedly differently. And I know it sucks, but you can't regret telling someone how you feel. It's always a gamble when you love someone. That's what makes it so great but so damn scary."

We hovered in the kitchen, taking turns devouring the cookie stash. It felt like it could have been ten years ago if it weren't for how grown-up Sarah looked now. Here was my married baby sister, finally in a position to give me dating advice.

She swallowed and said, "Shit, I feel bad for basically telling you to go for it at the wedding."

"Don't. I would have done it anyway. I was sure she'd felt the same." These cookies were good. Maybe I'd get the recipe off Mom.

"So was I!" Sarah said, disappointed. "You should have seen the way she looked at you. I thought it was obvious."

I threw an arm around her shoulders for a brief hug. "We both did."

"You're here!" Mom's first move when she entered the kitchen was to pull the tin away from Sarah and me. "And you'll ruin lunch if you keep eating these."

"Hi, Mom." Her hug was comforting.

Dad was a few steps behind her. "Jackson, this is a surprise. I didn't know you were coming over."

"It was a spur of the moment decision."

He brought me in for a hug. "I'm glad you're here. I wanted to talk to you about something."

"Actually, I have something I need to talk to you about, too."

I followed him into the small back room he'd turned into an office, although he used it more for reading. As such, the space was cluttered with books and journals on every surface, a moat of words surrounding the two worn armchairs that sat by the window.

Dad settled into one, and I followed suit, already planning how I would propose this to him. I could guess how this conversation would go, knowing dad, and my best approach would be not to allow him to derail me.

"I got some good news today," I said, pleased when Dad indicated to go on. "So, you'll remember that when I signed on for the show originally, it was a long shot. None of us had any sort of fan base, and no one knew how popular the show would be, so I took what they offered, which wasn't much, but more than I had been getting at that point."

He nodded. "I remember."

"And I think I've told you before that as the show has gotten bigger, they've refused to change our contracts, even though they're making a lot of money off of us right now."

He nodded again.

"Well, we finally managed to secure an increase, and I wanted to use the money to help you and Mom—"

"No."

"Dad," I started, but he didn't let me continue.

"No, Jackson. It doesn't matter how you were planning on finishing that sentence because there's no way your mother and I will accept your money."

I pushed forward in the chair, sitting on the edge, determined to convince him. "Look, I know how much you guys struggled with money when Sarah and I were growing up, and that doesn't even come close to what you had to do to support me through my career. And you're both still working. I want you and Mom to be able to retire. Enjoy some time together. And now I'm in the position to look after you for a change—"

"Jackson. I said no." I went to protest, and he cut me off with a gesture. "It's not your decision when we stop working. We'll do that when we're good and ready. And you can forget the idea that you owe us anything. Yes, we worked hard to keep a roof over our heads and to help you when you first started out in LA, but we're your parents. That's what we do. The whole point was to make sure you and your sister could plan for your futures. Your own families."

It was clear that there was no room for further discussion, and I accepted it only because I had half expected it before I'd said anything. Dad's convictions were the foundations on which I'd built my own, so I couldn't blame him for not taking my money.

Still, I had hoped. There were always other ways. Christmas. Birthdays. Mom.

I'd work it out.

Now that he'd closed the door on my offer, Dad changed tact. "You know, I was hoping the reason you'd come over, beyond wanting to see us, of course, was to talk about your plans with Audrey."

Resigned, I sank back into the chair. "That would be difficult. We've, uh, split up."

The only response he provided was an astute raised brow, which he always employed when he was disappointed and wanted you to explain yourself.

He would have made a great actor.

"It's probably for the best. My job comes with certain expectations that aren't exactly fair on whoever I date. Audrey ..." How did I want to put this? "She'll be better off with someone whose life isn't complicated with press and publicity."

"Is that what you want?"

"No. But that doesn't stop it from frustrating me. I love Audrey, and I absolutely want," I hesitated, "wanted. A future with her. But …"

It was hard to discern my thoughts from those that Audrey had raised. How had she so succinctly put it? *You don't know what a real relationship is.*

She, unfortunately, had a point. "The timing wasn't right. Just because I wanted it to work doesn't mean I'm in the position to give her what she needs."

"Jackson, dear, where on earth did you get a ridiculous idea like that from?" Mom had materialized in the doorway and wore a look of disbelief. "While it's certainly very noble that you're worried about providing for her, it's very selfish."

They weren't to know that Audrey had made that choice herself by walking away. "I didn't mean—"

Dad cut in. "You don't think I did all that on my own, did you? Your mother worked just as hard, no, harder, to provide for you and Sarah."

"It was an equal effort," she said with a kiss to his temple. Then she returned her attention to me. "It can't be one person shouldering it. It's a partnership."

"And if she doesn't want to be with me?"

Mom's tone was tender and caring. "Love is hard. And when you've met the right person, it doesn't always fall into place. It hasn't always been flowers and rainbows with your dad and me. There were times, in the beginning especially, when I didn't know if we'd last. But we worked through it. Together."

34

AUDREY

"This is nice. It's been a while since we had a girl's night. I was starting to forget what you looked like."

I know Tiff didn't mean it as a slight, but I couldn't help feeling a little guilty anyway. Outside of our Saturday mornings and text conversations, we hadn't spent much time together in the last few weeks.

Just another aspect of my life I'd been neglecting.

"I know, I'm sorry. I didn't mean to disappear."

Her look shifted from joking to concerned. "Hey, I was joking. Everything ok?"

"Sometimes, I hate that you know me so well."

"Is it wine bad or ice cream bad?"

"It's not anything bad. I'm just … missing Jackson and feeling like the world's biggest idiot."

"Ok, well, from the sounds of that, I definitely need some form of chocolate. Come on. I'll bake while you talk."

Somewhere in the time that I'd known her, Tiff had decided the best way to hash out a problem was by baking. Her wizardry over recipes extended across all mediums, it seemed. While I, on the other hand, decided I could learn a handful of dinners to whip up on short notice, leaving the fancy stuff up to the five or so decent takeout places near my apartment.

Tiff's kitchen was hardly more than a single long counter, but she made the most of it. She patted the only spot on the bench where overhead cupboards hadn't been installed. "Sit. Talk."

I popped up onto the counter and watched while she dug out bowls, spoons, and a variety of ingredients, throwing them together with practiced ease. She measured nothing, which gave me mild anxiety, but had never been an issue for her. I sat silently, her calm movements relaxing me.

It had been almost a week since Jackson and I had broken up, and I still felt the gaping hole left by him. The congealed mass of my regret had settled in my gut, sneaking its grip through my insides and squeezing my lungs.

"Ok," Tiff said when the silence had dragged on long enough. "I'll start. He's a jerk, and we hate him."

I shot her a look. "We don't hate him. We hate me for hurting him. And we hate you for introducing us." I was only half-joking.

Immediately, she pointed the wooden spoon at me. "Hey! You're about to pull off an incredibly successful launch of a delicious new spirit, and I'm fresh off my fourth consecutive win as bartender of the year." I half-heartedly rolled my eyes, but she continued, "So you can stop that pity party right now."

There was a loose thread along the seam of my jeans, and I pulled at it, lazily curling it around my finger. "I'm just trying to wrap my head around it. It wasn't that long ago you were convincing me to stop dating and start looking for something casual."

Tiff looked regretful. "Don't remind me."

"No, that wasn't—I just meant that everything happened so fast, I'm only just processing it all now."

It was just meant to be a fun little fling. An escape.

How had he so completely weaved his way into my every thought?

"Before Jackson, my biggest issues were the latest shipping error, arguing with that cocky shit from Liquor Kings about stock orders, and price gauging. Now, I can't stop thinking about him. Wondering what he's doing. Wanting to see him, hear his voice."

"You love him." She said it so matter-of-factly. With the same conviction Jackson had the other night.

I thought about everything that Jackson had done for me without asking for something in return. Even when I was holding back, he was patient, giving me space or time or a distraction. Even on our first night together, when we were little more than strangers, he had made sure I was comfortable every step of the way, always checking I was ok before he kissed me, touched me.

"I do."

There was no denying it. My biggest regret was not telling Jackson when I'd had the chance. Now, I wasn't sure I'd ever get to.

The now familiar ache spread through my chest, the weight of my attachment making itself a home within me. He had burrowed his way into my heart, and honestly, I wanted him there.

"Then why break up?"

"Because I'm an idiot, remember?" At her unimpressed look, I recanted. "You saw me that day. I was a mess. We talked about the interview, and then he said he loved me, and I just. Freaked out. Stopped listening. I got defensive and said some really stupid things just to hurt him."

"Call him. I'm sure he feels the same way."

I watched as Tiff filled a half dozen muffin trays with the gloriously chocolatey batter. "What if he doesn't? I want to apologize, but I'm not sure he'd even want to hear from me again."

Which was the hardest part. Because as much as I loved Tiff, she wasn't the person I most wanted to talk to about this. The only person I wanted to talk to, the one person whose opinion I wanted on all this, was him.

She popped the tray into the oven and leaned her hip on the counter. "Then you move on."

This was a card Tiff usually played with her clients. Played devil's advocate to see what side of the fence you fell on. She said it was the best way to uncover your innate desires. And it worked.

The very idea of moving on caused my heart to cry out like a petulant child throwing a tantrum in a grocery store aisle.

I didn't want to move on.

I wanted to be with him.

Damnit.

Why did he have to go and be all funny and charming and utterly frustrating to the point where he had buried himself in my heart and found a home there?

Why did I have to be so utterly pigheaded not to see what was important?

The problem from the beginning was that I'd been trying to avoid all this nasty feelings business.

It had felt like the safest option at the time. An arrangement, built purely on sex, that wouldn't—couldn't—hurt me.

And then along came this amazing, caring man to ruin it all.

Except he hadn't been the one to ruin it.

While we'd been together, I never told him what I was feeling, that I was scared and fragile and why. I had just pretended I was ok, that I could deal with this on my own, and I thought I'd just figure it out in time.

I couldn't forget the look on Jackson's face when he said those three little words and I didn't say them back. God, I was such an asshole. If only I'd told him sooner, maybe I could have saved us both some heartache.

But I'd been selfish. And now I was miserable.

The last thing I ever wanted to do was hurt him.

I needed to apologize.

I'd lost count tonight of the number of times I'd almost texted him, but I couldn't bring myself to say those words via text when he deserved to hear them in person.

It probably would have been easier if I could get angry about it.

I wanted to. I wanted to hate Jackson for wanting more. I wanted to hate myself for getting into this stupid arrangement in the first place. I wanted to hate Brad for ruining love for me.

But I couldn't.

Because I'd loved what we'd had.

I missed him, goddammit. I missed his friendly, joking texts during the day. The sparkle in his eye when he was teasing me. His strong hands and solid, reassuring presence against me while we slept.

Tiffany draped an arm over my shoulders and rested her head against mine. "I'm sorry it didn't work out."

I closed my eyes against the tears that threatened to escape. "Me, too."

"Will you be mad if I confess something?"

"Probably not, even if I want to be."

"I thought you were good together. I know I never saw you at the beginning with Brad, but I saw enough, and I've never seen you so happy than when you were with Jackson. I really hoped it would work out for you two."

I went to reassure her, and she looked pained. "What's wrong?"

"You should be angry at me. I introduced you. I pushed you together."

"I'm not angry at you," I groaned. "I'm angry at me. I wasn't ready."

"You are ready."

"Tiff—"

"No. You don't think you are, but that's just because you're scared. Love isn't supposed to be easy, Auds, and I know I don't really know what I'm talking about because the longest relationship I've had lasted three weeks, but I don't want you to miss out on something wonderful because you feel like you don't deserve it or some bullshit like that." She pulled back and spoke with more vulnerability than I had heard from her before. "It's a leap of faith, Audrey. One I've always thought you were so brave for taking with Brad, Don't let one bad experience stop you from leaping again. Not when you want to so badly."

I wasn't quick enough to stop the tears from falling.

"What you want, Audrey?" She asked.

The million-dollar fucking question.

I loved my job. I was damn good at it, too. I wanted the launch to go well. But if I were honest, I wanted what David had—that balance between work and achievement and love. I wanted someone to come home to who would celebrate my wins and support me through the losses.

I wanted to hire a team to take over the day-to-day work so that I could focus more on the planning and event side. I wanted to start canvassing for new brands again; I couldn't remember the last time I'd had the time to research and travel. I wanted to talk to Tiff about establishing a series of annual events that could serve as a platform for marketing new bars, new spirits, and the talents of upcoming bartenders. And I wanted Jackson by my side as I did it.

I wanted to spend Sundays having brunch with Jackson and Sarah and travel out to have dinner with his parents. I wanted to be standing by his side when he got the accolades he deserved, spend lazy mornings in bed reading through scripts with him, and wake up enveloped in his arms.

Damnit, I loved him. More than I could even fathom and definitely more than I could put into words right now.

And I walked away.

But had I messed it up completely?

"I want him. I love him. I wish I could tell him that. I wish I *had* told him that."

"Then make it right."

"How? What do I do?"

"What do you want to do?"

I needed to see him. I needed to tell him how I felt.

I needed to get him back.

"I want to get him back. At the very least, I want to apologize and make sure he knows how I feel about him."

"What do you have in mind? I'll have you know; I'm very good at arranging coincidences."

"I think we're going to need help for this one," I said, dialing the one person I hoped could help me.

35

JACKSON

It had been a week since seeing my parents, and I wanted to reach out to Audrey, but I had no idea what to say. Everything I typed never felt like enough.

I wanted to salvage this. But I didn't know how.

So I focused on work instead, getting to the set early for extra hours of training or just hanging around with the crew, and on one occasion, shadowing Naomi while she worked. Seeing how everything came together was fascinating, and I had started to think about asking Bryson what my chances were of directing an episode next season if we got picked up again.

On top of that, Addison Michaels had asked me to come to New York for the day to run screen tests with the rest of the film's main cast.

The test went smoothly enough. It was always a bit nerve-wracking meeting people the first day, not to mention I'd fought hard for this role, and I still wasn't convinced that Addison wouldn't realize he'd made a mistake and change his mind. He'd been upfront that he was giving me a chance but that I hadn't been his initial choice.

We'd run some lines but mostly spoke in a small group about the characters and themes. Addison, I was surprised to find, had a calm, insightful manner when talking to us actors. He was articulate and precise, even when he told you to change something he didn't agree with, but he also genuinely listened to our opinions and would work it into the dynamic if he liked it.

All said and done, it was a great day, but I was happy to be on my way back home.

It was the first Sunday in years that Sarah and I didn't have brunch together, so I called her as I waited at the airport for my flight back to Chicago.

It took me all of twenty minutes to bring Audrey into the conversation. I wanted to believe I was strong enough to have one moment where she wasn't at the front of my mind, but who was I fooling. Ever since I met her, I found myself thinking of her at odd times of the day, then almost every day, until there wasn't anything I did or anywhere I went that didn't bring her to mind.

I'd had to stop myself that very morning from texting her a photo of a corgi that had been checking out of the hotel. With its owner, of course. The point being that the dog was wearing a raincoat, and the first person I wanted to tell was Audrey.

"And you haven't spoken since that night? Is there a reason you haven't talked? Or tried to sort things out?"

"What can I do? I put myself out there once, and she walked away. And what if there's nothing I can do? We said some pretty raw things to each other."

There was a pregnant pause before Sarah asked, "Would you take her back if she wanted to?"

"In a heartbeat. I still love her, you know? As much as it hurts, I want to run over there and just forget this happened. That probably sounds ridiculous, but it's the truth."

"It's not ridiculous, Jace. You can't help how you feel."

"Thanks. I'm sorry we missed our brunch this morning."

"Actually, I have an idea. I just discovered this great little Italian place downtown. What time do you land? Do you think you could meet me there by seven? You owe me for all this free relationship advice I'm giving you."

I chuckled and checked the time. "I think I can make that. Text me the name of it, and I'll let you know if I'm running late."

"Can do. And hey, I think everything is going to be alright."

"Thanks, Sarah. See you tonight."

Tht evening, I searched for Sarah as I entered the quaint and cozy restaurant. Traffic from the airport had made me an hour late getting home, but I'd texted Sarah, then threw my suitcase in the room and forgone a shower to make my way here, so it was only thirty minutes past when I'd agreed to meet her.

Hopefully, she wouldn't give me too much grief for it.

She hadn't texted me back after I let her know I was on my way, which wasn't unusual, but something still felt off about it. Like I was walking into an ambush.

When I spotted the familiar soft waves and expressive eyes, I realize that's exactly what this was. And I had just walked right into it.

Audrey was seated at a table tucked away in a corner where the lights were the dimmest, but I would be able to pick her out in the dark. I was walking towards the table before I realized I'd started moving, and she stood when I get close.

When I didn't immediately sit, we were left to stand awkwardly in greeting. I didn't know why she was here. I didn't know why I was here. Except that Sarah tricked me into this meeting. And I'd absolutely have a word with her about interfering tomorrow.

Right now, I was torn between relief and disbelief.

Audrey's smile was somber, but even her obvious anxiety couldn't distract from how beautiful she looked. "You can leave if you want. I would understand if you don't want to see me."

I did want to see her. It was all I'd been able to think about, and here she was. But why? "I'll stay."

We sat, and a server came by to take our order before departing, leaving us in suitably awkward silence.

My instinct was to talk, open the conversation up, but I resisted. She had orchestrated this with Sarah, so she should talk first. The last time I put my cards on the table, we'd broken up, so as hard as it was to sit across from her and not tell her I wanted to give it another shot, I knew I needed to wait and see what she had to say first.

Besides, what if I read this all wrong? What if this was some sort of breakup post-mortem? But then, Sarah wouldn't have agreed to that, surely.

It isn't until after our drinks arrived that she steeled herself with an exhale and started.

"You have to know I love you, and I'm sorry. I would never forgive myself if I didn't tell you that. I feel terrible that I let my fears stop me from saying that as soon as I could."

She watched me across the table, and I was aware that I hadn't moved. Hearing the words that I so desperately hoped for sent my heart into overdrive, but I knew it would take more than that to fix things. I took a swig of my beer just to break my stillness, and she took my silence as a sign to continue.

"You were right that night. It wasn't about the interview. Or the Instagram post, or any of it. I," she squeezed her eyes shut for a moment, "I appear to have some issues letting people help me." I felt my lips twitch around an aborted smile. She wasn't wrong.

"I can't excuse how I acted that night. I should have talked to you, told you how much I was struggling. I was so wrapped up in the past and trying to protect myself that I messed up. I kept thinking that having anything more than casual would mean ending up where I was before, which is ridiculous, I know. That I had to choose between this life that I'd built for myself and you, but that was selfish and stupid, and that's on me."

Hope began to stir within me. Hope that we could salvage this.

"And I'm so sorry I used your past relationships like that. I was trying to hurt you, and I was wrong. If anything, you're better off for not having the same baggage as I do."

Audrey's eyes shined in the low light, glassy from unshed tears. "No one makes me feel like you do. No one ever has. I don't want to lose you."

My continued silence hadn't broken, but not because I didn't want to speak. Instead, I had found myself awed speechless because this amazing woman was laying her heart out to me.

"I didn't think I could feel like this. I thought it was something out of a script you'd probably hate. How could I ever believe in a million years that some incredible guy would come into my life? You seemed too good to be true. So I told myself to just enjoy it while I could. Because I was convinced it wouldn't last. Couldn't last."

After this, because I already knew I was going to accept Audrey's apology and make this work, I would find that asshole of an ex and make him apologize for ever letting this woman feel an ounce of heartbreak.

She reached across the table to place her hand on mine. "I want this. All of it. I love you. And I understand if you can't forgive me, but I needed to say it and ask if you still felt the same."

36

AUDREY

He was silent for a moment, and I realized that this was what I had put him through after he'd said the words. How cruel that must have felt, and I endured it now as penance for the hurt I'd caused him.

Tiff had told me to take a leap of faith, but right now, it felt like I was walking up to a cliff and throwing myself off the edge, hoping it worked out.

Finally, he said, "I love you, too. And I want us to be together, but …"

My heart stuttered in my chest when he paused, and in the millisecond before he continued, I imagined all the worst endings that could possibly come after. "But I can never forgive you for hurting me" … "But I'll never be able to look at you again" … "But I'm moving to another country just to get away from you."

All of them were increasingly ridiculous, and thankfully, I was put out of my misery before I spiraled any further.

"But I have some things I need to say first." He gently squeezed my hand, an added reassurance that this wasn't going to end badly. "I know you said it wasn't about the interview, but it was for me. I hated that I made it sound like you weren't anyone important when you are the most important person to me. I don't think there's anything I wouldn't do if you asked me."

"You're an incredible woman, Audrey, and I want everyone to know how insanely lucky I feel to be with you. I want to be there next to you as you accomplish brilliant things. I want to help you accomplish them. Although, I promise only to help when you want me, too. It turns out I have some issues with fixing other people's problems for them." He offered me a small smile, which I returned, knowing that while things weren't going to be perfect—I'd still want to take care of my own problems, and Jackson would still want to solve them for me—we would have each other.

"And I never should have thrown your ex in your face like that. I was hurting, but that's no excuse."

My focus narrowed to the caress of his thumb across my knuckles and the quiet emotion in his voice. The light sharpened the shadows of his cheekbones, making him look otherworldly. But beyond how handsome he was, I loved how generous, caring, and thoughtful he was.

"I want you to know what I was scared of. I have been terrified that I couldn't be the man you need, the man I *want* to be for you."

My lips pursed in regret, aching to take back the hurtful words I'd carelessly thrown at him when we'd fought.

"I shouldn't have let you walk out that night, but I'm almost glad you did because it made me realize I never want to let you go again."

Instinctively at his words, I tightened my grip on his hand. I didn't plan on letting him go anywhere. "I can't believe I ever made you question how I feel about you. I love you, Jackson. I should have told you as soon as I knew."

"I wanted to. At the wedding. I thought it would scare you off."

"To be honest, it probably would have. But I would have wanted to say it back."

Jackson leaned in, lifted our hands to his lips. "I'm sorry if I ever pushed you too fast."

"You didn't."

He challenged me with a look, and my cheeks flushed with a

familiar heat. The last aches of tension seeped away, knowing we had gotten over the worst of it. He was here; he wasn't going anywhere; we could work this out.

I couldn't contain my smile. "Ok, maybe a little. But I wanted you to. I needed the push. I know I'm not that great at opening up, but I promise I want to be honest with you. When I'm with you, I feel more like myself than I ever have before. You've let me just be me, and I never thought I would find that."

Jackson's focus on me was intense and unwavering. "I still don't know what I did to deserve you."

I swallowed against the rise of emotion, blinking in the low light. "You don't have to do anything. I just want you."

He opened his mouth to speak, paused, then continued. "I've spent a long time believing that I needed to be ready, that I needed to have enough to offer someone else. More than just myself. But I didn't think about what I wanted in a relationship, and I know now that I don't want something one-sided. I want a partner."

"I want that, too." More than anything.

I opened my hand to cup his cheek, and he turned to kiss my palm. "I want to make this work. But I can't promise you I know what the hell I'm doing."

A choked snort escaped me. "I think it's fairly obvious I'm not an expert either."

"So we work it out together."

"I'd like that."

Our eyes locked, and I felt lighter as I released a heavy breath. God, I was so lucky. I might never stop feeling grateful for this gift. For this man.

I lost track of how long we spent just taking each other in, but eventually, he smirked. "Sarah obviously helped you set this up."

"If it makes you feel any better about it, she promised to track me down if I hurt you again."

He laughed, and it was the best sound I'd ever heard. I hadn't realized how much I needed to hear it again.

"So what now?"

As if on cue, my stomach growled, reminding me that I hadn't eaten in hours. I'd been too nervous earlier. "I don't know about you, but I'm starving. I've been waiting here a while."

"Nervous?"

"I was either going to pass out or puke."

Another laugh. "And now?"

A hunger of another sort flared in me. "Now, I need to kiss you and eat something. And not necessarily in that order."

"I see where I stand." He joked as he leaned across the table towards me, meeting me halfway in a searing kiss.

All too soon, my senses were overwhelmed with the smell of cheese, garlic, and freshly baked bread, and I tore myself away from Jackson, moaning in pleasure at the food that had been placed on our table. Our gazes met, and my stomach flipped in joy as it finally sunk in that we were ok. He was here. He still loved me and wanted to be together, and I hadn't lost him.

"I'm not used to feeling like this. I'm not always going to get it right, but if I mess up or stumble, I'd rather do it by your side than anyone else's. I couldn't. I have all this love for you inside of me and nowhere else to put it if you aren't here."

I continued because, now that the flood gates had opened, I didn't want ever to close them again. I was an idiot for keeping my feelings hidden from him in the first place. "You know what the worst part was? Life kept going on, and the one person I wanted to share it with wasn't there, and it was my fault. I was scared that I'd wake up from this incredible dream to find out I'd made you up in my mind."

He reached across the table to hold my hand, and that simple touch sent shivers across my skin. "I felt the same way."

"Really?"

"Audrey, I've never met anyone like you before. I never thought I'd understand what it meant to want to share the rest of my life with someone until I met you. I was just as scared that this was too good to be true, but that's what made me realize how much I love you."

"Do you think it'll ever stop feeling that way?"

"I hope not."

I watched as he shuffled his chair around the table until he was seated next to me.

He stared deeply into my eyes, leaning in close. My breath hitched as I let myself fall into those turquoise blues, murky in this light, or perhaps it was the force of the passion I see reflected at me.

My own eyes closed as he cupped my cheek, and I instinctively leaned into his touch. His lips were feather-light on my other cheek before hovering by my ear. "Tell me again."

I opened my eyes and tried to convey every ounce of love I had for him. I placed a kiss against his palm. "I love you." Then I leaned in to kiss him.

I planned to say it again and again and continue until he knew it was real and forever. And then I'd continue because I never wanted to stop telling him.

37

AUDREY

Wow.

I ... wow.

How many weeks had I been agonizing over tonight? How many hours had I put into pulling everything together?

As I looked around at the eclectic mix of high chairs, bar tables, and barrels, I couldn't be prouder. Winnie had absolutely made a great call in using Jeff's handy work to solve our last-minute hire issue. After we'd banded together, everything had gone relatively smoothly.

Guests were everywhere, mingling now that the official tasting had ended, and I was pleased to see most of the sold-out crowd had stayed behind to purchase more drinks and talk with Jeff and Julie about the distillery.

Tiff and I were celebrating with a pitcher she'd thrown together before relieving herself of her bar duties. I'd told her that I hadn't intended for her to work tonight when I'd asked her to curate the drinks list, but she'd insisted that she needed to oversee, and I didn't fight her. Who else would understand the need to make sure your hard work was honored?

"The decor is better than the bar. Maybe I should think about a revamp," Tiff said, admiring the brass accents and greenery I'd arranged to decorate the bar tops. Everything harkened on natural, earthy elements; to marry in with the oak touches.

I'd done rather well if I did say so myself. Not out loud, of course.

"Agree that you've done an amazing job," Tiff said as she poured me another drink, "or I'm cutting you off." Damn, she knew me too well.

I took a sip of my drink, my smirk catching on the rim. "Yes, you're doing a real good job of that so far."

She placed a jug of water down. "There. Responsible service. Now can you please just admit that you did an amazing job tonight? I mean, just look at this place." She motioned to the room, where at least half of the crowd was still milling about, laughing and talking. Somewhere in there were Jeff and Julia, as happy as I'd ever seen them. I could just about spot Julia's wild curls from my bar stool.

I rolled my eyes, but it was likely ruined by my wide smile. "Fine. It went well."

She cleared her throat, but I remained reserved. "Ok! It went really well."

"You're impossible, but whatever. I know you're amazing, and so does everyone else here. Even if you can't admit it."

I blushed under her praise. Tonight really had been amazing; better than I could have hoped for.

Two strong arms wrapped around me, followed swiftly by Jackson's silky voice. "There you are."

He'd been commandeered by some fans earlier, and Tiff and I had left him to dazzle them, but I was glad to have him back. It had barely been a week since we'd gotten back together, and I was feeling especially greedy.

"Tiffany, can you do me a favor? I need a photo with the most beautiful woman in the room."

"Why wouldn't you," she said, taking his phone while he pulled me into his side, kissing my temple as she took a few photos. Too many photos.

"Ok, enough!" I laughed and squirmed in his grasp, turning to look at him because that's what I always wanted to do when he was near me.

His lips brushed my ear. "She's right, you know. Everyone knows how amazing you are." I buried my blush into his shoulder.

When he took his phone back, he immediately set about posting it to his accounts, the fifth one of us tonight. Surely his fans would be over us by now.

I was ecstatic.

My heart soared further at the caption he added to the photo:

Lost my heart in Chicago. If found, please return to Audrey Adams.

He tasted like rum and bitters when I pulled him in for a kiss.

David was beaming when he came by to say goodnight, pulling me into a congratulatory hug. "Great job, kiddo! I just spoke with Jeff and Julie, and they are thrilled. They're excited to get going on the next thing."

"Thanks, David. I'm glad you finally helped me get out of everyone's way. Tonight wouldn't have worked out if you hadn't."

His hand on my shoulder was firm, reassuring. "Don't for a second dismiss your efforts here, Audrey. This is all you."

"As nice as that is, I think Winnie and Jet feel that they could have worked for someone less frustrating."

He scoffed. "Don't tell them that. In fact, I don't think I've seen them happier. It might have taken you a minute to get there, but in the end, you were leading them the way that I knew you could."

I wasn't wearing waterproof mascara. I couldn't cry without it running everywhere. How dare he.

Seeing my apparent distress, he pulled me into another quick hug and then excused himself so that he could get home to Nicky.

The goodbyes came in quick succession after that.

Jeff, who looked happy but also like he'd rather be away from all the noise, made sure to shake my hand once more before they slipped out. When Julie hugged me and said, "We knew you could do it," I'd had to bite my lip to stop it from trembling.

Why was everyone so set on making me cry tonight?

The worst culprits had surprisingly ended up being Winnie and Jet, who rounded out our little group as among the last to leave. Jet quietly thanked me for the experience but mentioned he wasn't sure he wanted to continue after this year ended. I told him to keep in touch once he knew what he did want because I might have some contacts that could help him. He seemed shocked at this offer like I'd just told him he'd won the lottery.

Winnie, sweet, smart, going places Winnie, had been the one who finally broke my defenses. But how could I not feel overwhelmed when she told me that she'd really looked up to me and she'd requested David assign me as her mentor as long as that was ok with me.

As long as that was ok … Was she kidding? I'd never been called someone's mentor before.

"Of course, that's ok!" I said, wiping my damp lashes with my index finger and grimacing when it came back black. "And I promise to let you do more from now on."

"As long as I can keep learning from you, I'm happy," she replied. "David was right when he said we'd be learning from the best."

I cleared the lodge in my throat. One of us was going to have to leave soon, or I'd be a blubbering mess.

Jackson saved me, sweet and proud. We caught up to Tiff as she flirted with a very perky woman with a bright pixie cut, and I saw Tiff swapping numbers with her before we said goodnight.

The train home was uneventful, exhaustion finally hitting me. I burrowed into Jackson's side, my head tucked into his chest as we rode the few stops home, and I closed my eyes, breathing him in and feeling completely at peace.

I couldn't possibly ask for a better night.

By the time we walked into his apartment, he was the only thing keeping me upright. The bedroom was too many steps away, so I threw myself onto the couch, groaning at the relief of finally being off my feet.

"Just think," Jackson said, removing my shoes, "we have to do that all again in a couple of weeks when the new season premiers."

I groaned louder, though it was mostly swallowed by the cushion smashed into my face.

His voice was suddenly very, very close, and very, very low. "Do you know what you need right now?"

My lips curled against the cushion. Sleep. A foot rub. Your mouth on me. All of the above?

I mumbled something that could barely be considered words then heard his answering chuckle. "Come on. I owe you a bubble bath."

"Can't. Too sleepy."

"Oh?" He proceeded to test my theory by lowering himself onto me, plastering himself to my back, nibbling on my earlobe and the soft skin below. "Or maybe there's something else you'd like?"

His fingers deftly worked my shirt out of my pants, fingers dipping under the waistband as they teased the now uncovered skin. I writhed under him and was rewarded with a hum of appreciation low in my ear before he was suddenly pulling himself off the couch. I whimpered at the loss, flipping onto my back to glare at him.

"Oh, good, you're awake." He was entirely too amused for my liking.

Whatever retort I had in mind was replaced by a long yawn, one that forced my eyes closed. It was immediately followed by a second.

Jackson chuckled again. "Alright, sleepy. You've convinced me."

A featherlight kiss passed over my lips as he helped me off the couch, and I let my eyes drift close as he maneuvered me into the bedroom, my legs absentmindedly moving as the energy faded away from the rest of my body.

Only when I was nestled under the covers did I realize I'd lost my pants somewhere along the way. Jackson was a long line of heat and stone behind me, and I melted into it, threading our fingers together once his arm was anchored around my waist and our palms were pressed together at my heart.

Where he lived. Where he belonged.

EPILOGUE
AUDREY

10 Months Later

My phone rang as I finished applying my lipstick. I didn't need to see the caller ID to know who it was. "Hey, I thought you were working tonight?"

"I am. That's why I'm calling. Are you free to lend a hand? I'm down a bar bitch."

"Oh, no, I am not falling for this again." I pulled the phone away from my ear, calling out in the direction of the bathroom. "Uh, honey?"

"Mmm?" Jackson sauntered into the room, adjusting his cuffs, looking every bit like the movie star he was. The movie premiered in a month, and the hype had been growing since the trailer dropped. My man was officially "hot property." Not to mention smoking hot in his suit. I didn't hide my low groan of appreciation as he walked over and pulled me into his arms.

He smelled amazing. That tantalizing mix of cologne and *him* that made my toes curl.

We were running late. I knew that. And yet, I really wanted to be naked with him.

"My eyes are up here, beautiful." He winked at me, and it was almost painful not to drag him over to our bed.

"Ugh, I can taste the sickening sweetness from here. You two disgust me." Tiff's taunting effectively brought my attention back.

Innocently raising my eyebrow to Jackson, I asked, "Is there any reason Tiff is asking me to lend her a hand at the bar tonight? The same night as our anniversary?"

"I don't know. It might be because we planned a small surprise party."

"What the f—" I held the phone away to save my hearing. It was no use; Tiff's loud exclamation could be heard even from a distance.

I laughed as I brought it back. "Oh, did I forget to mention that Jackson told me?"

"Seriously, what the hell! It was meant to be a surprise."

"I think we've had more than enough of those in our relationship, thank you very much. So you can stop trying to come up with ways to meddle."

"Excuse you. I believe I'm still the one who got you two together in the first place."

"How could I ever forget when you're constantly reminding me."

"Whatever, just get your asses here already." And with that, she hung up.

Jackson pulled me close. "How disappointed was she?"

"Extremely, but she'll be over it by the time we get there."

He still gave me butterflies, even after a year. Sometimes at the oddest times. It could be waking before him, curled against his back, basking in the steady warmth and protection I felt there. Or when I perched myself on the tiny counter in our bathroom to watch him shave in the morning, and he would lean in to kiss me wetly on the cheek, smearing cream on the way. But especially when we went to events because if we were ever separated and our eyes met across the room, my love for him overwhelmed me. Like beginning all over again. I honestly couldn't stop being grateful for having him in my life. By my side.

"And how annoyed do you think she'll be about this?" He

grasped my left hand and kissed it, the warmth of his lips a contrast against the cool gold band that now adorned my ring finger. Thin and delicate, with a single small diamond embedded in the band. It was understated and pretty, but with a fragility that I fell in love with the minute I saw it. It had only been twenty-four hours, and I had to keep reminding myself it was real.

We hadn't told a soul yet, deciding to wait until the party tonight. The day had been incredible, and while it was a small form of torture to not immediately call everyone and let them know, being able to celebrate alone with Jackson was a memory I'd cherish for the rest of my life.

Which might not be too much longer once Tiffany killed me for not telling her.

"She might actually murder me. Or you. I wouldn't put it past her."

"At least I'll die happy." He leaned down and kissed my cheek.

My giddiness hit a new high when we made our way into The Basement and were greeted immediately by our closest friends and family. The bar was closed to the public tonight, and we'd filled the space to celebrate a mix of occasions. Jackson's film didn't premiere for a month, and my birthday had been two weeks ago, but getting everyone together was a mammoth affair, and we had figured one giant party with everyone would be our best bet.

I lovingly stroked the lone ring on my left hand. Not to mention the latest good news we had to announce.

It took far too long to get to the bar. You'd think we never saw anyone with the way they were slapping Jackson on the back and wrapping me up in hugs, even though we worked and talked to most of them every day.

Tiffany wasn't behind the bar tonight, but she was the first to hand me a drink, a short tumbler of honey caramel liquid, one of her latest concoctions, which she'd so hilariously named "the set up" as a tip of her cap to her successful matchmaking. No matter how often I told her, she would not believe it was simply a stroke of luck, countering that she had dealt a hand of fate for Jace and me.

Debating with her was fun, but I actually liked the name and the drink, and it was my usual anytime I visited the bar. Which wasn't as often as before, but she happily conceded the time to Jackson as she was busy with her own relationship these days.

I held my glass in my left hand, tilting the ring outwards on purpose, but no one had picked up on it.

Fine. Guess subtlety was overrated anyway.

I got Jackson's attention with a pointed elbow to his side, and he protectively wrapped a hand around my waist before cupping his mouth and yelling over the music.

Most of the room turned to face us, and those who hadn't, turned once they realized where everyone was looking.

Now faced with telling everyone, I was grateful Jackson was holding onto me. Otherwise, my legs might have given out. I gripped his hand where it rested on my side, and he squeezed me tightly in response.

"I just wanted to thank everyone for coming tonight to celebrate with us. There's been a lot to celebrate recently, and you've all been here with us, so I won't go over it all again now."

"Good!" came a shout from the back, sending a wave of chuckles through the room.

"But there's one thing I'm especially thankful for. A year ago, I met the love of my life, and I can't imagine having anyone else by my side right now." Jackson turned to me, and even though he'd already proposed and I'd already said yes, those same butterflies stirred up in me again. I swallowed against the lump in my throat and held his hand tighter as he continued. "And for some unknown reason, she feels the same way, so last night I asked her to marry me."

Sarah was the first voice I heard, loudly whooping from nearby, and it started a chain reaction of cheers in the room. A loud male voice called out, "She said yes, right?" I was fairly sure it was Jackson's Dad, but I couldn't tell over the collective congratulations thrown at us. I did manage to call back, "Of course I said yes!" I held my hand up, which was promptly grabbed by Sarah and nearly yanked out of its socket as she admired the ring. Mrs. Ward then grabbed my hand out of her grasp to hug me and welcome me to the family.

Ok, I was definitely crying now.

Tiff was immediately by my side with a napkin because she knew me like that. She hugged Jackson while I dabbed at my eyes, and when I was done, she crushed me in a hug and spun me around. "You're lucky I love you, or else I'd be pissed you didn't tell me."

"I am lucky," I breathed out, too emotional to think of a witty retort.

"Shit, Hannah is going to hate that she missed this!"

"I'm happy to see you happy, by the way."

She hushed me. "It's only been a few weeks, don't make a big deal out of it." But I could tell she was a little head over heels. "Oh! I didn't tell you, apparently Harry is selling the bar."

"What? To who?"

"His brother. I've never met him, but as long as he stays out of my way, we'll get along just fine."

"Good luck."

She let me go as Wes hugged Jackson next to us and called out, "Toast!"

Tiffany threw up a hand. "Wait! Wait! I just learned sabrage! Give me a second." She then proceeded to run behind the bar and pull out a fucking sword from under the counter, resulting in a wolf whistle from Wes. She gave him the finger with her other hand before picking the bottle of champagne off the counter.

Everyone collectively took a step back.

"Alright, screw the lot of you. I'm about to be a badass."

Honestly, I shouldn't have been surprised when she casually held the bottle up, gave the cork one, two, three baby taps with the blade, then, in one clean, confident swing, popped the bottle open, immediately depositing the now overflowing champagne into the waiting glasses.

She passed Jackson and me a glass first, smiling smugly, though her eyes were a little glassy. I'd tease her about it later, but for now, I was trying my hardest not to burst into tears myself.

A couple of hours later, and the party was in full swing. I'd been nursing an espresso martini for the last twenty minutes, too busy watching Jackson as he chatted to David. David had this habit of using his hands wildly as he spoke, something I was fairly sure he'd picked up from Nicky, causing Jackson to keep moving his glass out of the way.

The fact that he hadn't put his drink down or made some passive aggressive comment to David about his hands made me so happy that this kind, considerate man was who I got to spend the rest of my life with.

As I contemplated the fantastic future we had in store, I overheard Tiff mention she was out of napkins and needed to get to the office to restock.

"We'll get some more!" I quickly latched on to Jackson's jacket on my way past and pulled him along. "Come on, handsome."

As soon as the door closed behind us, I backed us up to the desk, sat on the edge, and tried to get him between my legs. He stood firm, just out of reach, looking very pleased with himself, even as he denied me. "Baby, everyone's waiting."

"Let them wait. You're driving me crazy in this damn suit." I pulled again on his jacket, trying to get him close enough to kiss, but he was stronger, and he knew it.

"David was just telling me about the sister bar that you signed and how big it is for the business."

"Mmm." I looped my fingers through his belt hooks and pulled again, encouraged as he stepped minutely closer, though still not close enough.

His hands ran up my bare arms, sounding amused. "And it looks like I got that voice acting job for the next Disney film. Terry said they'd call me about it this week."

"Sure." My hands felt up his chest, running over the ridges of his muscles underneath, my gaze following, stopping only when I noticed his raised eyebrow and amused expression.

He was biting his lower lip. Definitely on purpose. He knew what it did to me. "I'm starting to think you only want me for my body."

"But what a body it is."

He took another step forward. He was between my legs now but still frustratingly out of reach of my lips. I could stand up and close the distance, but part of the fun was the tug of war.

And knowing he would eventually give in.

"And what about the rest of me?"

I locked eyes with him, giving him a look of clear and utter adoration. He blinked, transfixed, and I knew I'd won.

"Every part of you is amazing, and every day we spend together, I find new things to love about you. But if you don't hurry up and kiss me right now, I'm going to go out of my mind."

He did just that.

ACKNOWLEDGMENTS

A huge thank you to my ex-husband/roommate/friend who is the antithesis of Brad and also was my sounding board during the conception of this book. He will also say he chose the title, which... Ok, I'll give him that one.

To my close friends and family, who have supported my decision to do something crazy like write a book! And will now have to either (gasp!) read it, or pretend to. Please know that it's ok if you didn't finish it, or skipped the sexy parts. And dad, if you didn't skip the sexy parts, please don't tell me.

Huge thanks to the brilliant Bailey from BaileyDesignsBooks for her cover design. She was an absolute JOY to work with, and took what I can only describe as my vague description of what I wanted and turned it into something beautiful. I can't wait to see what we create for Tiff's sequel!

This book wouldn't be half what it was without the incredible work of my editor. Thank you Olivia, for making this book better and making me a better writer for it. Your advice was crucial to moving the story from okay to great, without ever making me feel like a complete idiot.

And to every single person who made it this far, and read the book. I cannot thank you enough. No matter what you thought of it, I never once while writing it, thought that one day anyone might actually read it. It means so much that you took a chance on this fluffy little romance, and if you liked it that is all the more special to me.

ABOUT THE AUTHOR

Dani McLean is an emerging author of sexy, snarky stories featuring kickass women who can't quite get their shit together, and the irresistible but confused men who fall in love with them.

Born in Melbourne, raised in Perth, Australia, Dani loves to read, write and travel. She loves Hallmark movies because they're unintentionally hilarious, she's been on enough terrible Tinder dates to fuel countless books; and when she isn't conducting unofficial wine tastings in her pyjamas, she's devouring all things romance.

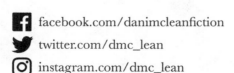

facebook.com/danimcleanfiction

twitter.com/dmc_lean

instagram.com/dmc_lean

CPSIA information can be obtained
at www.ICGtesting.com
Printed in the USA
FSHW012109170521
81544FS